THE SIMULACRUM

THE SIMULACRUM

BY
BRAD D. SEGGIE AND
LINDA W. YEZAK

Linda's Dedication

*Dedicated to my dad, Jim, who awaits
us in the Kingdom. I miss you.*

Brad's Dedication

*This novel is dedicated to everyone who understands
that novels (not platforms) sell novels.*

*To the rise of self-publishing and the imminent
death of the legacy gatekeepers.*

And to all the writers in the struggle.

Linda's Acknowledgments

To K.M. Weiland, Michael J. Scott, and Kimberli Buffaloe for their keen eyes, superpower abilities, and vital words of wisdom, a very special thank you. Y'all rock!

And to my gift from God, my husband, Billy, thank you for enduring my crazy schedule and moods. Love you!

Brad's Acknowledgements

To Ed Keener and Jake Welland, who read the novel and provided positive feedback. You have no idea how important you were!

To pilots Len Zink and Pastor Joe Johnsick, who were kind enough to provide an expert eye to the aviation scenes. Thank you both!

To Kim Camp, who was kind enough to read through my first attempt at a novel and to provide feedback. Much appreciated!

To Terry Burns, the only literary agent who saw any value in this novel. Thank you!

And to my wife Angel, who gave up a lot of family time to allow me the time to write. I love you!

(Are you scanning the credits? Why isn't your name there?)

PROLOGUE

HE CREPT THROUGH the moonlight shadows of the trimmed hedges, scrunched low to the manicured lawn, and eased toward the back of the house. Somewhere nearby a dog barked, and he froze, his eyes riveted to the splash of light spilling out of the windows and landing in bright rectangles on the deck. His latex-gloved hand tightened around the grip of his Glock. His nerves yanked taut, and he felt the heightened awareness he'd experienced in a different neighborhood, a dirtier, hotter neighborhood where the language was as strange to him as the people who spoke it.

What had happened in Kabul over a dozen years ago was war, an evil that no longer touched his life. In Kabul, everyone was a potential combatant, and many had felt the bite and burn of his sniper bullets an instant before meeting Allah in person.

But he'd never killed an American.

He clenched his jaw, let the urgency of his mission course through his veins and flush out the icy shards of doubt.

This American needed killing, deserved to die. The scientist posed a threat to everything the ex-Marine had dedicated his life to. The only way to save all he'd worked for was to eliminate the threat. Execute the old man, as was once done to all traitors of the faith.

He sucked in a cold breath, steeled his nerves.

He melted into the darkness on the back deck of his victim's large colonial home, stepped silently past the wrought-iron patio furniture and padded loungers arranged for casual conversation. How often had the scientist spread his lies while roasting marshmallows on the fire pit?

Heat burned in his chest, warding off the chill of the night and driving him on his mission. He edged forward for a peek through a crystal-cut window.

Inside, Dr. Wayne Oakford hunched over his laptop at the kitchen table, his fingers flying over the keys. A half-eaten sandwich and a sweaty glass of tea sat at his right hand. Bare feet peeked out from his lounging pants, and a dark blue t-shirt covered his thin torso. The silver-haired scientist looked harmless enough, but his weapon was words, and those words posed a threat to the entire scientific community.

At close range, the ex-Marine wouldn't need more than a single shot to end Oakford's life, and the suppressor would prevent the neighbors from hearing a thing. He placed a gloved hand on the brass knob and slowly twisted. The door opened without the slightest squeak, and he stepped over the threshold, not making a sound until he stood opposite Oakford in the kitchen.

He leveled the gun at his target. "It's time to stop working, Dr. Oakford."

The old man looked up. Confusion clouded his eyes, instantly replaced with alarm as the gun apparently registered in his brain. He shoved back from the table, his chair toppling to the hardwood floor behind him, and raised his arms over his head.

"What do you want?" His voice trembled, his hands shook. His face looked pale in the blaze of the overhead light. "Do you want money? I have money! It's in a safe in the basement."

"This isn't about money. It's about science. You were warned."

A gleam of recognition flashed across Oakford's face, and he lowered his arms. Even with a gun aimed at his chest, he dared to smirk. "You're too late. I've already spoken with somebody from the Academy. I revealed everything."

"Nobody will believe it."

"Oh yes, they will," Oakford said. "I provided proof that can eliminate even a shadow of a doubt."

CHAPTER ONE

MARY DILLARD SMOOTHED her clammy hands down her satin-clad thighs, then curled her fingers into a fist. Her nerves were betraying her. Confident women didn't have sweaty palms.

She pulled her shoulders back, adjusted the silver chain of her sequined evening purse over her shoulder, raised her chin—all the tricks to make her appear more confident even though her knees knocked beneath her gown. She'd dressed to the nines before, this wasn't her first time. But it was the most important. The position of Director of Development at the National Academy of Sciences was at stake. It could be hers, if she could just shed her nerves and cross from the marbled entry of the neoclassical mansion into its grand hall beyond.

Laughter rang out from the hall, accompanied by the rich chime of quality crystal. Mary urged her rooted feet forward in time to catch Dorothea Lodge, the hostess and her boss's wife.

"Mary, dear!" Mrs. Lodge air-kissed each cheek, then locked arms with her. "So delighted you're here. Come meet everyone."

She drew Mary into the sea of jewel-toned gowns and sparkling diamonds, dark tailored suits and freshly shaved cheeks. Manly, earthy colognes vied with feminine flowery, spicy perfumes, both low key to the savory scent of roasted pork loin wafting from the kitchen. White-gloved men and women in black servers' uniforms weaved around furniture and cliques, serving hors d'oeuvres of bacon-wrapped scallops and crab-stuffed mushrooms. And Mary's legs threatened to morph into boiled linguine with every step she took.

She barely heard the names Mrs. Lodge announced, barely saw the people she pointed out, until one particular name overpowered the blood pounding in her ears: Robert Quigley, the largest of the Academy's large contributors. He'd already written a hefty check this year, and scoring another donation from him would be quite a coup, bound to make Dr. Lodge take notice of her and offer to give her the directorship permanently.

If ever there was a time to shine, this was it.

"That's just the man I want to see." She drew up to her full height and freed herself from Mrs. Lodge's grasp. "Excuse me, please. I'd like to catch him before he disappears into the crowd."

Mrs. Lodge winked at her. "Go get him, dear. See if you can't shake another sizable check out of him. He can afford it."

Mary shot a nervous grin at her hostess, then made her way toward him, pausing just long enough to lift a crystal flute of liquid confidence from the silver tray a server presented. She crossed the room and took a sip of the champagne. The familiar bubbles tickled and burned as they drifted over her tongue and down her throat. Quigley ceased his conversation and watched her with open appreciation. That ego-boost was all the encouragement she needed.

She slipped beside him and smiled. "It's about time I get to meet you. I hear you're one of the Academy's best friends."

"You have me at a disadvantage." His voice was deep and silky, with a hint of thickness that came from one too many cocktails before dinner. "Have we met?"

"No." She offered her hand. "I'm Mary Dillard, interim director of development."

Instead of shaking her hand, he tucked it in the crook of his arm and began to stroll with her to the far side of the room, away from those he'd been speaking with. "Shame about Howard."

"Yes, it is." Howard Sheldon, the former director, had been stricken with cancer and was currently hospitalized, a fact that both broke her heart and provided her with this opportunity for advancement. "He was a terrific mentor."

"I'm sure he was," Quigley said, then lifted a smooth brow. His chocolate brown eyes held a teasing sparkle. "So, I suppose you're after my money. What kind of inducement will you offer to finagle a second check out of me this year?"

The question—and its implications, made obvious by the tone of his voice—startled her back to her champagne. What a jerk! Did he think they'd find a spare bedroom in the mansion where she would perform for pay? Not in this lifetime, buster!

But she couldn't afford to get on his bad side, either.

She schooled her features to her best contemplative expression—brows drawn, slight frown—and tilted her head. "I'll have to think about that."

He lowered his lips to her ear. "I could give you some suggestions."

"I'm sure you could." Her laughter sounded fake to her own ears; no telling how it sounded to him. The heat rising to her cheeks in response to the amusement in his eyes infuriated her. She was blushing like a ten-year-old. Sophisticated women didn't blush. Her confidence wilted like a rose out of water. Getting more funds out of this womanizer proved trickier than she'd thought.

He paused before the door to the library, where Dr. Rutherford Lodge and others were gathered in front of the TV.

"Tell you what," Quigley said. "Why don't you come out to my little summer home next Friday, and I'll write you a check guaranteed to land you the directorship."

She gawked at him. Had she been that obvious?

"Don't look so surprised, honey. A man in my position is accustomed to solicitations by those who want to advance their status, even from women as beautiful as you." He patted her hand. "Now, say you'll come. We can have dinner on the deck over the water. It'll be perfect."

Red flags popped up everywhere in her brain. "I don't want you to have to go through all that trouble. You could just mail a check."

"Nonsense! Besides, I want to show you something special. It's really quite impressive."

"I'm sure it is, but I have plans next Friday. Perhaps you'd consider a morning appointment? Say, around ten?"

His lips tightened for a moment, then he nodded. "Of course, you probably have a date. Ten is just fine. We'll have brunch—"

"Mary, come here." Dr. Lodge waved her into the library. "You need to see this."

"What is it?" With a slight smile offered to Quigley, she eased her hand from his arm and entered the masculine warmth of the library. A diversion from the leech was just what she needed. She'd have to walk a tightrope to get what she wanted from him without giving him what he wanted.

Dr. Lodge pointed at the television. "Look."

Her uncle's face appeared on the huge plasma screen—the professional photograph he'd used for years. She'd fussed about his needing a new one, a shot that more represented him at sixty-five, but he never took the time.

Oh, no. This had to be about Paluxy Man, and she was in the wrong company if it was. No one in this room—in this entire house—would be sympathetic to Uncle Wayne's cause. Ever since he found that fossilized skeleton, he'd been publicly questioning the theory of evolution. People were calling him a closet creationist, and worse. If she hadn't known better, she'd have sworn he was trying to destroy his standing in the scientific community.

"Turn it up," someone said, and the volume rose loud enough to be heard in the next room.

"Tonight, sixty-five-year-old Wayne Oakford, a leading paleontologist for the Smithsonian, was apparently murdered in his home in Vienna, Virginia."

The stark words punched Mary in the stomach with the full force of a blow from a heavy-weight boxer. Uncle Wayne was dead? Murdered? She clutched the back of the nearest chair and stared at the TV through stinging eyes.

The screen split: her uncle's picture on the left, a solemn female reporter standing in front of his Colonial home on the right. Yellow crime scene tape cordoned the entire property; blue lights flashed to red and back, reflecting off the house's white painted facade; an army of professionals milled about, clustered together, went inside, came out. Detectives, cops, others she had no clue of their functions. So many people.

The camera focused on the somber face of the young reporter. "The only thing local police are willing to share during this ongoing investigation is that Dr. Oakford suffered from a single gunshot wound ..."

He'd called her earlier, just as she was leaving for the party. She'd been running late and let his call go to voice mail, with a promise to herself she'd get in touch with him first thing in the morning. What if he'd called for help? What if she could have saved him?

She yanked her cell phone from her evening bag and scrolled until she found his message.

"Call me back as soon as you can. You won't believe what's going on."

Her breath caught in her throat. Whatever was going on had gotten him killed.

*

Behind the wheel of her BMW hybrid, Mary burned the highway between DC and Virginia. She needed to know what the cops had discovered. Needed to know if Wayne had left any clue of what he'd hinted about over the phone. Needed to make sense of him being dead. She pounded a fist against the steering wheel. He couldn't be dead! He was the only family she had left.

She slowed as she entered the Vienna city limits and drove by rote to her uncle's house, which was still surrounded by crime-scene tape and cops. A white Ford hearse backed onto Uncle Wayne's driveway and parked. Mary's heart lodged in her throat. More than the blue flashing lights, more than the yellow tape, that hearse drove home what she had been denying since she left DC.

She choked back sobs and concentrated on the scene at her uncle's house. Several uniformed officers surrounded one man in regular clothes. If he was the head honcho, he was the one she'd come to see. She parked the Beamer across the street and strode toward him as quickly as her evening gown would let her.

An officer held up his hand and stopped her at the tape. "Sorry ma'am. I'll have to ask you to stay outside the line."

"But I have to go in!" She couldn't keep a tearful plea from her voice. "He was my uncle. I'm his only living relative. Please. I need to know what happened."

"Let 'er through," the plainclothesman called to the officer. He waved her toward him.

The officer lifted the tape; she dipped her head under and hiked up her skirt high enough to walk with a decent stride.

"I'm Detective Tom Gifford." The plainclothesman's tone was bland, but authoritative. His gaze scoured her from head to toe, then back to meet her eyes. "You're the niece?"

"Yes. Mary Dillard. What happened?"

"Looks like he surprised a burglar. We caught the guy breaking into another house a block over. C'mon." He took her by the elbow. "We'll do a walk-through, and you can tell me if anything is missing."

As they turned toward the door, the staff from the medical examiner's office rolled a gurney down the walk and toward the hearse. Mary's knees threatened to buckle under her.

Detective Gifford's strong arm held her up. "You okay?"

"I want to go to him," she whispered, unable to take her eyes away from the white-sheeted figure on the gurney.

He shifted her away from the sight, but she continued to watch over her shoulder. Her heart ripped in two, and she whimpered with the pain.

Detective Gifford turned her to face him. "Miz Dillard, there's nothing you can do for him now, but you can help us. Let the M.E. do what he has to, clean your uncle up before you see him. I'll take you to him myself as soon as we're through here. Okay?"

She slipped her lower lip between her teeth and nodded.

At the front door, the detective handed her pairs of disposable shoe covers and latex gloves, then donned a pair of each himself. When she was ready, he led her on a tour of Uncle Wayne's home—the home where she'd played hide-and-seek with Aunt Clarice and attended Easter and Christmas and birthday parties. The home she'd run to when her parents were killed; the home she'd brought her first serious boyfriend to.

She clamped her hand on Detective Gifford's forearm, unable to move a single step. The memories flooded her mind, and she needed to take a moment to force them aside.

"I'm sorry," she muttered. The detective had been so patient with her.

"Take your time."

She drew a deep breath and released it slowly through her lips. "I'm ready."

From room to room nothing seemed amiss. Valuable artwork still adorned the walls; first editions of Steinbeck, Hemingway, and Dickens had been left untouched in the bookcase; Aunt Clarice's collection of antique Hubbels and Fabergé eggs still shone from curio cabinets. The burglar was apparently a tasteless amateur looking for the more mundane things. But in the den, the sound system and TV still where they'd always been. Just what had the burglar been after?

"Nothing's been touched," she announced. "I don't see anything missing."

Detective Gifford scrubbed a hand across the back of his neck. "Well, we haven't been to the kitchen yet. Maybe he was after the silver."

"Then I need to see the kitchen."

"Just a word of warning, ma'am. That's where he was killed."

Mary stared at him a moment as she let the words sink in. Then she tightened her lips and nodded. "Okay, then I definitely need to see the kitchen."

Men and women Mary didn't know swarmed in Aunt Clarice's once-orderly kitchen. Fingerprint powder covered virtually every soapstone surface. Voices murmured, pens scratched over pads. A photographer snapped pictures of the bloodstain on the parquet floor.

Uncle Wayne's blood.

She swallowed the urge to cry and shifted her focus to the hutch which housed Aunt Clarice's china and silver. Nothing seemed to be missing here either. She peeked through the door just to the right of the hutch—Uncle Wayne's office had been ransacked. His desktop computer was missing, as was his laptop. Unless he'd left it at his office. No, that would be uncharacteristic of him. He'd never leave it behind. Research materials were missing, files were gone. It didn't make sense. "Are you sure this is the work of a burglar? Did you find the computers?"

"Not yet, but give it time. He may have handed them off to an accomplice." Detective Gifford guided her out of Wayne's office and toward the back door. "Even if that's all he got, computers are a top commodity. We figure Dr. Oakford caught the man before he'd gone too far through the house and got shot for his trouble. The guy probably decided to skip out with the computers before someone came to investigate the gunshot."

"Well, it could've happened that way, I suppose." But what would a burglar want with files of paleontology notes?

CHAPTER TWO

I N THE EARLY morning quiet at Hadley Scientific, Val Gordon cradled a limestone femur in his arms and baby-stepped across the laboratory. When he reached the stainless steel counter, he eased the bone inside the XN-17 and closed the lid. The apparatus whirred into life and within moments began transmitting a wire frame image of the fossil to his computer screen, slowly filling it with color and texture.

Yawning, Val rubbed his sore eyes. After a sleepless night, the steady hum of the fan tempted him to grab a quick snooze. Instead, he sipped tepid coffee from his Semper Fi mug and drowsily watched the computerized version of the femur take shape on his screen.

His family had been asleep by the time he'd made it home last night. He kissed each daughter's cheek, undressed, and settled in next to his wife. Without waking, she curled into him and brought with her the reminder that the brutality of his former life was over.

What he'd done had left him sleepless and uneasy for hours. He'd reevaluated everything he stood for, the work he did for the furtherance of science. But in the end, he returned to his core belief. Science was worthy of his total devotion.

Morning hadn't changed his mind.

He treated himself to a fresh cup of coffee, then returned to watch the bone he was making continue to develop on the screen.

Creating bone replicas out of plaster wasn't unusual; natural science museums all over the world requested replicas for display. But this bone, a special request from La Musée d'Histoire Naturelle in France, came complete with a rush order. He couldn't allow his sleepless night to alter his five a.m. to seven-thirty p.m. schedule, or his grogginess to interfere with the precision required to replicate a femur.

He went to the coffee maker and poured another cup, then started another pot. He was in for a long day.

After a while his computer beeped, signaling the image's completion. The high-resolution, three-dimensional femur rotated slowly in full color on the screen. Val removed the fossil from the XN-17 and laid it on a thick felt pad beside a series of similar bones.

A red light blinked above the door to his lab. The security monitor showed a lanky man in a dark suit leaning over the keypad just outside the door. The lock gave way with an ominous click, and Chancellor James Darbyshire, a redheaded man with sharp features and a no-nonsense gaze, swaggered through the heavy metal security door, brandishing a newspaper.

"'A burglary gone wrong,' police say." He peered over his glasses, a victorious gleam in his eyes, and slapped the paper down on the counter. "Color me impressed. I never should have doubted you. I trust you have all of his files?"

"I got everything, but I have some bad news. Oakford said he'd already met with someone from the National Academy of Sciences. Said he revealed everything." Val squared his shoulders and braced for the Chancellor's reaction.

"Everything? Including Paluxy Man?" At Val's nod, the Chancellor drew his brows to a deep V between his hazel eyes. "Who?" His voice thundered through the quiet lab.

"He wouldn't say."

"We must find out." With a hand on his broad forehead, the Chancellor paced in front of the door. "This is a catastrophe. I can only imagine what he exposed with that big mouth of his."

"He did more than talk," Val said. "He gave his contact the skull."

The Chancellor stopped and squinted at him. "What skull?"

"*The* skull. Paluxy Man's skull."

"They didn't find one. That's why there's a plaster replica at the Smithsonian to complete the skeleton."

"Well, apparently they did, and now it's in the hands of someone who could blow our whole operation."

"I don't believe this." The Chancellor's face boiled, his thin copper beard submerged into the red tide. "What makes you think there's a skull?"

"He told me."

"When?"

"Last night."

"What, when you had a gun at his head?" He barked out a laugh. "You point a gun at me, and I'll tell you I know the way to the leprechaun's gold. Anything to keep you from pulling the trigger. He was buying time."

Val clamped his mouth shut and ran a hand over the buzz-cut he'd worn ever since his time in the Marines. He'd seen Oakford's expression as he revealed the skull's existence. The man hadn't said it just to buy time, but arguing the point with the Chancellor would be useless. The Chancellor seemed convinced he was right.

"Besides, the paleontologists at the dig would've sent it along with the body, right? Was it on the inventory list?"

Val shook his head.

"Well, there you go. It doesn't exist." The Chancellor clapped him on the back, then turned to go. Over his shoulder, he said, "We still have to find whoever he spoke to. That's a keg of dynamite we can't allow to explode."

Val frowned. If he was right about the skull, and it was in the hands of an expert, that powder keg might have already exploded.

CHAPTER THREE

AS MARY PUSHED her cart toward the cashier at the Whole Foods on P Street, she felt an unfamiliar emptiness. Her trip to Whole Foods was normally a highlight of her week. The store was packed with some of the brightest, most educated citizens of the city. They were loading their carts with whole grain bread, organic fruit, and artisan cheese, and she felt great to be among them. Some people might feel a sense of community by attending a church and find comfort in the same solemn rituals. Mary felt a sense of connection by performing secular rituals: reading the Washington Post and the Sunday New York Times, listening to public radio, and shopping at Whole Foods. The intelligentsia were like honeybees, working independently but in unison within the hive of the city.

It normally was one of her favorite things to do on a Saturday morning, but Saturday had been spent in tears and restless sleep. She'd never even changed from her pajamas. Sunday was no different. And today, while everyone else worked their important jobs, she wandered the aisles at the store with no clear idea of what she wanted.

She'd seen her uncle's body at the medical examiner's Friday night, made the positive identification. Instead of the terror-stricken face frozen in death she'd expected to find, he'd looked as if he were enjoying a peaceful snooze. In a way, she'd found that comforting.

What she hadn't found comforting was the report the police had made to her the following morning. They'd called to inform her that they had indeed captured the killer, a mentally deranged man living in downtown homeless shelter. The murder weapon or any of the possessions taken from the house weren't in his possession, but he'd confessed to the killing.

The police were satisfied with that, so why wasn't she? Who was she to question the police? They were experts in solving crimes. Who was she to challenge them?

In the check-out lane, she handed the cashier her reusable shopping bags. The cashier, a tall waifish redhead with dreadlocks and Celtic tattoos, whipped her Rainforest Alliance coffee across the scanner and dunked it into a bag.

Outside the store windows, a commuter bus idled at the red light, sporting an ad along its side. Need help? Call me. Gunnar Schofield, Detective for Hire. His eyes in the larger-than-life image seemed to capture hers, assuring her he could help, assuring her nothing would be too difficult for him. She'd seen his commercials on television before, too, and had always garnered the same impression.

She'd never be satisfied with the conclusions the police had reached about her uncle's murder. Maybe she needed to give Gunnar a chance to prove them wrong.

"That'll be a sixty-three and seventy-two cents." The clerk's voice yanked Mary's attention back to the store and her purchases.

Mary swiped her card, paid for the groceries she'd gathered absent mindedly, and carried her bags out of the store.

As she was walking to her car, she heard the Tri-Tone sound coming from her cell phone. She pulled it out and looked at the screen. Seven new voice mails! She scanned the list; the calls went back over the last three days. She clamped her jaw. What if she'd missed an urgent work call? They all seemed to be personal calls. One caught her attention. It was another voicemail from Uncle Wayne on the night of the murder.

"You're not going to believe this …" Uncle Wayne had phoned her only two hours before he died. According to the call, he'd been convinced another scientist was out to get him.

Mary shoved her bags in her car and used her smart phone to find

Gunnar Schofield's office. There was no way a poor deranged man murdered her uncle. She wanted the truth.

*

The bell over the door at the Schofield Detective Agency chimed, and Mary lowered her copy of *Cosmo* to glance across the cluttered waiting room. A man in a paint-spattered t-shirt and blue jeans danced through the doorway with a cassette player blasting an old Eagles' song in one hand and a paper bag in the other. He clicked off the player, slipped it into his pocket, and dropped the sack in front of his matronly receptionist.

She looked up from her keyboard with a wry smile. "What did you get this time?"

"Cathy, you gotta see this." With all the flair of a vaudeville magician, he whipped a tool from the bag and held up a hand to wave off any comment she planned to make. "I know what you're thinking. Just your standard adjustable wrench. But you're wrong." Grinning, he twisted the handle, and its head began to spin. "How about that?"

Unimpressed, she resumed typing. "Another toy to add to your collection."

"Go ahead and laugh—" he pointed the wrench toward the hallway— "but that leak in the bathroom is history."

Mary tilted her head. So this was Gunnar Schofield. Out-dated, dressed like a janitor. He didn't really resemble the images she'd seen of him on the side of the bus and on TV. The only way she recognized him was by his goatee and slightly crooked Roman nose. He looked better in the silk suit he'd worn for his commercials. Surely his detective skills weren't as archaic as his choice in music.

He finally noticed her and leaned closer to Cathy, but didn't bother to lower his voice. "Who's the girl?"

"Mary Dillard. New client."

"Didn't you tell her the office is closed?"

"She told me." Mary dropped the Cosmo on the magazine table and rose to extend her hand. "But I insisted. My case is urgent."

He ignored her gesture. "Yeah, they all are. Look, the office is closed. I'm heading down to Miami for sun and sailing. Call me in three weeks."

Of all the things he could've said, she wasn't expecting that. "Can't you postpone it?"

He looked like she'd slapped him with a wet fish. "Postpone my vacation? It's spring break! Do you know what South Beach is like during spring break?"

He made a show of checking her out. His mocking eyes took in her Gloria Vanderbilt jeans and ballet flats, her blonde hair pulled into a functional ponytail trailing down her back. When he finished his assessment, he smirked.

She rolled her eyes and crossed her arms. "South Beach will still be there."

"Yes, but spring break won't."

"Look, just give me five minutes of your time. I'll make it worth your while."

His face hardened. "My vacation is not negotiable."

"Everything's negotiable, Mr. Schofield." She raised her chin a notch. "I'll pay double your normal rate, plus expenses."

Cathy stopped clacking on the computer, her fingers with their fuchsia-painted nails hovering just over the keys. The room grew silent enough to hear the street vendors hawking pretzels and hotdogs outside. Gunnar exchanged glances with his secretary, then swiveled his eyes back to Mary, suddenly all sweetness and sunshine. "Well, now. If you're willing to pay double, it must be something serious. And heaven knows I'm a sucker for a damsel in distress. Let's talk in my office."

Mary smiled. For once, money trumped bikinis–especially the amount of money she'd just promised him. She followed him down a short hall lined with credentials and awards in cheap metal frames.

When he reached the door, Gunnar paused with his hand on the knob. "It's a bit messy. I wasn't expecting clients."

Inside, Mary was struck by the smell of stale Chinese food from the takeout box on his desk. The rest of the room didn't match Gunnar's silk-suited TV image at all. Pillows and sheets were strewn across a Murphy bed. A half-eaten bag of Nacho-Cheese Doritos adorned the window sill, and stacks of files littered the floor.

She brushed off a layer of dust from a thick oak chair and perched on it.

Gunnar dropped into his leather desk chair, snatched the take-out box, and dunked it into the trash. "I can never resist the General's chicken." He locked his fingers behind his head and rocked back in his chair. "All right, tell me what's so urgent that you'd pay me double."

"I need your help investigating a murder."

Gunnar's eyes sparked. She'd finally nabbed his attention.

"My uncle, Wayne Oakford, worked for the Smithsonian as a paleontologist. Last year his research team found a fossilized human skeleton together with a dinosaur …" She tilted her head. Just how much did he know about the scientific world? "Are you familiar with Paluxy Man?"

"Can't say that I am," he said. "I almost subscribed to Archeology Illustrated, but then I learned they don't have a swimsuit issue."

"Mr. Schofield, if I wanted lame humor, I'd watch Conan." Her lips tightened. He wasn't taking her seriously. She should just renege on her offer and walk out right this minute. But he was the only detective she knew of, not that there weren't others in DC, but she was here. Might as well give the man a chance.

She leaned forward on the hard chair. "When my uncle said the human and dinosaur were found together, the creationists jumped all over it. A teacher in a public school in Borden, Ohio, began telling his students that humans and dinosaurs lived together—a coexistence that is totally impossible according to science, but the teacher cited this find and my uncle's conclusions as evidence. This has caused such an uproar, even the ACLU is involved." She searched Gunnar's eyes for a hint of recognition.

He gave her a blank stare.

"It's a national news story! You'd have to be a hermit not to know about it."

"What does it have to do with the murder?"

"Uncle Wayne left me a voice message saying another scientist was framing him, trying to convince his colleagues that Paluxy Man isn't real and that he'd committed fraud."

"Did he?"

"No! My uncle was a man of integrity." She straightened her spine. "He ended the voice mail by saying his life was in danger. And sure enough, two hours later, he was murdered."

"Have you told the police about the message?"

"Oh, yes. But they believe they've already identified the killer–some poor homeless man who probably confessed just to have regular meals and a roof over his head. They patted me on the shoulder and said they'd give the case the attention it deserves." She still seethed about it. The detective hadn't even listened to her about the paleontology files; he'd insisted they had their man.

Gunnar steepled his fingertips. "Let me get this straight. You want to pay me—no, pay me double–to investigate a murder that's already been solved?"

"They have the wrong man. I'm certain of it. I believe Uncle Wayne was killed by another scientist, probably a guy named Ted Cranston. They worked together on the Smithsonian's research team. They had a huge fight over Paluxy Man. Cranston called Uncle Wayne's credibility into question with his comments and accusations." She jabbed her finger on his desk. "He's in the field with his team right now. They're at the McIntire Ranch, just north of Paluxy, Texas."

"If he's in Texas, how did he kill your uncle?"

"Maybe he flew back. Maybe he hired an assassin. How should I know?" She wasn't about to allow him to dismiss her suspicions with logic. "I bet he had something to do with it, and we won't know what until you confront him."

Gunnar raised a brow. "You want me to drive to Texas?"

"Actually, I was hoping we could fly. We'll go together."

"Not gonna happen. I work alone."

"My money, my rules."

"Uh-uh, sweetheart. Your money only bought you my vacation time."

"I must go! We're talking about my uncle's reputation!"

"No, we're talking about his murder. It's too dangerous."

She slumped back in the chair with her arms crossed and glared at him. But he had a point.

*

Gunnar walked Mary to the office door and held it open for her. "I'll spend the afternoon doing a bit of research, then leave out of here around nine in the morning. If this Cranston guy is our man, we could have this tied up before the end of the week."

"I sure hope so." She nodded at Cathy and left.

Gunnar shut the door behind her, then whipped her check out of his shirt pocket and, with a flourish, presented it to Cathy.

Cathy's brows shot up. "Is that for the full amount?"

"Nope. This is just the advance. I almost feel like a heel for taking it from her."

"Shove it out of your mind." Cathy patted a pile of bills on her desk. "She saved our bacon."

Gunnar winced. "How bad is it?"

She studied the check, then rummaged through the bills, and separated four from the stack. "These are three months past due. We can pay 'em off and still have some to spare."

"Pay yourself first. You deserve it."

"Oh, don't worry. I will." She smiled, but then turned serious. "Are you okay?"

He picked up the mail and flipped through it. "Sure. Why wouldn't I be?"

"Don't tell me you didn't notice. Your new client could be Becky's sister. Spittin' image of her when she was younger."

He'd noticed, and for some reason had responded like a jerk. Even after two years, his heart was still raw from his wife's death, and seeing someone who resembled her had startled him into bad behavior—like he was angry that anyone would dare look like her. But Mary didn't act like Becky. Their personalities were entirely different. Ultimately, that difference was what made him decide to take the case. Well, that and the money.

"I'm fine." He tapped his index finger on the bills. "Work your magic on these, okay? I've got a skeleton to research."

"What about that drip in the bathroom? What about your fancy new wrench?"

"I'll take care of it."

In his office, Gunnar fired up his computer, and the old contraption sputtered and moaned into life. He could get a new one, but as long as it worked, it suited him fine. Just like his old cassette player. He wouldn't trash it until the last of his tapes broke.

In the length of time it took the computer to bring up background information on Ted Cranston, Gunnar fixed the leak.

CHAPTER FOUR

"SORRY ABOUT YOUR uncle." Dr. Lodge patted Mary's shoulder as he walked past her toward his putter in the corner. "When's the funeral?"

"The medical examiner's office won't release him yet. Apparently it takes longer when someone was murdered ..." She clamped her mouth tight. The word still got to her, still threatened to bring tears to her eyes.

Dr. Lodge turned to give her a sympathetic smile. "I'm surprised you even came to work today. I know you're going through a rough time."

"I'm fine, and I'd rather work. There isn't much I can do anyway." She shuffled the papers in her hand, landing on the month's itinerary. "We meet with some of our key contributors at the offices of Strickland Dunn Friday."

Lodge gripped his putter and hunched over a golf ball on the burgundy short-shag carpet. He lined up his shot to a white plastic cup eight feet away at the end of a synthetic practice green. With his knees slightly bent, he wiggled his ample rear end and stole a glance at Mary. "How do I look?"

"Like a pro." More like a hefty walrus, just as he always looked when he practiced his putt.

He tapped the ball, and it rolled across the practice green, rimmed the hole, and landed with a rebounding clatter inside the cup. "This putter makes all the difference. I may break seventy this spring." He propped his club back in its corner. "Strickland Dunn is the firm working on *Carson v. Borden School Board*, isn't it? Why are we meeting with them?"

"It was Howard's idea. He figured if the attorneys spoke with our contributors face to face and explained how the defendant school board could actually lose this case, they'd be more generous. The ACLU thought it was a good idea, too."

"Winning a creationism case is a given. Howard is a brilliant man, but the law is clear on this."

"The lead attorney for the defense told him the suit could go either way. In the prior cases, instructors in public schools were teaching religion. But Carson was relying heavily on Paluxy Man as scientific proof, so his claim that he wasn't teaching religion may sway a jury."

"Yes, but we have an ace in the hole, something the attorneys don't even know." He ambled over to his desk and sank into the chair. "Paluxy Man will be discredited long before the case goes to trial."

"What do you mean?"

"I didn't want to be the one to tell you this, but you're going to find out soon enough, and it probably should come from me." Clasping his hands on top of the mahogany desk, he gave Mary a look she couldn't interpret—half-sympathetic, half-victorious. "A scientist examined the skeleton at the Smithsonian. It seems that Paluxy Man wasn't a man at all, but a monkey."

"I heard about that. It's ludicrous." She waved her hand in dismissal. "He's probably just a jealous attention hound who wants to discredit my uncle. What proof does he have?"

"Scientific proof." Lodge leaned back in his chair. "Wayne's photographs and measurements don't match the actual fossil."

She frowned. "How could the pictures not match the fossil?"

"Photoshop, maybe?" He shrugged. "The scientist wrote an article. You can read it yourself in this week's *Proceedings*."

Her stomach twisted. She had been assuming Uncle Wayne's calculations were incorrect–they would've had to be for him to conclude dinosaurs and man coexisted–but the idea he'd falsify evidence never crossed her mind. He was simply incapable of such deceit. An article in the National Academy of Sciences' official publication would carry serious weight. It would destroy Uncle Wayne's credibility. She couldn't allow it. "My uncle didn't fake anything–he wouldn't! You can't let them publish that article!"

"I'm as surprised as anyone. A year ago, if somebody had suggested Paluxy Man was a hoax, I never would've believed it, but the facts speak for themselves. The truth will come out in the end. It always does. If the Academy doesn't publish it, somebody else will."

"But what if it's not the truth? What if he is being set up?" Mary rattled off the contents of her uncle's voice mail.

"So you think he was framed?"

"Yes. And it's obvious from the voice mail he knew he was in danger."

"Everybody loved Wayne. Why would someone want him dead?"

"I don't know, but I'm going to find out. I've hired Gunnar Schofield—"

"You hired Schofield?" His belly jiggled with his laughter. "He has that cheesy commercial that runs between get-rich-quick schemes and miracle weight loss pills."

Her cheeks burned. "I checked him out. He has fifteen years of experience. He wouldn't have been around that long if he didn't know what he was doing."

"Oh, I'm sure he's caught hundreds of cheating husbands. Found countless missing cats. But do you really think he's the right person to speak with scientists about paleontology?"

"He's not going to speak about paleontology, he's investigating a murder. He leaves for the dig site in Texas—" she glanced at her watch— "in less than an hour."

"If I were you, I'd go with him. See what you can find out about what they really discovered out there. Take some time off and fly to Texas. Trust me, the Academy won't shut down if you're gone for a few days."

"What about the article?"

Dr. Lodge rubbed his chin and stared into space for a moment. "You'll have until the end of business Thursday to convince me that Paluxy Man was human. If you don't, the article runs Friday morning."

"But this is Tuesday! You're only giving me two days!"

He shrugged. "Guess you'd better get moving then."

*

Within ten minutes of talking to Dr. Lodge, Mary slid behind the wheel of her Beamer and sped from National Academy of Sciences' parking lot. She whipped out her cell phone and dialed the Schofield Detective Agency. It was already eight forty-five, and Gunnar had said he'd be leaving at nine. Even if every street light turned green and every senior citizen stayed home, she couldn't possibly make it there in time.

After four rings, the call clicked over to the answering machine. "You have reached the Schofield Detective Agency. The office is closed ..."

"No, no, no! Cathy, are you there? Pick up!"

No response. When the machine beeped, Mary disconnected and kicked up her speed.

Twenty minutes later, she slammed to a stop outside the agency and double-parked in the street, flashing her hazards. She marched through the doorway. "Where's Gunnar?"

Cathy looked up from her work. "Good morning to you, too."

"I'm sorry—yes, good morning. I need to speak with him. Is he here?"

"You just missed him. He left a few minutes ago."

"Can I have his cell number?"

"He doesn't have one." Cathy lifted a brow over her white cat's-eye glasses and smiled wryly. "Mr. Schofield doesn't *do* cell phones."

"You're kidding, right? This is the twenty-first century!"

Cathy shrugged, but the look in her eyes told Mary she'd argued the point with him before—and lost.

Mary crossed her arms and tapped her foot on the worn industrial carpet. "I really needed to speak with him before he left."

"If you hurry, you can catch him in the garage down the street."

She'd passed that garage two blocks away, across from a sketchy-looking hotel that probably charged by the hour. "Thanks."

"You'll find him on Level 4A with Sheila, if they haven't left yet."

"Sheila?"

"He never goes on a case without her."

Mary flew out the door and down the sidewalk, running through the brisk spring breeze. When she reached the parking garage sign, she rounded the corner and raced up the incline.

She was less than five feet from the gate when an engine's squall ripped inside the structure. The gate arm shot up and a black motorcycle blasted out, barreling down the ramp. An instant from impact, Mary dove to her right, smacking her arm against the wall. She held it as she slid down to the concrete.

Tires squealed on the pavement, and the bike stopped cold. A man in Wranglers and a black leather bomber jacket vaulted from the seat and ran to her, yanking off his helmet as he came.

Gunnar.

"Are you okay?"

"You nearly killed me!"

"You were running up an exit! Didn't you see the sign?" He threw his hands in the air. "What are you even doing here?"

"I needed to talk with you. I would have called you, but guess what? *Mr. Schofield doesn't do cell phones!*"

"That's right. I don't." He reached for her hand and pulled her up. "What do you want to talk about?"

"I'm coming with you."

"No you're not. I work alone."

"So you said." She glared at him. "But I guess you forgot to mention Sheila."

He gave her a puzzled look.

"Cathy told me all about her."

"Oh, really?" A grin stretched between his cheeks. "What exactly did she tell you?"

"She said you two work together on every case."

Gunnar walked over to his bike and smacked the seat. "This is Sheila—a 1984 Harley Davidson Softail."

"Oh, that's perfect." Mary strode toward him. "Have you ever heard of a little thing called truth in advertising, Mr. Schofield?"

"Yep. Why?"

"You should deliver what you show in your commercials. I was under the impression I was hiring a professional."

"I am a professional."

She jabbed her finger toward the bike. "A motorcycle made in 1984? I wasn't even born in 1984!"

"Yeah. You're a regular spring chicken. What's your point?"

"A professional would use dependable transportation." She tilted up her nose. "He wouldn't put his faith in something that's old and unreliable."

Gunnar strode toward her, tension crackling with every step. "Let me tell you something, sweetheart. Sheila's a Harley. Harleys don't get old, they become classics. When you were playing hopscotch and collecting Hello Kitty, Sheila and I were solving cases."

"Oh good grief, you're not that much older than me. And you could certainly get more reliable transportation."

"Sheila's reliable," he growled.

"So you're planning to drive that … thing all the way to Texas?"

"Sure, what else would I do?"

"Fly!" Mary shot a hand in the air to punctuate her point. "Like any normal person with a long distance to go in a short amount of time!"

"I'll make it in plenty of time on Sheila."

"Yeah, if you ride all night. It's a twenty-two hour drive!"

"Right. I'll be there about this time tomorrow. Plenty of time, just as I said."

She smirked. "If it doesn't decide to break down along the way."

"We've been all across the country, and she's never let me down." He returned to the bike and straddled it. He settled the helmet on his head, then lifted the visor. "You want to come down to Paluxy, suit yourself. I won't insult Sheila by offering you a ride. I'll be waiting at the McIntyre Ranch tomorrow morning at nine o'clock. Don't be late."

He started the bike, throttled the engine, and roared down the street.

Mary set her jaw and watched the middle-aged biker take a curve. What had she done?

*

Wearing a filtered mask and protective ear muffs to drown out the high pitched wail of his sander, Val squinted through the dust while he sanded a few centimeters off a limestone humerus. Once he was satisfied he'd shaved off as much as he dared, he turned off his orbital sander and waited for its droning whine to fade into silence. He draped the ear muffs around his neck, lifted the bone off the felt pad, and dunked it into a bucket of sterile water. The bone wasn't finished. The head of the humerus was still too large, and at least a centimeter needed to come off the medial epicondyle. But he would go no further with the sander. From this point, the bone required precision detailing. Time for another scan in the XN-17.

He removed the bone from the water and set it aside to dry. As he rose from his stool, his desk phone rang. He pulled his dust mask below his chin and answered.

"Good news," the Chancellor's voice boomed. "I've found her."

"Who?"

"That woman Oakford talked to. Drop what you're doing. We're taking a road trip."

"I can't just leave. I have too much to do. I'm under a deadline!"

"No, you're under the orders of the Headmaster. We both are. You're coming with me."

Val resigned himself to the trip. There was no arguing with the Headmaster—not that he could. He was too low on the totem pole to dare such a confrontation. When the Headmaster issued an order, he expected it fulfilled–and no one yet had defied him.

"Where are we going?"

Val retrieved his orders, then hung up. Thirty minutes. The Chancellor had given him only thirty minutes to straighten his lab, get home, and pack his gear.

No point in straightening the lab.

CHAPTER FIVE

AN ARMADILLO SCURRIED across Mary's lane. She jerked the wheel left and jammed the brakes, squealing them on the blacktop. Her rental car came to a stop in the wrong lane. She panted to catch her breath and pressed a hand against her pounding heart. A quick look over her shoulder assured her of the animal's safety.

She hated Texas.

After spending her post-college years in business suits and heels, working with museum curators, wealthy contributors, and university professors, she'd actually been looking forward to seeing a live scientific expedition. Real paleontologists out in the field, digging fossils from the ground, brushing away the dust, cataloging finds with the sun beating on their backs. The way Uncle Wayne had done. She'd thought it would be fun. But after two hours in the Texas Hill Country, she was ready to go home.

She stepped on the gas and steered back into the right lane. Only five more minutes to the ranch.

Just over the hill, Gunnar leaned against a rusty pipe-rail gate. Not far from him, his motorcycle rested on its kick stand.

Mary pulled over and stopped. As he sauntered toward her rental car, she lowered the passenger window. "Are you sure we're in the right place? The GPS shows the ranch to be a half-mile down the road."

"I'm not going to the ranch." Gunnar jerked his thumb toward the sign hanging next to the gate behind him. CTU Excavation Site. The gate opened to a truck-rut road, which curved behind a stand of cedars. "Of course, you can go on down to the ranch if you'd like."

Mary shot him a scathing look. "Just move so I can park."

He stepped away from the car only to return again once she'd repositioned it and shifted the gear to park. He said, "Those trees are pretty dense, but I could make out a building a couple of hundred yards back. I figure that's where we need to go."

"That's fine. Just give me a second."

She climbed from the car, pocketed her keys and lip balm, and tossed her purse in the trunk next to her overnight bags.

Gunnar smirked. "You've got to be kidding me."

"What's wrong?"

His gaze dropped to her feet. "You're wearing those to a ranch?"

"They're boots." Italian leather boots to be exact, with clunky two inch heels and side zippers. And they looked fabulous on her.

He snorted. "This is going to be fun, I can tell already."

She smirked at him. "You'll probably need the excitement to keep you awake. Have you looked in a mirror?"

"I'm here, aren't I?"

She slammed the trunk shut. "I just hope you're not so tired you can't do your job."

"Don't worry about me. You just worry about keeping your balance on this rocky soil." He worked the latch on the gate, and the gate swung open with a rusty squeal.

Mary started down the path. "See? I'm walking along just fine."

"Yeah, you're Grace Kelly on level ground. Just wait till we hit the hills."

The rugged terrain shouldn't make any difference. These boots were comfortable, snug on her feet, and sturdy enough to handle anything. But she wasn't going to argue foot fashion with this bearded macho-man beside her. There were more important things to discuss.

"When we meet Dr. Cranston, I'll do all the talking."

"Oh, so you know how to interrogate a suspect? What on Earth do you need me for?"

"I'm not here to do your job for you, but before you get him all defensive with murder questions, I need to ask about Paluxy Man."

"Do you want to find the killer or—" Gunnar clamped a hand around her arm and yanked her off the path. "Listen."

His whispered command was harsh. She held her breath and strained to hear what had set off his alarm bells. The river rushed in the distance, and the leaves rustled in the crisp breeze, but nothing sounded dangerous. "What am I listening for?"

He squinted, staring into the lacy curtain of evergreen. "Someone's in the woods."

A rifle shot sang out, echoing against the hills.

Mary's heart hammered in her chest, and a jolt of adrenaline surged through her veins—but her legs wouldn't move.

Gunnar launched his body over hers and pinned her against the rocky ground. His own gun dug into her until he rolled off and pulled it from the shoulder holster beneath his jacket.

"Run!" He shoved her away, then fired into the woods.

She scrambled through the trees and found a gray, weather-beaten building. A padlock secured the door.

Another report rang out, and she scooted behind the building.

Gunnar returned fire, then dashed to her side.

"Who's shooting at us?"

"I can't tell. He must be camouflaged." He flashed her a look as he ejected the clip from his gun. "Did you tell the ranch owner we'd be coming?"

"No, there's no reason for him to know."

"Except he may not want strangers trespassing on his property."

"You think he's the one shooting at us?" That didn't make sense. "Why would he, when he has a whole group of scientists on his property?"

"Point taken. Do you think it's Cranston?"

"He doesn't know we're here."

The nearby rustling of dry leaves and cedar branches yanked Mary's nerves taut.

Gunnar took another clip from his pocket and jammed it in his gun. He whispered, "I'm short of ammo. I can't hold him off long."

"What do we do?"

"We have to go forward. Run as fast as you can. I'll cover you."

She looked down the washed-out road. After ten yards it veered sharply to the left. The trees were too dense to see where it went from there.

A blast from the woods.

"Now! Go!"

She sprinted as gunshots cracked behind her. Her boots weren't made for running. Why hadn't she worn her Nikes? She cut left at the bend, darted down a straight away, and followed the road as it curved to the right–then skidded to a stop a foot from a white-water river. Trees, boulders, and brush blocked the shoreline in both directions. There was nowhere to run. A two-seater kayak bounced with the waves at the water's edge.

Rapid footsteps raced behind her. She whipped around as Gunnar sped through the trees to the shore.

He bee-lined to the kayak and pulled the line securing it to the riverbank. "Get in!"

"I can't swim."

"Then stay in the boat!"

She climbed inside. Gunnar pushed off, hopped aboard, and snatched the paddle.

The kayak shot through the rough rapids. Gunnar worked the paddle but the river seemed to have control, pulling them forward. The light boat bobbed and rocked as the icy water splashed them.

Another crack of the rifle.

Mary jerked her head around. A man in grease paint and military camo emerged from the woods a hundred feet away and spotted them. He raised his rifle.

"He's on the shore! He's going to shoot!"

Gunnar paddled furiously, maneuvering the kayak through the rapids, around rocks and tree branches. The boat dipped and rose, muffling the rifle shot and carrying them farther away from the shooter.

"Did we lose him?" he shouted.

She looked back. They'd rounded a bend in the river and the clearing was no longer visible. "I think so."

Suddenly the kayak caught in a ferocious eddy. Around and around it spun before breaking free and sending them downriver backwards. Mary twisted to see where they were headed.

A massive boulder broke the water's surface only a few yards away.

"Gunnar, look out!" She shifted forward just as the kayak bucked, plunging her headfirst into the rapids.

CHAPTER SIX

VAL LOWERED HIS rifle and glared downriver. He'd missed. The kayak was gone. His kayak.

He turned and shoved his way through the cedars back to the old shed, leaving a stream of vulgarities in his wake. If he'd had time to check his scope before they left, he never would've missed the first shot. He'd just been wasting ammo. Moving targets were difficult in the best of circumstances, and these weren't the best of circumstances.

Sniper 101: Sight in your scope. Any idiot knew that.

He pulled out his cell phone, checked the signal, and called the Chancellor. It rang three times, then a familiar voice said, "Darbyshire."

"She got away."

The Chancellor was silent.

"She's with somebody," Val said, "and he's armed. The guy shot back at me. They made it to the river and took off with the kayak."

"Did they get a good look at you?"

"No."

"Were there any witnesses?"

"Just the three of us. Should I track them on foot?"

"No, leave her be for now."

"Just let her go?" Having her on the loose could jeopardize everything they'd worked for, everything they'd done. "Let me track them. I'll get them both before they reach Cranston."

"No, this may be for the best. We can take care of them later. I want to talk to Cranston after the woman does, find out what she knows."

"All right." Val's jaw tightened. "What do I do now?"

"Get back to the highway. I'll pick you up later and we'll call the Headmaster. See what he wants us to do." The Chancellor grumbled, "He's not likely to be happy."

Val snapped his phone shut and scowled. No, the Headmaster was not likely to be happy. But the Headmaster should've given him more than thirty minutes' notice that his sniper skills had become necessary.

No telling when the Chancellor would arrive to pick him up, and he had no intention of squatting in the cedars to wait—any more than he intended to let that woman and her trained Chihuahua roam around scot-free without at least gathering a bit of intel.

CHAPTER SEVEN

A ROUGH HAND TAPPED Mary's cheek and a baritone voice called her name. "Come on, kiddo. Wake up."

She opened her eyes and squinted toward the source of the voice. Gunnar knelt beside her, soaked and dripping. His jacket was off, exposing the gun-butt snapped into his shoulder holster and his wet t-shirt clinging to his rather impressive muscles. A metal cross dangled from his neck chain.

She blinked and looked around at all the faces staring at her, then met Gunnar's eyes. "Where am I?"

"We're at the McIntyre Ranch, deep in the heart o' Texas. You tipped out of the kayak, and I had to dive in to drag you out."

"Last I remember, someone was shooting at us. Who was it? Who would shoot at us?"

"Don't know yet, but it wasn't Ted Cranston." He nodded toward a broad-shouldered man kneeling at her left. "You'd know better than me who wants you dead. Any ideas?"

"No one, unless …" The thought crossing her mind made her heart jump. "But how would he know we're here?"

"Who?"

"Whoever killed Uncle Wayne. Maybe he's after me, too." She swallowed. The possibility was too real, and it drove home the point Gunnar had tried to make–this would be a dangerous mission.

"Then we'll just have to get him first, won't we?"

Dr. Cranston offered her a hand up. "I was sure sorry to hear about Wayne. He was a good man."

"Yes, he was." She felt a little weak and water-logged after being tumbled in the rapids like a load of dirty laundry, but with the help of Dr. Cranston and Gunnar, she managed to stand on wobbly legs.

A young, college-age redhead approached and looked her over. "We need to get you into some dry clothes. You're about my size. Let me see what I can come up with."

"Bring them to the mess, Holly." Dr. Cranston turned Mary toward a tent in the center of camp and supported her as they walked toward it. Over a dozen smaller tents surrounded the main one on a level rise protected from the north wind by a cedar forest and situated just yards from the river.

A crowd of fifteen kids—college students probably—parted to allow them through.

Someone from the group clapped his hands for attention. "Okay, everybody, show's over. Let's get back to work."

Dr. Cranston held open the tent flap and, with a hand on her back, guided Mary through. "I'll heat some soup guaranteed to warm you up."

Inside the cavernous main tent, Dr. Cranston led Mary to a bench at a molded-plastic picnic table. Backpacks, boxes, and expensive Yeti chest coolers lined the sides near the tent flap. At one end was a camp kitchen complete with a Coleman stove; at the other end, a tan canvas partition divided a segment from the main tent.

In a few moments, Holly entered with a change of clothes and a pair of white tennis shoes, and handed them to Mary. "I hope they fit okay."

"I'm sure they'll be perfect." Mary accepted the bundle with a grateful smile. Her wet clothes had given her head-to-toe goosebumps. "Thank you so much. I'll get them back to you as soon as I can."

She went behind the partition into what appeared to be Dr. Cranston's private quarters and laid Holly's clothes on the thin mattress of an aluminum cot.

On the other side of the canvas, Gunnar cleared his throat. "Thanks for your hospitality."

"Not a problem." Dr. Cranston said. "Just glad we were in the right place at the right time."

"Well, it's more than that, Dr. Cranston. We were looking for you. So you heard about Wayne Oakford?"

"Call me Ted." From what Mary could hear, Ted was preparing the soup, rattling pots and bumping around in the camp kitchen. "Yeah, we got the news on the ham radio. Terrible. Just terrible."

Mary yanked off her boots—now ruined—and listened as Gunnar introduced himself and told Ted who she was.

"I'm sorry about your uncle," he called, then addressed Gunnar. "How can I help you?"

A soda top popped. "You worked with him, didn't you?"

"Yes, we worked together. We came out here last year as part of a research team."

"You've been living in a tent a whole year?" Gunnar sounded incredulous.

"Oh, no." Ted chuckled. "This is a different expedition."

"When did this one start?"

"About three weeks ago."

"And you've been here the whole time?"

"Yes. I have." Ted's voice took a cautious edge. "Why do you ask?"

Mary drew her lips tight and dressed faster. Gunnar was supposed to wait until she'd asked her questions before he started in on the man. If Ted clammed up because of him, she'd never get her chance. She pulled on Holly's Central Texas University sweatshirt over jeans that fit a tad too snugly, then wadded her wet clothes into a bundle and left them on the tent floor. Then made a beeline dash through the canvas opening. "This feels so much better. Is that soup? It smells divine. Is it ready?"

"Well, look at you. Holly's clothes seem to fit you just fine." Ted rose from the table and moved to stir the soup.

Mary grabbed the opportunity to skewer Gunnar with her eyes; he shrugged.

Ted tapped the spoon against the pot rim. "The soup's left over from lunch, but it should still be good."

He gathered a couple of spoons and blue tin bowls, then ladled the soup for them. The man was attractive—muscular and tan, evidence he'd spent as much time in the field as in the lab. Only a salting of silver in his thick brown hair hinted at his age, which appeared to be around forty-five. He didn't seem the type to kill anyone or hire an assassin. Still, she needed to discover if he was trying to discredit her uncle.

She sat at the table across from Gunnar. Ted placed the steaming bowls in front of them. The soup seemed more like a basic stew—large chunks of beef, potatoes, and veggies swimming in a thickened stock. For a moment, the robust scent lifted her from her seat and settled her back in Aunt Clarice's kitchen, fifteen years younger and hungry for the savory blend of bay leaf and Worcestershire sauce in the tomato base of her aunt's hearty stew.

This one tasted flat.

Dr. Cranston asked, "Do you want something to drink?"

"I'll have what Gunnar's having."

Ted handed her a Diet Coke from the ice chest and settled on Gunnar's side of the table.

Mary opened the can and offered Ted a sweet smile. "I bet the Smithsonian sent you and Uncle Wayne here last year to examine the man-tracks."

Gunnar passed a glance between the two. "Man-tracks?"

"That's what the creationists call them," Ted answered. He seemed to relax, and his voice took on a professorial tone. "About a hundred million years ago, dinosaurs left footprints in Paluxy's limestone river beds. We can still see the impressions, some clearly dinosaurian, but others appear to be human. Christian fundamentalists claim the tracks are evidence that humans and dinosaurs coexisted, which is preposterous. Many of the human-like imprints were actually made by metatarsal dinosaurs. A substantial number of the tracks did appear to be human footprints, but scientists discovered they had been carved on, treated with chemicals, or otherwise altered in ways that invalidate them as evidence. Of course, the creationists denied having altered the footprints–well, draw your own conclusions. Anyway, yes, the Smithsonian sent us here last summer to examine those prints. But everything changed when one of our researchers stumbled upon the fossilized skeleton that we call Paluxy Man."

Mary opened her mouth to redirect Cranston from his lecture to her questions, but Gunnar jumped in ahead of her. "Wasn't Oakford the leader of the research team?"

"On paper." Ted gestured toward Gunnar's empty bowl. "Want more?"

"Is there enough?"

"Sure." Ted took up the bowl, leaving Gunnar with the spoon, and stepped to the camp stove to ladle more.

Gunnar twiddled his spoon between his fingers. "Did you resent that?"

"Resent what?"

"Oakford leading the research team."

"No, not at all." Ted placed a full bowl in front of Gunnar and raised a questioning brow to Mary.

She glanced at her half-empty bowl. "I'm good for now."

Ted resumed his seat and stretched his long, denim-clad legs to the bench opposite him.

"I'm not sure I buy that," Gunnar said, with his spoon hovering over the stew. "You're the head of the geosciences department at Central Texas University, right? The entire research team is comprised of paleontologists and students from CTU, and you want me to believe you didn't resent an outsider taking over?"

He'd done his homework. This was the first sign Mary had seen that Gunnar truly was a professional–outside of the gun strapped to his shoulder. But what was his angle? Did he still consider the professor a suspect?

Ted's brows dipped. He crossed his arms over his chest. "Naturally, I had assumed I'd be the team leader, but since the Smithsonian was funding us, it was their call—just like with this dig. Last year, Wayne had formal leadership, but in practice we shared all the decision making."

Gunnar swallowed and said, "So, you shared the responsibility, but Wayne got the credit for finding the fossil."

Ted's neck flushed crimson. "I resent what you're implying. Yes, Wayne got the credit for everything, but I wasn't unhappy with the situation. We wouldn't have found anything if the Smithsonian hadn't made it possible. I was grateful for the opportunity to work with Wayne and to be a part of such a significant discovery. And I still am."

Mary studied his face. With his brows drawn and his arms crossed, he looked angry and confused and maybe a bit defensive. But he didn't look guilty. Maybe he didn't have anything to do with killing her uncle, but he had one more hurdle to jump before she could consider him totally innocent.

She lowered her spoon. "Last winter, Uncle Wayne told me you two had a big fight over the publicity he was getting."

Ted swiveled his eyes between her and Gunnar. "Is that what this is all about? Our little disagreement?"

"The way Uncle Wayne described it, it didn't sound like a 'little' disagreement."

"Well, yeah, we fought, but I wouldn't call it a big fight. We argued about the publicity, like you said, but just the publicity. Not about getting credit for the find." Ted dropped his feet from the bench and sat up straighter. "I was unhappy with some comments Wayne made—and to a cable news channel, of all places! He implied right there on camera that a human and a dinosaur may have coexisted." He jabbed a finger on the table to accent each word.

"You said he 'implied' it, not that he said it. Maybe you just misunderstood Uncle Wayne's statement."

"Oh, no. His implications were strong enough for anyone to jump to the wrong conclusions." Ted crossed his forearms on the table and leaned forward. "Those kinds of comments are damaging to science, especially when they come from such a well-known and respected paleontologist. It plays right into the hands of the creationists."

"Did you ask him to stop talking about it?"

"I asked him to be more cautious in his public statements. Look, nobody can deny that we found the human fossil we now call Paluxy Man in the same area as a dinosaur known as Ornithomimus. But it's ridiculous to suggest they coexisted. Dinosaurs became extinct long before humans ever walked the earth. The evidence is overwhelming on that point, and Wayne knew it as well as anybody."

"Wait a minute." Mary pushed her bowl aside. Dr. Lodge had mentioned having proof that the fossil wasn't of a human. "You're saying Paluxy Man was human, right? Not a monkey?"

"Not a monkey. Paluxy Man was definitely a homo sapien."

She frowned. "Before he died, Uncle Wayne said another scientist is claiming the skeleton was that of a monkey. He said this man is accusing him of intentionally misrepresenting it as being human. That wasn't you?"

"Of course not. The length and shape of the bones clearly indicate that it was a homo sapien. I've always maintained that."

"I don't understand." Gunnar leaned forward. "If you both agreed that it was homo sapien and that it was found with a dinosaur, then why the fight? Because he told the public the fossils were found together?"

"Not just that they were found together. He suggested they had lived together–at the same time. Which is preposterous. The Ornithomimus was from the Late Cretaceous period, which ended more than sixty million years ago. But with Wayne's comments about carbon dating, he left everyone with the impression the two coexisted."

"Carbon dating. I should remember that from high school science." Gunnar threw his empty soda can in the trash and waved toward the cooler. "May I?"

"Sure. How about you, Mary?"

"Please."

Ted gathered the empty bowls and deposited them in a pail of water. "Carbon dating is one of those things you forget if you don't have to use it." He retrieved a Coke for Mary and set it before her. "It's a way of measuring the amount of Carbon 14 in an object to determine its age. Carbon 14 is an unstable element and it breaks down over time. Every 5,730 years, the amount drops in half. That's called a half-life. The amount of Carbon 14 keeps getting cut in half, smaller and smaller until eventually there's nothing left. That's why you can't use carbon dating on something that's more than sixty thousand years old. At that point, there's virtually no Carbon 14 left to measure." Ted shifted his gaze back to Mary. "And that's where Wayne and I parted ways. We both wanted to carbon-date Paluxy Man, but Wayne wanted to test the dinosaur as well–which he did over my objection. And the test results indicated that both Paluxy Man and the dinosaur were six thousand years old."

Mary's jaw slackened. "A six thousand-year-old dinosaur?"

"Absurd, isn't it?" Ted said. "But it's a case of 'garbage in, garbage out.' When you find a homo sapien fossil in Texas, I think it's reasonable to use carbon dating to determine its age. But it's highly inappropriate to use the technique on a dinosaur fossil. The test results are unreliable when the object is millions of years old."

"Just a second, let me get this straight." Gunnar scratched his head. "You're saying Carbon 14 breaks down over time, and after about sixty thousand years it's almost completely gone?"

"That's right."

"So after millions of years, it's gone entirely."

"Of course."

"And if a dinosaur bone is millions of years old, it shouldn't have any Carbon 14 left in it, right?"

"Right."

"So how could the one Oakford tested have enough Carbon 14 to age it at six thousand years old?"

Mary glared at him. Was he trying to insult the man?

Ted hesitated with his response, and he shouldn't need to respond to Gunnar's impudence.

She jumped in. "Putting aside all these details, you and Uncle Wayne agreed the Paluxy Man fossil was of a human?"

"Yes, we did."

"Did anyone on the team think it was a monkey?"

Ted rubbed his chin, considering the question, then said, "There was one person, Eric Merrow. He's a graduate student at CTU. In fact, he was the person who found Paluxy Man. He saw the first bone—a portion of the ulna, if I remember correctly."

Gunnar raised his brows. "How did he feel about somebody else getting the credit for his fossil?"

"He thought he deserved greater recognition, but he's a kid. You know how kids are—full of themselves. In a sense, though, I can't blame him. Still, excavation is a team effort, and Wayne was the team leader. Eric shouldn't have been surprised that Wayne got all the media attention."

"Was he angry at Wayne?" Gunnar asked.

"There was some tension." Ted rolled his empty soda can between his hands. "They had a heated argument last summer—or at least Eric was heated. His voice practically echoed off the hills."

"What was it about?"

"The fossil, I'm sure. I didn't hear the whole discussion and don't know the details, but I'm pretty sure it was about Paluxy Man." Ted straightened in his seat. "Wait—I know where you're going with this, and I'll tell you right now–Eric did not kill Wayne. He's just not the type."

"Who knows what the type is," Gunnar said. "I'd like to speak with him."

"He no longer works for us. After his argument with Wayne, he got called away. Some family problem. But instead of taking a leave of absence he quit the team and moved back to his grandfather's house in Tennessee. I think he's working on his thesis there."

Mary clamped her lips together. Was Eric's decision not to return based on his fight with Uncle Wayne? Had he been that angry to leave a major dig and not come back? They needed to find him.

"Where in Tennessee?"

CHAPTER EIGHT

MID-AFTERNOON SUN BRIGHTENED the leaves of the scrub oaks and cedars. Mary followed a silent Gunnar up the rutted road back to their vehicles. He seemed to be mulling something over, unaware of her treading along behind him.

She wasn't too interested in talking either. Her boots were ruined beyond salvation, but she carried them, along with her bundle of damp clothes. If not for Holly, she'd be doubly miserable now. She'd obtained Holly's contact information so she could return the borrowed clothes, the pockets of which now carried the items that hadn't disappeared in the river—a tube of lip balm and the key to the rental car. At least she still had those. Something had gone right.

That Ted had agreed Paluxy Man was human served as a big plus, along with the fact that he couldn't have killed her uncle. But this left her with two unrelated questions juggling for attention: Who did kill Uncle Wayne, and why Gunnar was so confrontational with Ted. Once he became convinced Ted wasn't a killer, Gunnar had listened to him with a disbelieving smirk on his face. Infuriating!

She picked up her pace to walk beside him. "You were sure argumentative with Ted."

"Don't like the way I do my job?"

"You were arguing about fossils and carbon dating. That has nothing to do with the murder." She glowered at him. "I have until close of business Thursday—tomorrow!—to convince the president of the Academy that Paluxy Man was human. I'm going to need Ted's help, and you almost alienated him. I don't care if you are a creationist, keep your beliefs to yourself."

Gunnar squinted at her. "What gave you the idea I'm a creationist?"

"Aren't you?"

He shrugged. "I don't have an opinion one way or the other. Never thought about it. I'm an agnostic."

"Then why do you wear a cross?"

His hand went to the heavy metal now hidden beneath his t-shirt. "It was a gift from my wife, Becky. She, uh … she passed away a couple of years ago."

"Oh, I'm sorry. I didn't know."

They followed the path without speaking. Small animals rustled in the undergrowth, scurrying away from the danger of humans. A breeze swayed the cedars, bringing with it the faint sound of the river rapids behind them.

Gunnar had been married before. The discovery shouldn't have come as a surprise. He was certainly the age when most men had a wife and children. She'd just assumed … nothing. She'd assumed nothing of his private life. And she shouldn't. This was a professional relationship, which would end as soon as their case was over. His life beyond this case held no relevance.

Still, how awful it must've been for him to have lost his wife. Doubly awful if they'd had children.

She was about to ask him when he pointed up the road. "There's your car."

"Oh, good." After the day they'd had, she was ready to sit on something padded and rest her feet and legs, even if the car's leather seat wasn't really that comfortable.

She headed for the rental, but Gunnar held her back, gesturing for her to stay in the shadows. He crouched in the shade of a cedar, looked up and down the road, and studied the bushes on the opposite side from them. After a few moments, he approached her car and examined it—even squirming over the gravel to inspect the underside.

After he checked out his Harley, he waved her over. "It's safe."

"Do you think the shooter is still around?"

"No idea, but I don't want to find out the hard way."

Mary pulled out her key to pop open the trunk. She tossed the wet clothes inside beside her bags and grabbed her purse.

Gunnar pulled a map out of the bike's saddlebag and studied it for a moment. "It's ten hours from Dallas to Nashville, but it's a straight shot on I-30. We can be there by one in the morning."

Mary winced. "Can't we fly? It would save so much time."

He shook his head. "I'm riding Sheila."

"Leave it at the airport. You can pick it up later."

"I'm not leaving her anywhere. If you want to get there earlier and confront Eric alone, then do what you gotta do."

"Fine." His uncompromising attitude irked her, but after being used for target practice at the river, she wasn't about to enter another potentially dangerous situation without him. "We'll need a place to stay tonight." She climbed into the car and turned the key to gear up the GPS.

"What are you doing?"

"Looking for a hotel in Nashville."

Gunnar stuck is hand out. "Got your phone with you?"

Mary reached in her purse and pulled it out, holding it an inch from his grasp. "When are you going to get your own?"

"When they finally perfect it and stop upgrading every year. Which means, probably never."

*

Mary shot him what she must've thought was a withering glare, but Gunnar didn't wither easily. As she turned to her car's electronic gadgets, he poked in his office number. "Cathy? Glad I caught you. I need you to do something for me right quick."

"'Quick' like right this minute, or 'quick' like have it done by morning?"

"By morning is good. We're looking for a guy named Eric Merrow, and all we know is that he's in Tennessee—somewhere in the Nashville area—and lives with his grandfather, Jim. Can you get me an address for him?"

"Sure, no problem."

"Great, I'll call you in the morning. Anything else going on today?"

"Just the usual mail and bills …"

Her voice tapered off, and when she didn't continue, he prodded her. "What else?"

"You're being sued."

He snorted. "Won't be the first time."

"No, this one's different," she said, her voice strained. "It's a wrongful death suit, Gunnar. Becky's dad is suing you."

The earth stopped revolving; Gunnar's mind went numb, but he shook his head sharply and brought back the ability to think. Daniel Henderson thought he was responsible for Becky's death? Well, welcome to the club. He'd thought the same thing ever since it happened.

"Gunnar?"

"Yeah, I'm here." He ran a hand through his hair. "Call my lawyer in the morning. When I get to Tennessee, I'll leave the motel's fax number for you. Send the petition to me. I want to see what it says."

She agreed, and they disconnected. Gunnar held the phone to his chin and waited for the ache in his heart to subside. While Becky was alive, Dan Henderson had been like a father to him. But when he lost her, he lost his surrogate father too. And both left a deep void.

"Everything all right?" Mary asked.

"Yeah. We need to get rolling." He handed her phone back, then jammed his helmet on. "Where are we staying tonight?"

"I found a Hilton." She handed him a slip of paper with the address.

"Fancy place. Glad you're paying expenses." He straddled Sheila and cranked her engine, drowning his thoughts in the roar of her power. Before releasing all that strength, he shouted, "See you in the morning."

CHAPTER NINE

VAL WATCHED THE road through the trees at his designated pick-up point. His ears perked at the sound of a vehicle in the distance. Soon, it slowed to a crawl on the graveled shoulder. As it neared, he could see the Florida plates on the white utility truck the Chancellor had rented in DC. Val remained in the shadows until the Chancellor reached the property line and pulled over not far from where Mary's car had been parked.

That drew Val's mind to mistake number two—and he wouldn't take the blame for this one as he had earlier for missing his shots. If someone had clued him in about the target and the mission, he could've brought explosives and blown her up in the car. He could have at least cut the brake line. Had he known the car was hers, he would have.

It all went back to planning. A mission couldn't be planned in the short amount of time he'd been allowed. Intel had to be gathered and analyzed. Plans had to be prepared and examined for flaws. These alone were basic for a successful mission.

But when the mission was designed by civilians, failure could be expected.

The Chancellor gave a quick double-tap on the horn, and Val jogged toward him with his rifle dangling from his shoulder by its neoprene sling. He stepped through the fence, paused to check the road for on-coming vehicles, then trotted to the back of the van. He opened the cargo door to rest his gun in its case, then climbed into the passenger seat.

After a quick glance in the rearview mirror, the Chancellor eased back onto the road. "Sorry I had to keep you waiting. Took forever for Wayne's niece and that detective to clear out before I could meet with Cranston. Have to hand it to Schofield. He's thorough."

Val had watched the camp from the shadows while Schofield and Dillard were there, but he wasn't about to admit he'd tracked them against the Chancellor's orders.

He scowled. He'd been taken by surprise when Schofield returned fire that morning; he would not allow that to happen again. Sizing up his target would give him an advantage in the long run.

The Chancellor chuckled. "According to Cranston, all they talked about was Paluxy Man. Schofield even had the nerve to argue about carbon dating."

"They didn't ask about Oakford's death? That is what they were here for, isn't is?"

"Oh, they asked, but apparently they were quickly satisfied Cranston didn't have anything to do with it."

Of course. One would think it a no-brainer that a scientist in Texas wouldn't have killed someone in Virginia—or even have the necessary connections to hire an assassin. But as long as the dimwitted PI chased the improbable, Val was safe. He was probably safe anyway.

But another thought cluttered his mind. "Did you ask about the skull?"

"No. Why would I?"

"Just based on what Wayne said before—"

The Chancellor's jaw twitched. "There is no skull. I thought we settled that." He slowed at a vacant four-way stop, then turned onto the state highway. "Mary apparently didn't ask about the skull either, or Cranston would've told me. That means there is no skull to ask about."

Val gritted his teeth. Her not asking could also mean she knew about it and had no reason to ask.

The Chancellor glanced at him. "Ted figures they're going to Tennessee to see Eric Merrow next."

"I guess that means we're going to Tennessee."

"Not we. You. I'm catching a flight out of DFW and heading home. You're to continue on in the van." He pulled a slip of paper from his shirt pocket and handed it to Val. "Here's the address. They're looking for a grad student named Eric Merrow. Don't fail this time."

Val fisted his hands, then flexed and fisted again. Taking military orders from civilians grated the core of his soul as a Marine. But he was called to duty—not for the Chancellor or anyone else in the society.

For science.

CHAPTER TEN

"HOW WAS YOUR meeting with Ted?" Dr. Lodge's gruff voice on her cell wasn't what Mary wanted to hear first thing in the morning. "Is he the cold-blooded murderer you imagined him to be?"

She rolled over and blinked the clock into focus. Eight twenty. She needed to be up anyway. "No, I don't think he was involved. And he was working with his research team the last few weeks, so he has an alibi."

"What about Wayne's photographs of Paluxy Man? Did he shed any light on why they don't match the fossil?"

"Not directly, but he was there when the first bones were taken from the ground. He examined the skeleton himself, so he's an eye witness in Uncle Wayne's favor. I don't know why the photographs are wrong, but there's no doubt in Ted's mind that Paluxy Man was human."

"He said that?"

"Yes." She untangled her legs from the sheets and swung them over the side of the bed. "He said he'd always maintained that the fossil was of a homo sapien."

"That's a disappointment." Dr. Lodge's voice sounded deeper, strained. "I'd always had a lot of respect for him. I would hate to believe he and Wayne were involved in this together."

Mary bolted upright. Her grip on the phone tightened as she paced beside the bed. "Wait a minute! You think because he supports Wayne, he must be lying too? They both must be lying? That's quite a leap, Dr.

Lodge. A number of people saw Paluxy Man when it was taken from the ground, and except for one guy, they all thought it was human."

"Have you talked to the dissenter?"

She paused by the window and thrust her free hand through her hair. Sheila stood diagonally in a parking space below. "Gunnar and I are meeting with him today. His name is Eric Merrow. Do you know him?"

"I know of him," Dr. Lodge said. She could almost hear him smile. "And I think you'll find what I know to be very interesting."

*

At a corner table in the Hilton's dining room, Gunnar nursed his second cup of coffee. Too expensive, but it served its purpose—which was to slap him awake after a ten-hour ride and a four-hour sleep. Less than four hours, if he excluded time tossing and turning over the lawsuit Becky's dad had hit him with. The faxed copy lay on the table before him, twice-read through bleary eyes. Part of him understood what Dan was doing, the other part—the bigger part—knew Dan didn't have a leg to stand on. And since man is made of many parts, another part of him wanted to plead guilty to all charges, because that's how he felt. Guilty.

Mary rolled her suitcase to the table. She plopped her purse in the chair next to him and herself in the one across from him. "You look rough. What time did you get in?"

"Around one." He snatched the fax off the table, folded it in thirds, and shoved it in his jacket's inner pocket. "Great room. Thanks."

She quirked a brow at him. "You going to be okay to work?"

"Yeah, why wouldn't I be?"

"Like I said, you look rough." She waved the waiter over and asked for an espresso.

Gunnar rubbed his eyes. Mary was right. The man in the mirror this morning had looked rough. For once, looks weren't deceiving.

When the waiter stepped away, he tried to infuse a little more life into his countenance. Debatable whether he'd succeeded, but his voice didn't seem quite so dull when he announced, "We need to ride together today. I'll leave Sheila here."

"Really? Here?" A quart of sarcasm dripped from those two words.

"Hey, it's supposed to downpour all day, and I don't want to ride in the rain. With that article running tomorrow morning, I doubt you want to wait until the weather clears."

"If you had left Sheila at the airport so we could fly, we could've had our job done by now and got out before the rain hit."

"I told you, I didn't want to leave her at the airport. Besides, then I'd have to fly back to Texas to get her and ride home in the rain anyway. At least here, there's a car we can use."

"Logistics aside, I'm still amazed you're willing to leave her at the hotel." She tilted her head and regarded him a moment. "I'm beginning to think this isn't about Sheila at all. You're afraid to fly, aren't you?"

"Don't be ridiculous." He downed his coffee, cold and bitter now. "If we're going to do this, we'd better get cracking. Give me the keys. I'll drive."

"You're not on the contract as an alternative driver."

"Who cares? Who'll know?"

"I'll know."

The waiter brought her coffee. She smiled at him and gave an apologetic shrug. "Looks like I'll have to take this to go. Will you bring me a cup please?"

Once he stepped away, she added sugar to the brew. "Where are we going?"

He rattled off the address Cathy had sent him earlier that morning along with the other fax. Mary plugged the address into the GPS app on her phone.

The waiter returned with a waxed paper cup and a plastic lid, then poured her sweetened coffee into it. She thanked him as Gunnar reached for his wallet to pay the tab and leave a tip.

Mary stood, pulled out the keys from her purse, then slung the bag over her shoulder and grasped the handle on her rolling suitcase.

Muted thunder followed a crack of lightning visible from the lobby windows.

Mary smirked as she grabbed her coffee cup. "You can ride with me, or you can take Sheila in the rain. You driving the rental isn't an option."

Only the thought that she was paying him double—and that he didn't want to ride in what promised to be a deluge—made him keep a civil tongue in his head. He stood and waved a hand toward the exit. "Lead on."

*

As they drove east, out of the city limits, Mary said, "Dr. Lodge called this morning. He said the article coming out in tomorrow's edition of the *Proceedings* was written by this Eric Merrow."

"Have you ever heard of the guy before?"

"No, Uncle Wayne never mentioned him."

"Professional jealousy is as good a reason for murder as any." He wriggled in his seat and tried to stretch his legs in the small BMW hybrid, then scowled as he felt along the side of the seat. "Merrow may be just the guy we're looking for."

"Yeah, but why would he kill him, then turn around and smear his name in a journal?" She'd been trying to figure that one out since Lodge's call. "I mean, wouldn't that throw suspicion on him right off?"

"People do crazy things. Never know what to expect out of someone who's crazy enough to kill." He found the switch and pushed the seat back as far as it would go.

"I didn't get the impression from Cranston that he was crazy, much less a killer."

"Won't know until we've talked to him."

"That's true." Mary sighed. "Hey, would you hand me the green bag from the back?"

He reached behind her seat and pulled the bag to his lap. "What's this?"

"A little snack for the road. Organic apples. I picked them up on the way to the hotel last night." She twisted her head to grin at him. "Something you have time to do when you fly instead of drive."

"You're real funny, you know that?" He pulled one out, rubbed it on his pants, then took a bite. A light smattering of juice landed on his lip and chin. "You know, they've done studies, and organic, locally-grown food isn't any better for you than the regular kind." He held up his apple. "It just costs twice as much."

"It is healthier, Gunnar. In fact, they were talking about it on the radio yesterday."

"You shouldn't believe everything you hear on talk radio."

"I'm not referring to talk radio." Mary dug an apple from the bag. "I was listening to This American Life on NPR."

"That's talk radio," he said. "It's the other side of the same coin."

Mary rolled her eyes. "Not quite."

She turned onto a rough, pot-holed road leading to several houses spaced acres apart in the mountains. The spring shower pelted the windshield, and the wipers missed a wide swath with every pass, making it difficult to see. She slowed at the driveway to each house and squinted at the names and addresses on the mailboxes.

Gunnar pointed at a neglected, wood-frame shanty. "That's it."

She pulled over to the side of the road. The yard around the house was cluttered with rusted metal—old Coke machines, motorcycles, car parts. At the end of the driveway was a weathered homemade sign in faded red paint: PRIVATE PROPERTY. TRESPASSERS WILL BE SHOT DEAD.

Mary nodded toward it. "See that?"

"We're not trespassers. Trespassers are police, Jehovah's Witnesses, feds." Gunnar slammed the car door, tossed aside his apple core, and started up the driveway.

After a moment's hesitation, Mary pocketed the keys and joined him in the rain, keeping his body between her and the house.

The screen door popped open, and a tall, elderly man stepped outside. He level a double-barreled shotgun at Gunnar's middle. "Can't read?"

Gunnar raised his arms as if under arrest and flashed a smile. "Don't you remember entering the Publishers' Clearinghouse Sweepstakes?"

The old man cocked both barrels.

CHAPTER ELEVEN

MARY STEPPED FORWARD before Gunnar's sorry attempt at humor got them both killed. She swiped strands of wet hair from her face and peered up at the grizzled homeowner. "We're sorry to disturb you. This is Gunnar. I'm Mary. I work for the National Academy of Sciences. That's in DC. Well, you probably know that." Her words rattled out of her mouth with a machine-gun staccato, but she couldn't control them any more than she could control her knocking knees. "I need to speak with Eric Merrow. It's really important. Does he live here?"

"What do you want with him?"

"Just to ask about a fossil, that's all." She raised her hands in appeasement. The man hadn't lowered his gun, and with Gunnar glaring like a madman, she'd do anything to diffuse the tension.

Her stomach twisted and threatened to toss up what little of the apple she'd eaten on a river of the coffee she'd managed to down. She swallowed the nausea away. "He found a fossil last year, and I really need to ask him some questions about it."

"You mean Paluxy Man?"

"Yes. It's an incredibly important find—something that could rock the world if not handled properly." She hoped she was getting through to him, but he kept the shotgun up. "I don't mean to cause problems for him, I just need to speak to him."

Finally, he lowered the barrels. "He's not here. He's down in the

Manor Ridge coal mine, looking for fossils. Again. Says there's lots of 'em down there. Not dinosaurs or anything, just plants and bugs. Says they're important. He's writing a paper about 'em."

Gunnar lowered his arms. "How far is the mine from here?"

"Not far." He pointed down the road. "See that shadow down there, past the oak tree? That's the coal mine."

Mary shielded her eyes against the rain and looked where the man pointed.

Gunnar asked, "Open shaft?"

"Called an adit. Mine's horizontal. Abandoned back in the forties. They just left it that way. Never closed it off."

"Goodness, that sounds dangerous." Mary returned her attention to the man on the porch.

He shrugged. "Told Eric to stay away from there when he was young. But you know how boys are, they don't listen. One day he found a fossil in there. It got him interested in science, so maybe it was a good thing."

"Do you know when he's coming out?"

"Pro'bly not till late. He usually comes back 'round nine or ten, but he can be down there till midnight sometimes."

"Oh, no." Mary bit her lip. She had to report to Dr. Lodge by five to stop the article for the *Proceedings*. "Is there any way you can contact him? We don't have that much time."

"Then you'll have to go into the mine. He's not that hard to find. Walk down the main corridor. He should be working at the end, about a quarter mile or so in. Just don't go into the side shafts, and you'll be fine." He quirked a brow and squinted at them. "You got flashlights?"

They shook their heads.

He leaned his gun against the door frame and waved them along with a flip of his hand. "Come on. I got some in the shed. Be wantin' 'em back, though."

As they stepped around the debris, Gunnar asked, "You're Jim, right? Jim Merrow? Eric's your grandson?"

"Yep." He offered a thin, freckled hand. " 'em 'Scuse my manners. I'm not too fond of folks poking around up here."

Jim led them through the backyard to a wooden shed with peeling paint. He pulled a key chain from his pocket, flipped through a dozen or so keys until he found the one he wanted, then opened the door. Tools and equipment lined the walls inside the shed, and an old Murray riding lawnmower sat in the middle of the dirt floor.

Jim reached up to a shelf, pulled down a couple of black Maglites, and flicked each on. Strong beams brightened the back wall well enough to see the cobwebs. "That'll do."

"Yes, sir." Gunnar took them from him. "Thanks."

Jim propped a foot on the running board of the Murray. "Reckon I'd better warn ya, Eric's a bit unconventional 'bout getting his fossils out."

"Unconventional how?" Mary knew of only one way: pick, chisel, and patience.

"He don't got the temp'rament to noodle 'em out." Jim's face split into a wide, gap-toothed grin. "He blasts 'em out with dynamite."

Mary gawked at him. "Isn't that dangerous?"

"Don't seem to be. He's been doin' it since he was a kid, and he's still alive."

"But the destruction! How can he get any good fossil specimens if he's blowing them to bits?"

"No, it ain't nothin' like that. He uses a small blast to loosen up the larger rocks, then whittles out what he wants."

Gunnar asked, "No accidents?"

"None in ten years."

"Let's hope his luck holds," Mary muttered.

As they exited the shed. Gunnar jutted his chin toward the mine. "We just stay straight in the main corridor, right?"

"Straight ahead. Shouldn't be a problem."

*

"Huh. So this is the old Manor Ridge." Gunnar flicked on his flashlight and stepped into the adit. "I've never been inside a mine before."

Mary stood firm outside the entrance, rubbing her shoulders through her wet cotton shirt to ward off the chill emanating from the dark interior.

"What's wrong?" Gunnar asked.

"This whole thing is kinda creepy."

"We're exploring. Isn't that what paleontologists do?"

"I'm not a paleontologist. I have an office job."

"If it were up to me, your uncle would've been a bartender, and we'd be sailing around the Caribbean in search of his lost Piña Colada recipe. But you have to take life as it comes." He swept his arm toward the mine. "Shall we?"

Mary drew a fortifying breath and stepped forward into the mouth of the cave.

He gave her a smug grin and nudged her forward. He started walking. Mary held her shoulders back and marched along with her hand cramped around the flashlight. She tried to exude a confidence she didn't feel.

And Gunnar apparently knew it.

He draped an arm around her shoulders. "All this is your idea, you know. If not for you, I'd be on a beach in Florida."

"Yes. Tan and broke. Not a penny to spend on those sunbathing beauties you wanted to leer at." She smirked. "I'm paying you so well for this, you should be in here alone. I should be somewhere drinking Piña Coladas, waiting for you to bring Eric to me gift-wrapped."

"Yeah, right. I can just see you, Little Miss Prim-and-Proper, with a drink. You probably take teetotaling to a whole new level." Gunnar swung his flashlight down a side passage and lowered his voice to a whisper. "Like I said, it was your idea to come on this little jaunt, remember?" He studied the dark interior of the passage, then swept the beam behind them, shining the light back the way they'd come. His free hand angled for his gun, but he held still and listened.

"What's wrong?" Mary whispered.

"I thought I heard something,"

"There's nothing back there."

After a moment, he relaxed. "Probably just a rat."

She shuddered. Rats. Bats. Spiders. What other horrid creatures populated the dark?

She hated mines.

He turned his flashlight back to the main corridor. Mary matched his pace, staying close enough to bump him periodically as they walked. She didn't know much about guns, but she bet the one Gunnar carried could kill rats.

Deep into the mine, the passageway bent slightly to the right and then continued straight. They kept walking until Gunnar stopped again. "You didn't hear that?"

She tilted her head and listened but couldn't pick up anything over the rushing of her pulse in her ears. "I don't hear anything, and I don't believe you do either. If you're teasing me, cut it out. You're scaring me."

"I'm not teasing." He shined the beam behind them again.

They could see nothing, but at last Mary heard something—footsteps racing away.

"Eric?" Gunnar yelled. "Eric Merrow?"

No response. The sound of the steps faded, then silence closed casket-tight around them.

Gunnar held up a hand and hissed, "Stay here."

"Not on your life!"

He started jogging back the way they'd come, his light flashing wildly over the walls and floor of the cave. She stayed close behind him, her beam meeting and breaking from his in a frantic light show.

A deafening blast drove them back, slamming her into the hard rock wall.

She gave her head a sharp shake. The crashing of stone on stone hammered her ears and jolted her nerves, but in her dazed head, everything seemed surreal.

She stared dumbly up at Gunnar.

He jerked her to her feet. "Run!"

The mine shaft was collapsing with impossible speed. With each running step, she could feel the reverberation of the falling boulders.

Behind them, the old mine rumbled and moaned and crashed, blocking the entrance, filling the air with dust. In front of them loomed the unknown, dark and foreboding. Mary couldn't remember whether they'd stayed in the main tunnel or if they'd taken one of the side paths. Nothing looked familiar. She just kept cranking her legs, following the crazy beam of Gunnar's flashlight and trying to outrun the torrent of rocks behind her.

Ahead of her, the wooden beams shoring up the mine's ceiling cracked and groaned under the weight of the mountain. The stone walls around her began crumbling, slowly at first, grit and pebbles cascading to the cave floor. Mary darted past the area, frantic to escape before the larger rocks came clattering down.

Gunnar turned into the darkness of a side tunnel. "This way!"

Just as the beam above her gave way, Mary charged behind him. She kept running until something hit her and drove her to the ground.

Noise faded from her ears. Images swirled into a senseless vortex. Blackness enveloped her, easing both panic and pain.

*

Val drove the utility van from the mine, often flicking his gaze to the rearview mirror to watch the show. White smoke billowed out of the opening. The rumble of the collapsing cave walls resounded in his ears even with the truck windows up.

It was finished. No one could survive that crash.

With the death of Mary Dillard and her detective, the body count stood at three. Four, probably, if Eric Merrow was in the cave as his grandfather had said.

None of this was necessary. Only Wayne Oakford had needed to die. Oakford never seemed to understand that his actions were threatening more than a military operation or the reputation of a museum. His plans would have dealt a death blow to modern science. They had to stop him before he could do any harm. But the woman's death lay solidly on Oakford's shoulders. He shouldn't have brought her into this, forcing Val to kill her too.

But now with her death, all the loose ends had been tied. Almost.

The photographs needed to be found and burned. He hoped they were in with the files he'd taken from Oakford's house. Once they were destroyed, the only solid evidence of what had been found in Paluxy would be the skeleton replica on exhibit at the Smithsonian, and it supported the theory of evolution.

The replica was the only evidence unless Oakford's words were true, and he'd given his niece the skull.

Val frowned and smacked the steering wheel.

It wouldn't be long before people would start to wonder where Dillard had gone. At some point, the authorities would search her condominium. Her family would go through her belongings. If she had the skull, they would find it, and it wouldn't take long for someone to figure out it belonged to Paluxy Man. When they learned the skeleton on display at the Smithsonian had a skull that didn't match the fossil, people would start asking questions. He couldn't allow that to happen.

Oakford could have been bluffing, as the Chancellor suggested. Val could've read him wrong, misinterpreted his expression in the moments before his death. But, try as he might, he couldn't make himself believe that. Still, he needed to be certain.

If there really was a skull, the original pictures would show it. As soon as he arrived in DC, he would put the mystery to bed once and for all.

CHAPTER TWELVE

EVERY PART OF her screamed in pain. Bones, muscle—
even her skin.

Mary blinked and wondered for a moment where she
was. Only a sliver of light pierced the darkness and illuminated the dust
particles still floating in the air. She groped her immediate surround-
ings. The splintery roughness of a wooden beam seemed to be the only
thing between her head and a pile of rocks that lay in a heap to her left,
no farther away then her scraped elbow. Her head throbbed, and she
gingerly felt the knot forming on her temple. Nothing was broken, but
everything hurt.

A deep groan from the direction of the single weak beam cut the
silence.

Her heart skipped a beat.

"Gunnar?" She crawled toward the flashlight, grabbed it, and shined
it over the rubble. There was no sign of him. "Gunnar?"

What if he lay dying? What if he was terribly injured? What if he
was lying beneath the rubble? What would she do? What could she do?
She knew nothing of first aid. How could she help him?

If something happened to him, what would happen to her?

A moan came from behind her. She whipped around toward the
sound. Gunnar lay face down, sprawled out on the cave's dirty floor.

She scurried to him and propped the light on some rocks over him.
Carefully, she ran her hands over his ribs, his arms, in search of broken

bones—not like she could do anything about it if anything was broken, but she had to know. She was about to check his legs when he moved. "Are you okay?"

"I've been better." Wincing, he pushed himself upright and held his head with both hands.

"Can you stand?"

He shook his head—not as a negative response, but as if to shake off a dizzy spell. After a moment, he tried his legs. He swayed a bit before catching himself with a hand against the mine wall. With his other hand, he pointed toward the collapse. "Shine a light over there, will ya?"

Rocks and boulders had landed just so, well enough to block their escape. The support beams had snapped like wooden matches and lay embedded in the new rock wall. Mary aimed the light to the ceiling; only the two boulders below it held it up. If either were moved, this part of the cave would collapse too. Panic clawed her throat, and she sobbed.

They were locked in—barricaded! There was no way out!

She flashed the light hysterically along the rubble. Surely there was a weakness somewhere, a place to squeeze through. Maybe if they moved the smaller rocks. Maybe she could break through. Maybe …

She scuttled to the wall on her hands and knees and began tossing the stones behind her. She glared at Gunnar. "Why aren't you helping me? We've got to get out of here!"

"No—stop. It's too dangerous."

She screeched at him. "Help me!"

He grabbed her shoulder and yanked her back from the rock wall.

She landed hard on her backside and scrambled up to gawk at him. "What are you doing? Don't you want to get out?"

"Not that way. It's too precarious. If you move the wrong rock, the whole thing could crash in on us." He found his flashlight and shined it around the other walls, finding an open tunnel ahead to their left. "Come this way."

"That's just going to take us deeper."

"Or it may take us out. You never know." He started toward the tunnel.

She brushed herself off, grabbed her own flashlight, and caught up with him. Fear and anger chased each other through her nerves, and at the moment, anger was winning. "You'd think one of us would've had the sense to ask about other entries into this mine."

"Yeah, you'd think." His tone indicated he'd already kicked himself for not having the sense. "Right now, all we can do is explore and see."

"What about oxygen?" Fear had regained its lead. "Do you think we'll use up our oxygen?"

"I'm not going to sit here and wait to die. As long as I can breathe, I'm going to look for a way out." He kept marching; his footfalls echoed off the cave walls.

His determination did little to ease her fear, but she matched pace with him. What else could she do?

As they approached the mouth of the side tunnel, they found yet another tunnel farther ahead.

"We'll try this one, and if it's a dead end, we'll come back and try the other."

Mary nodded and continued to follow, keeping as close as possible. If he was afraid, she couldn't tell. His fear may be well hidden, but he was undoubtedly aware of hers–she'd made no secret of the terror welling up inside of her.

"I'm paying you a lot of money," she said. "I expect you to get us out of here alive."

"Don't worry. If I don't, I'll waive my fee."

Humor. At a time like this, he tried to be funny.

It helped.

"You were right. You should work alone. It's too dangerous."

For a moment there was no sound but their feet hitting the stone floor. Gunnar was probably thinking up some smart remark about having told her so—would've totally killed the mood.

But he surprised her. "Actually, it was nice having you here with me. Like the old days. My wife and I used to work cases together until she had to quit to take care of her dad."

"What was her name again? Becky? What happened to her?"

Again with the silence.

She waited for a few moments, then rested a hand on his arm. "What happened?"

Before he could answer, a dim light appeared from deeper in the tunnel and bounced slightly as it grew in strength.

Gunnar pulled her behind him, but she watched the light from around his shoulder until the beam shone directly into her face. She squinted and lifted her hand to shield her eyes.

A male voice called out. "Who's there?"

Gunnar reached for his gun. "Who's asking?"

"Eric Merrow." He stepped up to them. The beam from Gunnar's flashlight glinted off his glasses. He pushed them up with a finger. Dust and grit powdered his unruly dark hair. Although his body seemed in great shape, a hint of "science geek" clung to his studious face like moss on an oak. The only thing missing was tape wrapped around his black plastic frames. "What happened?"

"That's what I was going to ask." Mary grumbled. "Jim said you've been using dynamite down here."

"I didn't do this. I haven't used dynamite in weeks. And when I do, I use it surgically."

"Do you keep any down here?" Gunnar asked.

"Never."

Mary grabbed Gunnar's arm. "Does that mean someone's trying to kill us? Here? How did they find us?"

"We don't know that it's us they're after—we don't even know if this was deliberate."

"Of course it was! How could it not be?"

Eric stared at them with his mouth agape. "Who are you people?"

"We'll explain later." Gunnar waved him off and flashed his light down the tunnel. "We're going to have to figure a way out of here. No telling how much time we have until the oxygen runs out."

"You don't have to worry about that." Eric pointed toward the side tunnel they'd decided to come back to. "There's an air shaft this way."

The sheer confidence this science nerd exhibited as he strolled through the mine eased the tightness in Mary's chest. He led them through the mine, twisting down one tunnel, then turning to the next, with the familiarity of someone who'd done this all his life. Just as his grandfather had said.

The deeper they went, the air felt cooler, cleaner than the dust-laden atmosphere they'd left behind. Mary sucked it down to her toes.

A circle of light reflected off the floor ahead of them, and darkness gave away to duskiness. They'd reached the air shaft. Thirty feet above them, through a hole roughly four feet in diameter, sunlight winked through leaves in the forest. Gunnar aimed his light along the walls and caught the dull gleam of an ancient metal ladder, its lowest rung just two feet off the ground.

"That ladder is rusty." Mary studied it in the beam of her own Maglite. "You could get tetanus just looking at it."

Gunnar shoved his flashlight in his belt at the small of his back, then placed his hands on a low rung. He pulled hard, but the ladder held in place. "Not bad. Nothing to worry about."

"No telling how long it's been in here." Eric examined the braces fastening the ladder to the mine wall as far up as his flashlight would allow. "You think it'll hold?"

"There's only one way to find out," Gunnar said. "I'm the heaviest. I'll go first."

He tested the bottom rungs, then worked his way up. With every move, the ladder wobbled and creaked under his weight. Halfway up, a rung broke off and fell. Mary jumped back as it clattered to the floor near her feet.

Gunnar looked down. "Make sure you don't step on that one." He resumed climbing. The ladder ended about three feet from the top of the shaft. Keeping a grip on the rail, he stretched from the next to the last rung and tried to grasp the rocky opening. "Can't reach it from here."

Pebbles and dirt rained on floor of the shaft. Mary coughed and waved away the dust. She squinted up at Gunnar. "Come back down. We'll find another way out."

"No, if I can use this one last ..." He took the last step. The handrail didn't advance much farther, and he gave up trying to hold it as he reached for the opening. He balanced precariously on the top rung, then stretched once again toward the world outside. This time, his hands found a grip, and he hauled himself out.

After a moment, he reappeared at the shaft opening. "All right, Mary, you're next."

She stared at the ancient ladder with the gaping hole Gunnar had left between the rungs and the impossible two-foot gap it had left from one rung to the next. She shook her head. "No, I don't think so."

"It'll hold you. C'mon!"

She waved a hand in invitation to Eric. "You go ahead. Really. I insist."

Eric looked up at Gunnar

Gunnar gave him a tight-lipped nod. "Okay. Come on."

He climbed up the ladder without incident, and being taller than Gunnar, easily reached for the mouth of the hole. Gunnar helped him out of the shaft, then poked his head over again, looking down at her. "Okay, let's go."

Mary wrapped her arms around her shoulders. "Can't you two just go and get help?"

"Not on your life. The whole mine is dangerous now. You need to get out."

As if to make his point, the cave moaned—a not-so-distant sound.

Fear knotted her stomach. Chills chased each other down her spine. She shivered. "Okay. I'm coming."

She glanced over the ladder one more time. Two heavy men had made it and only one rung had tumbled. Apparently, the ladder was stronger than it looked. If they could do it, so could she. She began to climb, refusing to look up. Just one step at a time.

With every step, the ladder shuddered under her weight. She held her breath and stretched over the two foot gap Gunnar had left, and made it.

The mine rumbled with the crashing of yet another unstable section. The shaft walls trembled, shaking the ladder Mary clung to.

She slammed her eyelids shut.

"It stopped. It's okay now." Gunnar's voice penetrated her fear. "It's over. Keep climbing."

"No, I don't think so."

"Mary, climb! Before something else crashes again, start climbing!"

She gulped. Her legs weighed fifty pounds each. She wasn't sure she could move them. But she tried anyway.

One hesitant step after another. One rung higher. One rung higher still.

Above her, a bolt loosened with a nerve-racking squeal. Five feet from the top, the left side of the ladder had wrenched free from the mine wall.

Then the right side jerked loose.

The ladder fell backward; the top smacked the opposite side of the shaft and jolted her feet from their rung. She swung backwards and swayed over the hole.

Her screams lodged in her throat. Below her, at least twenty-five feet down in the darkness, was the rock-solid cave floor guaranteed to crumble her bones if she fell. She bicycle-kicked, trying to get her feet back onto the ladder.

"Hold on!" Gunnar stretched halfway into the tunnel and reached for the ladder, coming up short. "Eric, hold my legs."

With the few more inches allowed him, he grabbed the top of the ladder. His muscles bulged as he strained to pull it—and her—back into place.

Mary's feet found a rung, but she didn't dare climb.

"Give me your hand. I'll pull you up."

Terror froze her in place. "No!"

"I can't hold this forever. Grab my hand!"

She whimpered.

"Mary. Look at me."

She couldn't.

"Mary."

Cringing, and glued to the ladder with all the strength God gave her, she ventured a glance upward. The confidence in his eyes assured her, comforted her. She grabbed a deep breath and nodded, then tentatively reached out until she clasped his wrist with her left hand. When she reached with her right, the ladder broke free and clattered down the hole.

She dangled over the hole from Gunnar's sweaty grip.

CHAPTER THIRTEEN

THE LADDER LANDED on the stone floor with a metallic ring, and Mary's terror boiled into another scream. She swayed over the gaping hole, and her legs clamored, trying to find a foothold.

Gunnar grasped her hand with both of his. She clamped her free hand around his wrist.

"Hang on, Mary. Stop kicking!" he shouted. "Eric—pull!"

Slowly the two men hoisted her up toward the shaft opening. Her feet finally found purchase on the mine wall, and she climbed as Gunnar pulled. He latched a hand under her arm, then grabbed her other arm and pulled, dragging her out to the forest floor.

Once she was safe, she fell back onto a carpet of soft damp leaves and gasped for breath in the heavy forest air.

"You okay?"

Both men hovered over her, worry etched in their features. Mary closed her eyes to shut out their faces.

No. She was not okay. She'd been shot at, dumped in the rapids, blasted in a mine, and dangled from a rickety ladder over a thirty-foot death-drop. She was not okay!

"You're not gonna go all girly on me, are ya Dillard?" A sneer laced Gunnar's words. He pitched his voice higher, mocking her. "You gonna cry now? You wanna quit? Oh, boo-hoo!"

She impaled him with a glance. "No, I'm not going to quit, you cretin! And it takes more than this to make me cry." She scrambled to her feet and slapped the dirt and dead leaves off her jeans.

Who did he think he was? She'd like to see him dangle over death like that and see how he took it! He had some nerve. Lord hasten the day he'd done what she hired him for and they could part ways. The insufferable jerk!

She stopped brushing herself off long enough to skewer him again with the daggers in her eyes, but he was grinning at her.

"Nice to have you back, Spunky."

*

Eric pulled a kitchen chair from his grandfather's Formica-topped table and waved his hand, suggesting they do the same. The chairs were '50s-style molded-aluminum with yellow vinyl seats and backs. Mary's seat had been torn and feebly repaired with a gray swath of duct tape.

"Y'all want some sweet tea?" Without waiting for a response, Jim grabbed an earthenware pitcher and poured tea over ice in four tall tumblers.

Gunnar accepted a glass, then turned to Eric. "You're sure you didn't leave any dynamite in the mine?"

"I'm certain. The damp air would ruin it."

"Any idea who would want to blow you up?"

"Me? What makes you think I was the target?" Eric pushed his glasses back up and blinked in rapid succession.

"Not too many people know we're here."

Jim leaned against the countertop. "Maybe that Tom Flanders feller had something to do with it."

Eric twisted to face his grandfather behind him. "Who's he?"

"Some guy. He came by looking for you this morning after these folks left." Jim shifted a finger between Mary and Gunnar. "Tall guy, buzz cut, ex-military type. Tattoo of a square and compass on the back of his neck."

"Square and compass," Gunnar mumbled. "The symbol for the Masons."

"Said he was one of your professors from the university. He wanted to talk with you about Paluxy Man. I told him the same thing I told these two. He'd have to find you in the mine." Jim scowled. "This place is turnin' into a regular Grand Central Station. People showin' up outta the clear blue. Can't get a moment's peace."

"Grampa, I have no idea who you're talking about. I never had a professor named Flanders."

"He didn't look much like a professor, but how was I to know?" The old man peered out the grimy window over the sink. "The guy drove up in a white delivery truck with Florida plates. Should've known right then he weren't from Central Texas University. Why would he have Florida plates?"

Mary rested a hand on Eric's arm. "Maybe whoever killed my uncle is after you now."

"Your uncle?"

"Wayne Oakford."

Gunnar crossed his arms on the table and leaned toward Eric. "We're trying to understand what happened in the weeks before his death. We spoke with Ted Cranston in Texas. He said you didn't get along with Dr. Oakford."

Eric regarded Gunnar with owl eyes. "He said that? That's not true. Sure, we had our disagreements, but we had a good working relationship. I had a lot of respect for him. He was a brilliant scientist."

"That's strange," Mary said. "When we spoke with Ted, he claimed you were angry because Wayne took the credit for discovering Paluxy Man."

He shrugged. "It bothered me that he got the credit. When I brushed the dirt off that humanoid bone, I knew I'd made an important find. Then I got some bad news from my family and had to fly home. By the next week, the entire skeleton had been unearthed and packed for ship-ping, and Dr. Oakford was hailed the hero for finding it."

Gunnar raised a brow. "Bet that chapped your hide."

"A bit, yeah." He flipped his hand and rejected the idea. "But that's the way the system works. The leader of the field team receives the lion's share of the credit. He was the leader. He didn't do anything inappropriate."

Mary shook her head. "I don't understand. If you weren't angry, why write an article for the *Proceedings* claiming Paluxy Man is a fraud?"

"I didn't say Paluxy Man is a fraud. Nothing of the sort."

"Well, maybe 'fraud' is the wrong word," she said. "But doesn't your article say that Paluxy Man was just a monkey?"

"'Just a monkey'?" Eric's voice pitched higher. "Until Paluxy Man, scientists believed monkeys didn't arrive in the Americas until forty million years ago, and even then, they were isolated in South America. But we discovered a large New World monkey that lived in Texas millions of years before." He darted a glance from Mary to Gunnar and back. "Don't you understand the significance of this? It changes our entire understanding of primate evolution!"

Eric's grandfather threw his hands up. "Now you're getting over my head." He settled a measured gaze on Gunnar. "You convinced my grandson didn't kill anyone?"

"Yeah, I'm convinced. But I'm just as convinced he may be in danger."

"Why? Because of all this fossil mess?"

Gunnar nodded. "I haven't unraveled how big this 'fossil mess' is, but someone tried to kill us in Texas and Eric here. So it must be a pretty big mess."

"How do you know they weren't after you instead of me?" Eric asked.

"I don't, but like I said, no one knows we're here but Ted Cranston, and he's still in Texas." Gunnar gave him a direct stare. "Whoever blasted that mine may not be after you, but you need to be careful just in case."

"I'll see to it that he is." Jim pushed away from the counter, grabbed his shotgun from the corner, and headed for the door. "I'll be in the shed. There's more tea. Help yourself." The screen squealed as it slammed behind him.

"He's a bit protective. Thinks I don't have the sense of a turnip sometimes." Eric's lips curved into a self-deprecating grin. "I guess when I'm engrossed in my work, I don't."

"We need to talk about that article you wrote." Mary persisted. "What you're calling a monkey, Uncle Wayne called human. He is— was—a world-renowned scientist! Don't you think a man of his stature would know the difference between a man and a monkey? How can you possibly believe he'd make such a mistake?"

"He made a number of errors when he declared Paluxy Man to be homo sapien. Like the way he dated the fossil. By my calculations, Paluxy Man is at least a hundred million years old."

Gunnar nearly choked on his tea. He coughed and wiped the back of his hand across his lips. "A hundred million? Cranston agreed with Oakford that the fossil was only six thousand years old, and Cranston is the head of paleontology at CTU. You're saying two major scientists are wrong?"

"I don't see how either scientist can say it was only six thousand years old. The presence of the dinosaur found with it is enough to con- clude that Paluxy Man wasn't human. But it's not just the dinosaur." He pushed his glasses up again. "Look, we have a tool called biostratigraphy— we map out the earth's strata and determine age based on how close the object is to the earth's core. Paluxy Man was found in the stratum known as 'Lower Cretaceous.' That layer of soil dates between a hundred and a hundred fifty million years ago. And that means Paluxy Man is at least one hundred million years old."

"How do you know the age of the strata?"

"By using index fossils. Basically, if a species only existed during a short period of time and it left behind fossilized remains, we can use it to date the strata."

"So scientists use strata to figure out the age of fossils, and then use fossils to determine the age of the strata?" Gunnar snorted. "That's convenient."

Mary scowled at him. Was he going to argue with every scientist they talked to? Her end of this job entailed clearing Wayne's name. She'd hired Gunnar to find the killer. That was his function—not to argue over the science. Besides, what did he know?

He shrugged her off and focused his attention back on Eric. "What about carbon dating? Are you aware carbon dating proved the fossil is only six thousand years old?"

Eric barked a laugh. "Dr. Oakford carbon dating Paluxy Man was wildly inappropriate. I can't imagine what he was thinking!"

Mary shifted her glower his way. "I don't appreciate your tone." This kid was fresh from grad school. He didn't possess a thimbleful of the knowledge Uncle Wayne had accumulated in his decades in the field. "He may have made a mistake, but he still deserves respect."

"You're right. I'm sorry." The contrition in his eyes shifted immediately. "But the fossil is millions of years old. You just can't use carbon dating on objects that old. It's useless. The results aren't trustworthy, and he should've known that."

Mary shook her head. "Cranston said Wayne shouldn't have tested the dinosaur, but he thought it was okay to carbon date Paluxy Man because it's a homo sapien. And like you said, homo sapiens have only been around thousands of years."

"But it's not a homo sapien," Eric shot back. "You can put aside the strata, the index fossils, and every other way of dating it. Just look at the fossil. You can eyeball it and see it's not human–and definitely not a modern human."

"You're sure of that?"

"Absolutely." Eric bobbed his head; his glasses slipped. "When I was at the Smithsonian, I—" His face brightened and he held up a finger. "You know what? Let me just show you."

He went into another room and returned with some documents.

"Here. Look for yourself." He handed her an eight-by-eleven photograph of a hominid. "I took this picture at the Smithsonian. This is Paluxy Man's skull. Look at the size and shape of it. Notice the eye sockets and the relatively small cranial size. Look at the large protruding jaw. Does that look like a homo sapien to you?"

Mary gaped at the picture, and her mind went numb. She didn't need to study it to see what Eric meant, but she couldn't take her eyes off of it. "No, it doesn't. I'm not an expert, but it looks like a monkey. Definitely not human." She clamped her lips together and continued to stare. "But it's so obvious. Too obvious. How could Uncle Wayne look at that fossil and make such an elementary mistake?"

"I don't know. In the photographs he published, there's never a picture of the skull. The most important part of the skeleton, the clearest indication that Paluxy Man isn't human, yet Dr. Oakford never even mentioned it in his notes. In my view, if there's any indication that he intentionally misrepresented Paluxy Man, that's it–well, that and some things Dr. Freed said."

"Freed?" Gunnar slipped a notepad and pen from his pocket, and flipped through the pad for a clean page.

"Kevin Freed. He's a professor of paleontology at Vanderbilt in Nashville. They were scheduled to give a presentation about Paluxy Man at the National Paleontological Conference this summer. They were promising a revelation that would change our entire view of human evolution. But then, about a month ago, Dr. Freed backed out of the convention. He said he suddenly realized Paluxy Man wasn't human after all. That's what he told the media, anyway." Eric shrugged a shoulder. "He'd been relying on Dr. Oakford's photographs, but then he saw Paluxy Man with his own eyes and realized the photos were inaccurate. He never comes right out and says it, but if you read between the lines, he insinuates that Dr. Oakford may have engaged in some kind of wrongdoing."

Mary opened her mouth to protest, but Gunnar held a hand up. "Did Freed have any reason to lie about Oakford?"

"Like I said, it was an insinuation. He just pointed out that the photographs don't match the fossil. Same thing I'm saying. It's possible Dr. Oakford doctored the photos—"

"But why would he?" Mary demanded. "It doesn't make sense."

"Maybe he's getting paid by the creationists. That's where money is."

Her cheeks burned. "That's just ridiculous!"

"Sometimes money talks—"

She slapped the table. "No! My uncle wouldn't sell scientific truth for any amount." She shoved back from the table and stormed out of the room.

CHAPTER FOURTEEN

MARY SLAMMED THE car door and glared out the rain-spotted windshield. How was it possible? Uncle Wayne had taken a monkey fossil and told the world it was human? He'd told the creationists what they wanted to hear? No, not the Wayne Oakford she knew.

Eric's words echoed in her head: that's where the money is.

All her life, she'd believed Uncle Wayne was a man of integrity, a man of science. He didn't care about money, he cared about ideas. She pounded a fist on the dashboard. She still wanted to believe that. Believe in him. But how could he have unwittingly made such a monumental mistake?

No logical excuse came to mind. Maybe he was a fraud. Maybe she'd just have to face the fact he'd sold out. How could he?

She stared at the old house. On the other side of the picture window, Gunnar and Eric engaged in deep conversation. Had Eric convinced Gunnar her uncle was a fraud? And what did it matter what that gumshoe thought? Whatever Uncle Wayne had believed, he still didn't deserve to be murdered. Gunnar's job was to find the murderer.

Her cell phone rang, and she checked the screen. Good grief, it was Robert Quigley. Just what she needed. Steeling her spine, she answered.

"Hi, Mary," Robert crooned in a voice he undoubtedly considered sexy. "I just realized I never gave you the combination to the front gate. I'd hate for you to arrive in the morning and not be able to get inside."

"Tomorrow morning? Friday morning?" That couldn't be. She'd checked her calendar and had no appointments until the meeting about the Borden creationism lawsuit tomorrow afternoon.

"Yes, at ten, remember?"

She slapped her forehead. "I'm sorry, Robert, I completely forgot to register it in my Blackberry. I'm halfway across the country right now. Would it be all right if we rescheduled?"

"You're not trying to avoid me?"

"Don't be silly." She forced a laugh. "Why would I want to avoid you?"

"That's okay. I can take a hint." His voice wilted. "I'd planned to make a generous donation to the Academy, but if you can't make it tomorrow morning, I'll understand. There are plenty of foundations and charitable organizations in need."

"No, no, I'll be there." From the corner of her eye she caught sight of Gunnar coming out of the house. He shook hands with Eric and headed for the car. "I'll see you in the morning."

She ended her call as Gunnar opened the passenger door.

He slid into his seat. "Are you okay?"

"I'm fine."

"You don't look fine."

"He just got to me, but I'm okay now. What did I miss?"

"I got that Vanderbilt professor's home address." He looked down at his notes. "Dr. Kevin Freed. He lives just outside of Nashville, not too far from here. We can be there within the hour."

Mary cranked the engine. "I can't do that. I've got to fly back to DC. I have an important meeting tomorrow morning I'd totally forgotten about, and I can't miss it."

"But what about Paluxy Man?" He glanced at his watch. "There's still time."

"Time to what? Call Dr. Lodge?" She laughed. "Nothing's going to change. Eric told me everything I needed to know."

"So you believe your uncle was a fraud?"

Her shoulders slumped. "What choice do I have?"

"Was Ted was lying, too? Were they both in on it?"

She stared out the windshield. Ted had been telling the truth, she was certain of it.

He rested his arm along the back of her seat and angled toward her. "Look, if you need to be back in DC tomorrow morning, that's fine. Fly out tonight, take a red eye if you have to. But Kevin Freed was one of the last persons to see your uncle alive. He's a professor of paleontology, and I really need your expertise. It shouldn't take too long. Two hours, tops."

Mary took a deep breath and exhaled. "All right, what's his address?"

CHAPTER FIFTEEN

VAL SLID HIS key into the lock on Storage Unit 19, then rolled the orange door up on its track. This wasn't one of the temperature-controlled units. He'd seen no reason to take on that expense; besides billing anyone else would leave a paper trail. To cover his own hide, he'd signed the contract D. K. Brown.

He flicked on the light and surveyed the storage area. Preferring order to disarray, he'd hastily stacked boxes of Oakford's research material, taken from his home office, instead of tossing them in like his nerves and adrenaline had demanded that night. Still, he had no clue which box held the material pertaining to Paluxy Man. He grabbed one to sit on, then another to riffle through, and sliced through the tape of the second with his switchblade. Dozens of manila folders cramped the inside, all the tabs well-worn and the labels faded. He thumbed through them: quantum physics, spontaneous generation, primate evolution. Everything but Paluxy Man.

Several boxes and a couple of hours later, he stood and stretched, stepped outside for some air that didn't smell like dust and antiquity. Wasn't much better outside—hot concrete released the greasy odors of spilled motor oil, and there was no breeze to blow the acrid scent away. But the mid-afternoon sun felt good.

His cell rang; the display showed the call was from James Darbyshire.

"Yes, Chancellor."

"Where are you?"

"Here in DC. Just rolled in."

"You get the job done?"

"Yes, sir."

"Good." The Chancellor said, then disconnected. Rude of him, of course, but Val was used to it. Actually thankful for it this time. He didn't want to explain what he was doing. The Chancellor hadn't ordered this investigation and would no doubt disapprove of spending more time away from work chasing after things he didn't find important.

But Val did believe them important. If the original, untouched photos showed a human skull with the fossil, then the skull would have to be found. The Chancellor could no longer deny its existence.

Val rolled his shoulders to ease the tension and entered the dusky light of the storage unit. In the third box of this renewed search, he hit paydirt. He pulled a folder marked "P.M. Photos" from the rest of the files and rested it on the top of the box. They weren't originals, only photocopies. Not enough to convince the Chancellor, but they worked for Val.

The first picture showed Wayne Oakford and Ted Cranston sitting on the ground, apparently still in the field at Paluxy. Laid out on the ground between them was the skeleton, largely intact, except for a skull. Val slid the photograph to the back of the stack. The next showed Paluxy Man's ribs and spinal column. That was followed by a close-up of the skeleton's right hand. In the fourth picture, the skeleton was laid out on a blanket with each bone carefully in place.

In this photograph, the fossilized skeleton had a skull. A human skull.

So Oakford's dying words were true. He hadn't sent the skull to the Smithsonian. Instead, he'd kept it as proof. And he'd given that proof to Mary Dillard.

What had she done with it?

CHAPTER SIXTEEN

"SO, WHAT IF it's true?" Gunnar asked.

Mary shifted her gaze from the road ahead to look at him. "If what's true?"

"What if your uncle faked the fossil?"

She clamped her lips together. She'd barely allowed herself to think of the possibility, she certainly couldn't give voice to it. With a shake of her head, she dismissed the idea. "Like you said, Ted backed him up. Besides, that's not the kind of man I knew him to be."

"Folks tend to be different with family then they are in their professional lives." He rummaged in the snack sack, but apparently didn't find anything that appealed to him. He plopped the bag in the backseat. "Maybe the man you knew growing up kept secrets."

"You forget I became a player in his professional life too. My degree may be in literature, but my work experience is entirely in the field of science—well, at least the administrative side. But I did work with him, and not only that, I know his reputation. He was always held in high regard, well respected among his colleagues."

"Yet one of those colleagues wanted him dead."

"Yeah. I just can't figure out which one, but I don't know everyone. Just those he worked with in DC. Nobody from the field. I'd never met Ted or Eric. And I don't know this Dr. Freed."

The closer they got to Nashville, the more vehicles they encountered. Three lanes of west-bound traffic buzzed with speeders and slow pokes. Not a problem for someone accustomed to the DC insanity, but it contributed to the headache forming behind her left eye just the same.

She shifted lanes to get around a grandma.

"Whoever he is, I hope he'll be willing to talk to us." Gunnar stretched his legs and crossed strong arms over his thick chest.

An appealing image of him in his river-soaked t-shirt floated in her mind's eye.

Where had that come from? The heat of a blush rose up her neck. An attraction to him was pointless. After this job, he'd go his way and she'd go hers. She was his client; she'd paid him to hunt down her uncle's killer. It was a professional relationship. She should keep it that way.

She cleared her throat and returned her mind to the present conversation. "You think Dr. Freed wouldn't be willing to talk?"

"If what Merrow says is true, and Freed felt like he was being played by a fraud—at great risk to his own professional reputation—he may not be too keen about chatting with anyone associated with your uncle right now."

"Do you think he could've killed Wayne?"

"Won't know until we meet with him, but he's closer to Virginia than Ted was in Texas. It's not as improbable as it was for Ted. And if what went on between them really did damage Freed's reputation, he'd have motive."

"But we've definitely ruled out Eric."

"Definitely. But it would be interesting to know whether that blast was aimed at him or us."

Mary shuddered. The whole conversation seemed fodder for her headache. Time to talk about something else. "Tell me about Becky."

Gunnar raised a brow at her. "That's a sudden switch." But he sighed as if willing to accept it. "What do you want to know?"

"Well, things. You know—how long were you married, did you have kids, how old was she when she died? Things."

"Nosy, aren't you?"

"Look, we still have a long drive to Freed's place, and I want to talk about something other than bones and murder. The scale is tipped.

You know more about me than I do about you." She shrugged. "Share something."

He remained silent so long, she sneaked a peek at him to see if he'd chosen to ignore her. He stared out his window as the scenery flew by—beautiful scenery, but the tic in his jaw indicated he didn't see it. Thinking of his wife obviously brought him great pain, and for some reason, that seemed incongruous with the reckless, smart-mouthed jerk she was growing unwisely attracted to. She resisted the urge to rub his shoulder and tell him he didn't have to answer. Instead, she watched the road and waited for him to speak.

"She was thirty-eight," he said finally. "I had the last fifteen years of her life with her. No kids, we couldn't have them. But we were insepa-rable until her father fell ill and she had to keep a close watch on him." A sigh stretched the t-shirt across his chest. A wistful look stole into eyes that were usually sharp and cutting. "She was great. Smart, intuitive, funny. Not beautiful, really—not a classic beauty like some movie star or something. Her nose was slightly crooked, and she had a cow-lick she was forever fretting over. After we got married, we both suffered from newlywed weight gain. Her weight never came off, so she was a little chunky." He reached out his arms in a circle, as if to give her a hug. "But she still fit. Perfect fit." His smile harbored a tinge of sadness.

Her heart melted at the new image of this tough-guy beside her. A man who could love that deeply couldn't be all bad. "How did she die?"

The tic returned to his jaw as he clenched his teeth. "Plane crash."

He turned toward the passenger window. Conversation over.

CHAPTER SEVENTEEN

A T THIS MOMENT at Wright-Patterson Air Force Base, Hangar 18 held enough heat to bake biscuits, several rows of tarp-covered containers, and Major General Kipper "Kip" Hayden. In his thirty years with the Air Force, Gen. Hayden had been assigned many important duties. He'd worked at NORAD and at the Pentagon. He'd served as the chief of staff of the Air Force Systems Command during the Iraq war.

None of his assignments had been as important as this one. With a Patton-style fists-on-waist stance, he surveyed the rows. The public had no idea what was really going on at the base. Many of the professional UFO chasers claimed the "real" Hangar 18 wasn't at Wright-Patterson at all. They believed it was located at the Groom Lake facility in Nevada—a location popularly known as Area 51—and that it contained alien bodies and aircraft from a crash in Roswell, New Mexico, in the summer of 1947.

In fact, there had never been any evidence of aliens at the Groom Lake facility. Area 51 was a major testing ground for advanced military technology–or at least it had been until it became ensnared in the alien mythology. The cutting-edge technology that had once been tested at Groom Lake had been moved to an undisclosed location in Utah over twenty years ago. Any alien bodies or aircraft related to the Roswell incident–if there had ever been any–would certainly have been moved as well. The military maintained the same level of secrecy and continued to perform tests at Groom Lake, but only with planes and weaponry already in use. The site now served primarily as a distraction for the prying public.

But they'd had it right the first time. The hangar concealing secrets that could shake the world was indeed Hangar 18 at Wright-Patterson Air Force Base in Dayton, Ohio. What they got wrong was the nature of the secret.

Hayden's cell phone rang. The tone indicated it was somebody from Hadley Scientific. He'd been expecting this call. He answered, "General Hayden."

"Hey Kip, it's Val."

From his voice, Hayden could tell that something was wrong. "How's everything? Is the shipment ready for tomorrow night?"

"It's being readied. I'm not calling about that. There's an issue that's raised its ugly head."

Hayden clenched his jaw. "What's the issue?"

"We thought we had the entire skeleton of Paluxy Man. We don't. The skeleton had a skull, and it's not in our possession right now."

"Where is it?"

"Don't know, but I have a suspicion."

"Need help?"

"Might."

"Okay." Hayden wiped sweat from his brow. "We'll send in Blue Light."

CHAPTER EIGHTEEN

D R. FREED LIVED in a Norman Rockwell neighborhood. The stately homes with their manicured lawns weren't just for show—they were the playgrounds for kids of all ages and their accompanying pets. Mary slowed the car to twenty and kept an eye out for joggers, bicyclists, and tossed footballs. The scent of a backyard barbecue tickled her nose and made her stomach churn. Lunch seemed ages ago. Maybe it was. Had she eaten?

Gunnar muttered street numbers as they drove, then pointed. "Next one down."

Mary pulled to the curb in front of a two-story house. A gray pickup sat in the driveway with its tailgate down and at least a dozen fifty-pound bags of soil and mulch stacked in the bed. A short, stocky man with a bulbous nose and receding hairline eyed them as he approached the truck and hefted a bag to his shoulder.

Climbing from the car, Gunnar hailed him. "Are you Kevin Freed?"

"I am." Dr. Freed didn't stop but carried his load to a freshly dug flower bed around the trunk of an ancient oak. Gunnar grabbed a sack and followed.

Mary intercepted the professor on his trek back to the pickup. "Can you take a moment to talk to us?"

"Don't need insurance. Know who I'm voting for." He sidestepped around her. "Whatever you're selling, I'm not buying."

She scrambled after him. "I'm not selling anything. I just want to ask you about Paluxy Man."

Freed hesitated before reaching for another bag, but then he grabbed it, shouldered it. "I don't know what you're talking about."

Gunnar took another sack too and matched stride with him. "That's pretty feeble, doctor. Eric Merrow already told us you backed out of giving a presentation about it with Dr. Oakford this summer."

The man dropped the sack of soil next to the others, then turned suspicious eyes at them. "Who are you? Who sent you here?"

"Gunnar Schofield, private investigator." He shoved out his hand, which the professor ignored. "This is my client, Ms. Dillard. We're looking into the death of Wayne Oakford."

"Heard burglars killed him."

Mary stepped closer. "No. The police had it wrong. Someone in the scientific community killed him—or had him killed—and it has something to do with Paluxy Man. I know you know about it. I know you supported Wayne at one point. Can't you tell me what made you back out?"

He studied her a moment, then crossed his meaty arms over his ribs and glowered at them. "Back in January, Oakford invited me to assist with research on Paluxy Man and present with him at the conference in Denver. Then he monopolized the whole thing. He did all the research and writing, and kept me in the dark. That's when I started having second thoughts about working with him. Then in March, I took my family to the Smithsonian. When I saw the Paluxy Man exhibit, I was shocked. I realized right then that Wayne was misrepresenting a monkey as a homo sapien. You bet I backed out of the conference. Couldn't disassociate myself from him fast enough."

The impact of his words blasted into Mary's gut. Her chest felt hollow.

So it was true. For whatever reason, he had betrayed his science, his profession, his years of developing a reputation as a man of integrity. But why? It didn't make sense. "I can't believe Uncle Wayne would intentionally misrepresent a monkey as a human."

"He was your uncle?" Dr. Freed tilted his head and squinted at her. "Little Mary? You were just a kid last I saw you."

"We've met?"

"Years ago at a party Wayne and Clarice held in their home in Virginia. He talked about you a lot over the years."

"He was like a father to me."

The suspicion returned to his eyes. "Who sent you here?"

"Nobody," Mary said. "I'm just trying to find out the truth about Paluxy Man."

"And who killed Dr. Oakford," Gunnar added. He hooked his thumbs in his jeans pockets and raised a brow. "That little speech of yours sounded canned. Care to tell us what really happened?"

The professor's expression hardened. He glared at Gunnar, but then, the tight lines in his face softened and he nodded. "We'd better go inside."

He shot a glance up and down the street, then herded them up the front steps and into the house.

"You want to know what's going on, you have to promise me something." He closed and bolted the door, then ushered them from a formal parlor deeper into the house to a warm, cozy den lined with family photos. "Anything I tell you, you heard it from Wayne. You didn't hear it from me. We've never even met. Got it?"

Beyond confused, Mary could only nod. "What is it? What's wrong?"

"Your uncle was right." He flopped heavily onto the cushion of a plump, plaid chair, and waved his hand for Gunnar and Mary to take seats also. They sat together on a worn sofa and turned to face him. "Paluxy Man was a homo sapien. You can tell by the shape and cranial capacity of the skull."

"We've seen photographs of the skull," Gunnar said. "I'm no expert, but it certainly didn't look human to me. Looked like some sort of zoo ape."

"Where did those photos come from?"

"Eric Merrow. He took pictures of Paluxy Man when he was at the Smithsonian."

Freed flapped a dismissive hand. "Those shots are worthless. The skeleton on display at the Smithsonian isn't the real fossil. What you were looking at in his photographs was a fabrication made from plaster."

"The Paluxy Man in the Smithsonian is a fake?" Gunnar's tone registered his surprise.

"Of course. Human fossils are extremely rare. They're simply too precious to leave on display in museums, so reproductions are made out of plaster and displayed to the public."

"I guess that makes sense. A mock-up is fine for the general public. You can save the real fossils for the professionals."

Freed shook his head. "Even the professionals rely on the plaster casts. It's ironic, actually. Paleontologists love to write books and articles about human evolution. They come up with all sorts of theories and explanations, and they call themselves experts. But the truth is, most of them go their entire careers without ever seeing an actual human fossil, just chunks of molded plaster."

"But the casts are based on the fossils," Mary declared. Was the man serious? She'd seen the photo with her own eyes, and the thought that an institution as honorable as the Smithsonian would fake the mold was preposterous. "A plaster reproduction may not match the fossil exactly, but it must be very close. You'd have to be a professional to see the difference."

Dr. Freed raised his index finger. "But you're assuming the plaster skull is identical, or nearly identical, to the skull on the actual fossil." He interlaced his fingers and rested his hands on his belly. "Are you familiar with the dinosaur known as Brontosaurus?"

"Of course."

"Are you aware there's no such thing?"

"Of course there's such a thing." Gunnar scowled. "I've heard about them since grade school."

Chuckling, Dr. Freed shook his head. "The so-called 'Brontosaurus' was discovered in the late 1800s by a fellow named O.C. Marsh. What he found was actually the remains of an Apatosaurus. The skeleton was nearly complete except for the missing skull. That's not unusual–it's fairly common for a fossil to be found without its skull. Later, a few miles away, Marsh found a dinosaur skull and added it to the body of the Apatasaurus. But here's the problem: that skull actually belonged to a different type of dinosaur, which we now know as Camarasaurus. So Marsh put the Camarasaurus skull onto the Apatosaurus body and, *voila!*, we have a 'Brontosaurus.' This falsehood continued from the late 1800s until the 1970s. Scientists now know there's no such thing, but most of the public doesn't."

Gunnar shrugged. "Sounds like Marsh made an honest mistake—"

"—that was perpetuated for over a hundred years," the professor added.

"But it was still a mistake," Mary asserted. "Do you really believe a museum would deliberately display a plaster cast of a skull that didn't match the fossil?"

"Deliberately, yes, but not maliciously. Museums are businesses. They have bills to pay like everybody else. When folks go to a museum to look at fossils, they want to see complete skeletons. And like I said, fossils are often found without skulls. So what's a museum to do? They make a complete plaster cast. If they don't have a real skull to work from, they take an educated guess. Sometimes they get it wrong."

Gunnar shot the doctor a skeptical look. "Oh, c'mon! You're saying the very institutions we rely on to preserve and display natural science cheat? Make things up?"

"That's stated rather strongly, but yes. Consider what happened with Hadrosaurus, the first dinosaur skeleton to be displayed to the public, found in the early- to mid-1800s. The fossil was nearly complete but it didn't have a skull. Parts of the skeleton looked iguana-like, so they took a guess, created a giant iguana skull out of plaster, and plunked it onto the Hadrosaurus body. That plaster dinosaur was put on display in 1868 at the Academy of Natural Sciences in Philadelphia to 'educate the public.'" The doctor smirked. "Of course, we now know the

Hadrosaurus didn't have an iguana-like skull at all. In fact, it was probably duck-billed. But to this day, that iguana head remains on display at the Academy."

A door slammed somewhere in the house, and a woman's voice called, "Kev? Are you here?"

"In the den, Alice."

"There's a strange car at the curb—" Alice appeared at the threshold, windblown and looking as if she'd just arrived from a garden party, and caught sight of the two strangers in her home. "Oh, we have company."

Gunnar and Mary stood to greet her.

Dr. Freed waved a hand toward Mary. "You remember Wayne and Clarice? This is their niece, Mary Dillard, and her ... friend—I'm sorry, I forgot your name."

Gunnar nodded at the woman. "Gunnar Schofield, ma'am. Nice to meet you."

She smiled at him and then addressed Mary. "My goodness, you've grown to such a beautiful young woman." She wrung her hands. "I wasn't expecting company! We have some tea, I think, and a few peanut butter cookies left from when the grandkids were here."

"They aren't staying, dear." Dr. Freed gave Gunnar a pointed stare. "We're discussing some business, and then they have to run."

"Oh." Alice looked confused, but didn't argue. "Well, okay. If you need me I'll be in the yard."

"We won't be long."

She left, and Dr. Freed gestured them back to their seats. "Now where was I?"

"The iguana head," Mary reminded him. "Faked fossils."

"Mistaken fossils," he corrected her. "And, yes, sometimes faked. If the museum doesn't have the actual fossil skull, it needs to take a reasonable guess in creating a plaster one. And I think that's what happened with Paluxy Man. When Wayne shipped the fossils to the Smithsonian, he kept the skull. That forced the museum to take a guess and make a plaster one. Since Paluxy Man was found with a dinosaur, they naturally assumed it couldn't be human, so they made the skull of a lower form of ape. That would explain Eric's photographs."

"Wait—Wayne kept the skull?" Mary's nerves thrilled at the thought. "Where is it?"

Dr. Freed's lips tightened, and Mary could almost see him mentally weighing options she had no clue about. Finally, he clapped his hands on his knees and rose. "Follow me."

He led them down to the basement, which apparently served as the game room, judging by the dartboard on one of the walls and green-felted poker table in the center of the room. Tennessee Titan posters and Vanderbilt banners adorned the bare sheetrock, and a big-screen TV dominated a corner.

Dr. Freed rolled aside a metal shelving unit holding board games and books, and revealed a wall safe. He worked the dial, and the safe clicked open. Inside was a black metal case, which he set on the game table and popped off the lid. A fossilized human skull nestled on a thick layer of molded gray Styrofoam.

Mary's hands twitched to lift it from its bed and examine it more closely. "This is it? This is Paluxy Man's skull? It looks human. Wayne kept it?"

Kevin nodded. "He asked me to hold it with strict instructions never to hand it over to anybody but him. But now that he's gone, maybe he'd want you to have it." He gave them both a stern look. "But remember, I didn't give this to you. We never spoke. Anything you have, anything you've learned, came directly from Wayne. Got it?"

"Yeah, we've got it," Gunnar said. "What I don't get is that Wayne wasn't alone when they unearthed the fossil. He wasn't the only one who knows a skull was found. Doesn't keeping it violate some sort of protocol?"

"Big time," Mary said. "I can't imagine why he would risk it. If he was claiming he'd found proof of the cohabitation of dinosaurs and man, why would he want the evidence hidden?"

"Because he had more to prove than just the coexistence of two species." Dr. Freed pulled a chair from the table and sat. "An Australian creation scientist named Gary Babson contacted him and warned him that if he sent Paluxy Man to the Smithsonian intact, his fossil would be altered."

The professor settled back in his chair and steepled his fingers. "According to Babson, the United Nations initiated a secret operation in the 1950s called Operation Remnant, ostensibly to protect the human fossils from loss or destruction. Whenever one is found, it's sent to Hollister Baird, an enterprise the UN created to perform various services for the scientific community. Hollister Baird uses the fossil to create a plaster cast and returns the cast to the museum along with the fossil. But what the museum doesn't know is that they also make stone replicas to look like the originals." He leaned forward. "The museums think they're getting their fossils back, but they're getting the replicas–stone fakes– while the real fossils are shipped to military facilities for safe keeping."

"That's incredible," Mary said.

"There's more. Babson said whenever a human fossil is found that's inconvenient for the theory of evolution, Hollister Baird alters it. A human fossil goes in, an animal fossil comes out."

"Wayne believed that?"

"Not at first. But he was leery enough to keep the skull. And, sure enough—Hollister Baird made a monkey skull for Paluxy Man, and now everybody thinks it's a monkey fossil." He shook his head. "Your uncle kept the skull to prevent Paluxy Man from being misrepresented, but by doing that, he caused the very thing he was trying to prevent."

"Maybe." Gunnar said. "But if what Babson says is true, the human skull would've been altered anyway."

Mary shook her head. "But what Babson says isn't true." It couldn't be. She would have heard about it if it were. Wouldn't she? She turned her attention back to the professor. "Do you believe it's true about Operation Remnant?"

Freed looked grim. "Our presentation for the conference was fairly vanilla. The information had already been released to the public. Then Wayne caught wind that the plaster cast of Paluxy Man at the Smithsonian looked like a monkey instead of a human, and decided right then to use the conference to expose Operation Remnant to the world." He paused for a breath. His already grim expression took on a darker hue. "He was threatened. We both were."

Gunnar leaned forward. "Threatened how?"

"One of Wayne's 'friends' warned him that if we went forward with our presentation, we'd be killed. If we wanted to live, we had to retract the claim that Paluxy Man was human." He rapped his knuckles on the table. "We had to publicly declare that Paluxy Man was a monkey, back out of the conference, and never say a word about Operation Remnant."

"And that's what you chose to do."

Defiance glowed in Freed's eyes. "That's what I chose to do, yes. I'm involved in other work—important work—and don't want to risk it all by cracking open a hornet's nest." The fire died, and sadness took its place. "Wayne understood, but he said he wouldn't bend, wouldn't compromise his integrity. That was the last time I saw him. Two weeks later, he was dead."

"Do you know who made the threat?"

"No, but I'd have to assume it was somebody connected with Operation Remnant. Maybe somebody working for the United Nations."

"Who else knows Wayne kept the skull?"

"No one. Well, unless he told Artie."

"Artie?"

"Before his death, Wayne was working on his book with another person. He called him Artie. I don't know his last name, it never came up in conversation. All I know is that he's a quantum physicist. He was published in Physical Review Letters, I think—the most prestigious journal in the field of physics. Wayne mentioned he'd read an article of his and found it persuasive. That's one of the reasons he decided to work with him on the book."

"I don't get it," Gunnar said. "Why would you need a quantum physicist to help write a book about fossils?"

"I don't know."

"Any idea if there was bad blood between Oakford and this Artie guy?"

"I wouldn't know. I've heard they were working together out of Wayne's home right up until his death. For all I know, Artie might be the last person to have seen him alive."

"Anybody else who might have wanted him to disappear?"

"He said his book would be highly controversial. Probably make him a lot of enemies in the scientific community. But it was never completed, let alone published, and I don't know how many people even knew about it." He shook his head. "I don't know. I can't believe anybody would have killed him."

CHAPTER NINETEEN

THE SUN WAS setting by the time Mary and Gunnar walked out of Freed's house. She placed the box containing the skull in the trunk of her rental, then slipped behind the wheel and cranked the engine.

In the passenger seat, Gunnar reviewed a pocket notebook full of his scribbles. She peeked at the notes. He'd jotted them on the fly, but they were still legible. Barely.

He rubbed his chin. "I need to find the identity of Wayne's so-called friend, the one who threatened him."

"It was a scientist. That's what he said in his voice mail." She checked her rearview, then pulled onto the street. "But he never mentioned Operation Remnant or the UN or Hollister Baird. I wouldn't know how to start investigating those organizations."

"Me either," he admitted. "But if the last person to work with him was this Artie fella, then he's the guy I need to find."

"Great idea, but you'll be doing it alone. I have to catch the first flight back to DC. I can't afford to miss my appointment with Quigley."

"What about the article? Can you call your boss and get it pulled?"

"He leaves for the day at five o'clock. With the time difference, it's already too late."

Gunnar eyed the clock on the dash and winced. "Sorry."

"Don't be. I don't care about the article anymore." Mary grinned. "I have proof of Wayne's credibility."

"Yeah, the skull. You can't get better proof than that." He popped a fist on his knee. "I still don't get it. You saw how many people there were at that dig in Texas. How could anyone say the skull was a monkey's if there are witnesses that it was from a man?"

"Great question. And I wonder why Ted or Eric didn't say anything about it."

"Cranston may have assumed we already knew about it and didn't think to mention it. As for Eric, he said he'd been called away on a family matter. He left before the skull was dug out."

"So many unanswered questions. Was Cranston in on it when Wayne took the skull? Does he know about all this?"

"I wonder just how far 'all this' goes. Think about it—the United Nations, fer cryin' out loud." Gunnar scowled. "Somebody somewhere went to extremes to keep your uncle quiet and ruin his rep. How far up the food chain did that order come from?"

"I have no idea." Mary set her jaw. She didn't even know there was a food chain.

As the sun set and the darkness deepened, she turned on the headlights. At the next major intersection, she aimed the car in the direction of the Hilton and tried not to feel like such a minnow in this huge ocean she'd found herself in. How far up indeed? Everything Freed told them had taken her aback.

But her main concern was Wayne and his standing in the scientific community.

She raised her chin. "Uncle Wayne will be exonerated. Surely there are pictures of the entire fossil intact—skull and all. When I reveal those pictures and the skull, the Smithsonian will have to fix the plaster cast, and everybody will know he told the truth."

Gunnar twisted in his seat. "I'm not sure you want to do that. Somebody threatened to kill him and Freed if they didn't keep quiet. Apparently it wasn't an idle threat."

"That's because they were going to expose Operation Remnant." She shook her head. "I'm not touching that. I'll play dumb and say my uncle gave me this box a couple months ago, and I didn't think about it again until after he died. I'll say I was surprised there was a fossilized human skull in there, and naturally I wondered if it belonged to Paluxy Man. I'll take it to the TV networks and make sure they have photographs and video footage of what's clearly a fossilized human skull. Then I'll hand it over to the Smithsonian. After all that, everybody will know Uncle Wayne was telling the truth. And all the publicity will keep me safe. No one would dare touch me."

"Makes sense, I guess." He paused for a moment. "Do you think it's possible?"

"What?"

"That Paluxy Man might have lived at the same time as that dinosaur?"

"Don't be ridiculous." She glanced at him. Was he seriously considering the possibility? "The Earth's age and the theory of evolution are settled. Scientists are certain that dinosaurs and humans didn't coexist. They couldn't possibly have coexisted."

"What if they're wrong?"

"Are you kidding me?"

"What? They've never been wrong before?" Gunnar cocked a brow. "Must I remind you of the Brontosaurus?"

"Who are you to question an accepted scientific theory?" She glowered at him. "We're talking about the world's brightest scientists, people who've spent years in school studying evolution. They have PhDs. Nearly all of them believe in Darwinian evolution."

"Then how do you explain the dinosaur fossil they found with Paluxy Man? If your uncle was right—and it's looking like he was—they did, indeed, coexist."

She bit her lip. What little she knew about paleontology didn't provide an answer for this.

Gunnar tried to prop one leg on the other, but couldn't in the limited space. He stretched them in front of him. "Not that long ago, Albert Einstein came up with a theory that challenged the scientific consensus. He called it the theory of relativity. You know what they did? They laughed at him. They even put out a book called *100 Scientists Against*

Einstein. And you know how he replied? He said, 'If I were wrong, one would have been enough.' That pretty much sums up how I feel about your 'scientific consensus.' I'll take one man with the facts over a hundred eggheads any day."

"So now you're comparing yourself to Albert Einstein?"

"I'm not comparing myself to anybody. I'm no scientist, and I don't claim to understand what's going on here. But the more I hear about Paluxy Man, the more my Spidey senses tingle."

"That's fine," she said. "All I'm saying is if you question the theory of evolution, people will laugh at you."

"Oh, I'm not afraid of that." he said. "All the greats were laughed at."

"Yes. And so were the fools."

He shrugged. "The greats are people who do things most people believe are impossible. They come in two types. The first are smart enough to know it can be done. The others are just too stupid to know it can't. In the end, what's the difference?"

"Quite a bit. The 'stupid,' as you called them, just got lucky."

"Hey, luck counts." He grinned at her. "Regardless, they're both great. They both stand behind what they know is right instead of deferring to the crowd. It's called integrity."

"That's an interesting way of looking at things." She couldn't hold the sarcasm from her voice. She pulled into the hotel parking lot and stopped next to Sheila.

"I'm always looking at things from a different perspective. Something you should try." He got out of the car, but turned and leaned in. "Have a good flight."

CHAPTER TWENTY

GUNNAR WOKE WITH a start, his skin drenched in sweat, his lungs heaving, his heart hammering against his ribs. He focused on the desk clock opposite his Murphy bed. Seven-thirty. He'd hit the sheets around two, shortly after securing Sheila and going through his office messages.

Brody Carlisle wanted him to come in. His lawyer's summons had undoubtedly set off the nightmares. The fuel gauge, laughing maniacally and dropping lower and lower; the propeller dying, shrinking, disappearing entirely from the nose of the Cessna; the high-pitched squeal of the plane going down … down … down. And Becky fighting a writhing snake of a seat belt and screaming, "It won't latch! It won't latch!"

Those were her last words, and for a solid year, they'd echoed in his head. Like they were echoing now.

He shook the cry from his ears, if not his memory, and untangled himself from the sheets to go splash water on his face. He needed a shower and clean clothes, but Cathy would be in before too long, and he needed to talk to her, too. In a neat pile on his otherwise chaotic desk, the mail sat opened and prioritized, demanding his attention. Cathy had attached sticky notes to the bills, indicating which she'd paid in full and which in part—all thanks to Mary Dillard's impulsive offer to pay him double. Just her advance was enough to get him out of a heap of financial trouble.

The office door opened and shut, and the familiar sounds of Cathy settling in at her desk floated to Gunnar in the back. He grabbed his pocket notebook and strode to her desk to welcome her.

She studied him through her glasses. "You look like roadkill."

"Thanks. You look great."

"That's what a good night's sleep will get you. You should try it sometime." She hit the button on her computer, which whirred into life. "I bet you stayed here last night, right?"

"Of course."

"Gunnar, you have a perfectly nice home. Why don't you stay there? Especially after a long drive. Surely your bed is more comfortable than that thing." She waved toward the Murphy bed.

"I don't want to mess the house up too bad. It's on the market."

She snorted. "It's been on the market for two years. You're never going to sell that thing."

Gunnar looked away. She was right. As usual. Every time someone showed interest in the house, he'd declared it off the market and hidden the "for sale by owner" sign in the garage until he got the nerve to set it out again. It was the home he'd shared with Becky. He couldn't sell it. But he couldn't live in it either. Not yet.

He leaned against her desk. "Well, it'll do you good to know I'm on my way there now. Grab a shower and a change of clothes." He flipped through the pages of his notebook until he found what he'd written about Artie. "I need you to pull out your magic wand and find this guy. I don't have much to go on. He's a quantum physicist, maybe a professor. He may have written an article for Physical Review Letters, but I don't know when that would've been. 'Artie' probably stands for Arthur, but whether that's his first name or his last, I don't know."

"You're not asking much, are you? Anything else? Any other miracle you want me to pull off today?"

"Just a small one. Call Brody and see if you can get me in to see him within the hour or so."

Her gaze softened. "That's going to be rough for you."

"Yeah." He ran a hand through his hair. "Yeah, it is."

*

At the Riverside Café in DC, Val checked his watch and scowled. It was nearly eight-thirty. General Hayden had assured him that somebody from Blue Light would be there.

Blue Light was an Army Special Forces counter-terrorist unit established in the 1970s. Allegedly, it had been disbanded in the early '80s, when it was superseded by Delta Force. In fact, the unit had been assigned to the United Nations and continued to operate formally under the aegis of the Special Operations Command. They were involved in a number of international operations, but Val's only experience with them came from Operation Remnant.

A man with sharp features and a chiseled physique stepped inside the café and met his gaze. He approached the table. "You Gordon?"

"Yeah."

He stuck his hand out. "Major Terry Stark."

Val grasped the man's hand, then nodded toward the chair across from him. "Take a seat."

A slender, young waitress came, checking Stark out with obvious appreciation. She tossed her mane of dark curls over her shoulder and smiled at him. "What can I get for you?"

Maj. Stark winked at her. "You, if you're available."

She tittered and blushed. "Shift's not over for six more hours."

"Too bad." Stark snapped his fingers. "Guess I'll have to settle for an iced coffee."

When she walked away, he focused on Val, no longer the ladies' man. "Nice buzz-cut. If I didn't know better, I'd think you were the one in the military."

Val glanced at Stark's hair—not remotely military, and probably why women found him attractive. "They let you grow your hair out now?"

"It's required for some units. We need to blend in with the public." He read the menu as he spoke. "General Hayden says you heard the fossil had a skull. How'd you find that out?"

Val recounted the events of the past few days.

Terry frowned. He leaned across the table and whispered, "You killed Wayne Oakford?"

"Yes."

His frankness brought a drop-jawed response from the major. "Why would you do that?"

"He needed to be silenced. He was going to expose Operation Remnant."

"It's not your place." Stark snarled. "You know only Blue Light is authorized to use deadly force in support of the operation. Why didn't you call us?"

How to answer that? Val couldn't tell the major the United Nations wasn't the only organization he served, nor could he say the Headmaster had ordered the assassination.

He feigned contrition and shrugged. "I should have called the general. I guess I got carried away."

Terry leaned back, blowing out a minty breath. "Nothing can be done about it now. Where is the skull?"

"It wasn't among the things from his house. He hinted that he'd given it to someone, and we think the niece has it. Her condo's in Tyson's Corner. I'll bet it's there."

The waitress returned with his coffee. He smiled and flirted as he ordered a lumberjack's breakfast.

She left, and instantly, his gigolo persona disappeared. How he could turn it on and off made Val's head spin.

"We'll need to get inside." Stark kept his voice low.

"That shouldn't be a problem. I have a key." Val pulled a lock pick kit from his pocket just far enough for him to see.

He nodded his approval. "We'll also need to know when she won't be at home."

"She's dead." Val explained how he'd set explosives in the coal mine, locking Mary and her detective inside.

Stark scowled and shook his head. "You're a regular killin' machine, ain't ya?" He looked out the window, drumming his fingers on the table. "So you haven't confirmed that she's dead?"

"I destroyed the only entrance to the mine. There was no way out."

Stark skewered him with a pointed stare. "Are you absolutely certain she's dead?"

Val leaned back. "I suppose you can never be a hundred percent certain of anything. But if she's alive, it's all the more reason to get inside there as soon as possible."

CHAPTER TWENTY-ONE

ARY DROPPED HER espresso cup into the Beamer's holder, certain she held unrealistic expectations of wakefulness from the brew. After arriving home late the night before, she'd thought she would sleep like a hibernating bear, but worries about the case and what Gunnar might find kept her from sleeping well at all. She was groggy and heavy-headed, and the strong coffee offered little relief. By the time she reached the third floor office at the Academy, she still felt only marginally awake.

As she walked into the reception area, fifty-six-year-old Celeste Martling looked up from her desk. Celeste was supposed to be Dr. Lodge's assistant, but in the true nature of underfunded employment, she also served as receptionist and secretary for both Lodge and Mary. Why the petite woman put up with working three positions while getting paid for only one was almost as puzzling as why a creationist Christian like her would work for the Academy at all. But she had been there for over twenty-five years.

She gave Mary the once-over. "Looks like you could use a bit more caffeine."

Mary held out an arm. "Hook it directly to the vein." She strode toward her office. "I don't have much time. I'm supposed to be at Robert Quigley's in thirty minutes."

"That's a long way out. What are you doing here?"

"Hoping I have his gate code somewhere." She riffled through her top desk drawer, slammed it shut, and pulled open another. "He called me specifically to give me the code, then never gave it."

Celeste leaned against the door frame. "Too busy flirting?"

Mary smirked. "I see you've met him."

"Often enough to know to steer clear." She returned to her desk. "I think I have the code somewhere. Dr. Lodge has to go out there periodically."

"Maybe he should be the one going today." Mary closed the last drawer and joined Celeste at her desk.

"You're kidding, right?" Celeste clicked a few buttons on her computer. "When it comes to retrieving contributions for the Academy, Dr. Lodge is a strong believer that the job belongs to the young and pretty." She eyed Mary from under her brow. "Which means you."

"Apparently."

"Here it is." She scribbled down the number and handed the slip of paper to Mary. "If he gets to be too much for you, let me know and I'll call out the cavalry."

Mary grinned. "After all I've been through this week, I think I can handle the likes of Robert Quigley."

*

"Cable service!" Val yelled, then pounded on Mary Dillard's door again. He and Maj. Stark were dressed in brown maintenance uniforms Val had borrowed from work. Stark held a tool box.

"Use the pick," he ordered.

Val worked the lock and twisted the knob. After a quick look over his shoulder in search of nosy neighbors, he slipped inside, hurried Terry in, and closed the door behind them. He surveyed the floor plan. The door had opened directly into the living room, beyond which was the kitchen, just to the right of the staircase. Visible in the room to the left were a computer desk and a large filing cabinet. "Let's start in there."

He felt along the wall and flipped on the light switch. Heavy drapes covered the windows, blocking both sun and prying eyes. The room held shelves laden with books spanning the centuries. Shakespeare shared space with James Fennimore Cooper, who shared space with contemporary authors and poets like Maya Angelou. A small section on one shelf held books about green energy, evolution, and histories of the Civil Rights march. An overstuffed, wing-backed chair and its matching ottoman sat angled toward an electric fireplace; next to the chair stood a small side table holding a mug of stale coffee and magazines like *Archeology Today*, *Newsweek*, and *Cosmo*. A few plaques and awards lined the walls. Mary's graduate and post graduate degrees. Pictures of her with various renowned scientists. Val shifted each aside in search of a wall safe, but found nothing.

The filing cabinet was locked, but Stark popped it open with a small, flexible piece of metal. He pulled each drawer out far enough to see if a box were hidden in the back. "Nothing here."

Val rubbed his chin. "Where would she hide something that important?"

"Probably not here. More likely a safe deposit box."

"Let's hope not. That'll make it impossible to get to." He shook his head. "She may not have taken the time to get it to the bank. It's gotta be around here somewhere. Let's go upstairs."

Terry took the guest bedroom. Val entered Mary's room—a large area with an unmade queen-sized bed. A state-of-the-art treadmill faced a large, wall-mounted television on one side of the bed; on the other stood a modern dresser, black, and shellacked to a high sheen. A suitcase stood propped against the dresser. Val studied the airport tag. Tennessee. Yesterday. Through the bathroom door, he spotted an open cosmetic kit sitting on the counter. The glass shower door still showed signs of dampness.

He growled a curse and called out. "We have to hurry. She's still alive."

He moved to the dresser and jerked out the bottom left drawer. Soft sweaters and other winter garb shifted under his hands as he felt for the very bottom. Nothing. He tried the next drawer, and the next, until he'd felt through every silk and lace thing she owned. Still nothing.

The closet was to the right of the dresser. He pulled open the door, and a spicy floral scent greeted him—a smell that was both professional and all woman. Her clothes were hung with care and arranged by color; her shoes were lined perfectly underneath. Winter stuff on the left, summer stuff on the right. In front of him were a set of shelves holding purses and other female doodads—and something of particular interest to Val.

"Come in here," he shouted.

Stark appeared beside him in an instant. "Did you find it?"

"Take a look."

On the floor, under the shelves, rested a large metal safe.

Stark whistled. "We'll need a torch."

CHAPTER TWENTY-TWO

AT THE GATE outside Robert Quigley's ocean-view estate, Mary eased her car to the keypad. She typed the security code, and the ornate wrought-iron gates parted so she could pass. With her windows open to suck in the fresh Atlantic air, she drove up the winding, red-brick driveway until the mansion appeared between the pines. Opulent didn't begin to define the place.

As she pulled into the circle drive and parked, Quigley emerged from the stately front door and bounded down the stairs to greet her.

"Good morning." His voice seemed a bit over-exuberant. He helped her from her car and gave her a hug that lasted uncomfortably long.

She gently pushed him back while maintaining her practiced smile. "Good to see you, Robert. You have a beautiful house."

"Oh, this? It's just a vacation home. We call it our camp." He gestured toward the lawn. "Should I give you a tour of the property?"

"Sure."

Tucking her hand into the crook of his arm, he walked with her on the close-cropped carpet of St. Augustine grass and guided her around the side of the house toward the backyard. Stunning statues–Poseidon, Hera, Aphrodite, and others—were strategically placed around the perimeter of the property. Exquisite reproductions of life in cold, white marble.

"Those are beautiful," Mary said—more to be polite than truthful.

They were beautiful, but owning them seemed gaudy. A tasteful fountain, some sculpted shrubbery were more to her taste.

"Do you really think so?" He sneered. "They were my wife's idea."

Mary had heard the two were having troubles, but she wasn't going to be lured into a game of bash-the-wife. "She has great taste."

"Tolerable." He smiled and patted her hand. "There's one more you should see. My pride and joy."

They strolled toward the back of the property near the ocean. A long wooden deck stretched out across the edge of the lawn abutting the beach. Here, the land dropped sharply, and at either end of the deck, a wooden stairway led down to the shore. Sea gulls rode the air and cawed at each other. Rushing, white-capped waves whipped the beach, swiping the sand and whisking it back into the deeps. Sea oats nodded at the breeze, and the purple flowers of the railroad vine vied for attention with the dune sunflowers.

Mary lifted her face to the morning sun and sucked in the salty air. Despite the garish scene behind her, she could wake up to this daily.

Until they reached the deck and she looked at what was apparently Quigley's pride and joy. She bit her tongue.

"Isn't it magnificent?" He waved a hand to direct her gaze, as if she could miss it.

Below them, situated on the beach between the two sets of stairs, was an enormous statue of a man wearing a winged helmet and holding a caduceus. It must have stood thirty feet high.

"It's, um … it's amazing."

"It is, isn't it?" He grinned like a child with a new toy. "Ricardo Salvator, one of the world's greatest living sculptors, custom designed this just for our property. It's his magnum opus." His eyes sparked with mischief. "Do you recognize the god?"

"It's been a while since I studied Greek mythology, but if I had to guess, I'd say that's Hermes, the god of trickery and theft."

"'Trickery and theft,'" he repeated with a smirk. "Well, like any deity of the Greek pantheon, Hermes was a god of many things. But he's honored here as the god of science and innovation."

She nodded, studying the statue. Something about it seemed strange, something beyond the fact it marred an otherwise beautiful beach. She walked to the top of one of the stairs to see it from a different angle and touched a finger to her chin. "I realize this is a masterpiece, and it's probably just me, but it seems like the statue is out of proportion. It's top heavy. The head, the chest are too large, and his legs are too small."

He smiled and motioned for her to follow him. "Let's take a look from below and see if your opinion changes."

They walked down the wooden stairs on the right, then crossed the sand to stand directly in front of the statue.

"How about now?"

"That's amazing." And this time, she meant it. "It looks perfect from here. Everything is in proportion."

"It's called a simulacrum. If a large statue is sculpted in actual proportions and you view it from the ground level, you'll notice that the upper portions appear too small and the bottom too large. The ancient Greeks solved this problem by sculpting the top of the statue larger than the bottom. When you view a simulacrum from the intended angle, it looks like the real thing. Better than the real thing."

"I don't know what I think about that." She tilted her head. "If the statue symbolizes science, do you really want it distorted like that? You've improved its appearance by compromising its integrity."

He shrugged. "A statue is judged by how it looks to people, not how closely it conforms to an ideal." The wind picked up, and he folded his arms. "It's getting cold. Why don't we go inside?"

The wind felt refreshing to her, but she followed him to the deck, across the well-kept lawn to the house. They walked through French patio doors on the way to the kitchen and passed an indoor pool she instantly coveted.

The airy and spacious modern-rustic kitchen appeared to be every epicurean's dream with its massive stainless steel appliances. Cabinetry of polished maple lined the walls; the windows overlooked the ocean.

And a bucket of ice chilled a bottle of Korbel on the marble countertop.

"How about some bubbly?" Robert retrieved a couple of crystal champagne flutes from a wine hutch, popped the cork from the bottle, and filled the glasses.

"Isn't it a little early in the day?"

"You're quite right." He rummaged in the refrigerator for a carton of orange juice and added a few drops to each glass. "But it's never too early for a mimosa."

She gave him the smile he expected as she accepted the drink. How anyone could stand alcohol this early in the day—champagne or otherwise—she'd never know. But she needed the check he'd promised. If only she could figure out a way to shift the conversation to his donation.

With his hand resting against her lower back, he directed her into the living room and waved her to a seat on the tufted, ivory-leather sofa. He sat flush against her and gave what must've been his version of a roguish look.

She concentrated on her mimosa and tried not to roll her eyes. How much of this feeble attempt at seduction was she required to tolerate? The time to get down to business had long passed, and there was no delicate way to discuss money. She gave herself a mental shrug and plunged in feet first.

"So, you'd like to make a donation to the Academy?"

"We'll get to that." He sipped from his glass, regarding her over its crystalline rim with a barely concealed leer. "You know, I remember when I first saw you a few years ago, fresh out of college. I was struck by how beautiful you were. I have a son about your age, and I remember thinking the two of you would make a great couple." He fingered a lock of her hair. "Of course, that was years ago. He's in a relationship now, and I'm the one who's single. Did I mention that my wife and I are divorcing?"

"I don't believe you did." Good grief. The man was insufferable.

She rose stiffly, examined an antique figurine of Dionysius in a beveled glass display case, then perched on the hard cushion of a straight back Elizabethan chair across from him. "Now, is this going to be a corporate donation from Hadley Scientific?"

"Not corporate. Hadley likes to stay under the radar." He leaned toward her and rested his drink on the wenge-wood coffee table; his eyes never left hers. "Let's make it personal."

She broke eye contact first and looked at the fireplace dominating the wall to her left.

One more of his innuendos, and her nerves were going to snap. But if she wanted to leave the mansion with a fat check in hand, she needed to remain in his presence until he presented it.

She glanced at him. "It's funny. I've driven by the Hadley Scientific building many times. And every time I see the fence and the barbed wire, I think, wow, there must be something really interesting and important going on in there." She smiled at him then, hoping to appear fascinated. "What exactly does your company do?"

"Let me show you." He disappeared into another room and returned with a black briefcase, which he set on the coffee table and opened. Inside, atop a stack of papers, were a keycard and a blue ID badge shining from a black leather case. He reached into a pocket, pulled out a glossy page, and handed it to her. "This is the new brochure of some of the services we provide. That's really just a sample. We offer one-stop shopping for museums."

"Hadley Scientific," she read, "a division of Hollister Baird Enterprises." The company Kevin Freed had talked about! She willed her heart to stop pounding and glanced up at Quigley. "Your division makes plaster casts of fossils."

He looked at her sharply. "Where did you hear that?"

"From you, just then. 'One-stop shopping for museums.' Isn't that what you said? I've always wondered where the museums get those plaster casts."

"Hadley does lots of things, but let's not discuss business." He snapped the brochure from her hand and returned it to its pocket in his briefcase, then circled her chair until he stood behind her. "I'm flying to Miami in a couple of hours on business. Why don't you come along and we can talk about more interesting things on the beach?" He rested a hand on her shoulder and rubbed the side of her neck with his thumb. "I bet if you were able to secure a large donation for the Academy, it could put you on the fast-track for the director of development position."

"And I bet if your wife's attorney discovered how I obtained that donation, he would bleed you dry of every asset you own." She stood and smiled sweetly. "Now, if you don't mind, I won't take up any more of your time."

CHAPTER TWENTY-THREE

"**B**LOWTORCH WOULD BE too dangerous in here." Val waved his hand at the fine fabrics in Mary Dillard's closet. "I have a grinder and some wheels in the truck."

Maj. Stark gave him a skeptical look. "We need to go through at least an inch of steel. Do you think a grinder can do that?"

"I've done it before. It'll take some time, maybe an hour. But, yeah, it'll cut through steel."

"She could come back at any time."

Val shrugged. "That's a risk we'll just have to take."

Stark cocked a brow at him. "You tried to kill her once. You gonna try it again?"

"Nope. You made it clear that's your job." Val strode toward the hall. "Back in a sec."

He jogged out to the truck and returned with his grinder kit and a welding helmet. He put the helmet on and pulled the visor down. "Better get to it. Keep an eye out."

Stark stationed himself at the window and pulled the curtain back a fraction.

An hour later, Val turned off the angle grinder. After listening to the high-pitched squeal for so long, the ensuing silence fell like an eerie, heavy fog. Val lifted his face shield. "This wheel's pretty much shot. Hand me another."

Terry grabbed another from the kit and gave it to him. "How much longer?"

"Not much, I don't think. Everything okay outside?"

"Mail truck is coming. Folks will be checking their boxes before long."

"We should be done soon."

Val removed the shredded blade, replaced it with a fresh diamond wheel, and went back to work. When the wheel hit the safe's door, sparks again began to fly.

Finally, the squeal pitched higher as the last of the metal began to grind away.

He turned off the tool and removed his helmet. "It's open."

"Good." Terry joined him, squatting over the metal flak littering the closet floor.

Val looked inside the safe and grinned. "Now what might that be?"

He reached in and gently pulled out a black metal box. He took it to the dresser and opened the lid.

A human skull stared back at him.

"Let's get this to Hadley Scientific."

CHAPTER TWENTY-FOUR

AS GUNNAR ENTERED Brody Carlisle's office, the lawyer rose from his desk and stretched a hand toward him. "Hey, bud. You look rough."

"So I've been told." Apparently the shower and fresh clothes hadn't helped. Gunnar clasped his hand in greeting, then dropped into one of the chairs. "Too much work, not enough sleep."

Brody's office served as a shrine to all things aviation. Models of planes from barnstorming biplanes to the black Stealth Fighter were propped on stands or strung from the ceiling, disguising the fact that this spacious corner office encased a successful law practice. A polished, dark blue Corsair wing served as his desk, its propeller adorned the wall behind it. A pilot's chair bore the imprint of his backside. The display cabinet on the west wall was fashioned from the fuselage of some indiscriminate plane. Only a black-lacquered credenza, a couple of tufted-leather client chairs, and a heavily laden bookcase provided signs of conventionality.

His love of planes had brought him and Gunnar together years ago. Brody had been Gunnar's flight instructor and the guy he had turned to when his first disgruntled client sued him.

Resting his clasped hands on his desk, Brody turned sympathetic eyes on Gunnar. "This business with your pa-in-law affecting you?"

"A bit. Not that I blame him."

Brody's brows drew to a tight V. "You need to get over that. You weren't at fault. The very fact you were severed from the suit back then is evidence enough." He retrieved a file from the top of several which were neatly stacked on the wing. "He's suing you for mental anguish and loss of care and companionship."

"Well, he did have to get a home care agency to do for him what Becky used to." Gunnar shifted in his seat. "I know things have been hard on him, but why sue? Why now?"

"I don't know. He doesn't have a prayer. I have reports from the FAA and all the other investigators who were there at the time that say you weren't at fault. The problem was with the fuel injector system, but Becky's seat belt malfunction definitely contributed to her death."

Becky, wide-eyed in terror, struggling with the snake. "It won't latch, it won't latch!" Gunnar clenched his jaw.

"Why your father-in-law isn't suing them instead of you I'll never know, but it should be easy to get this thing dismissed. I'll draft a response and get it filed by end of business today."

"No, don't. Not yet." Gunnar rubbed his brow. "There's more to this than meets the eye. Dan knows he can't win. There's something else going on." He and Dan had been close at one time, before his illness, before Becky died. Gunnar needed to reestablish the bond between them. He needed to at least try. "How much time do we have to file the response?"

"Thirty days. What do you have in mind?"

Gunnar slapped the arms of the chair as he rose. "Gonna take a little ride. See what's on the old man's mind." He extended his hand to Brody again. "Don't know when I can get out there, but don't do anything yet, okay?"

"Just call."

*

Cathy had worked her magic and found Arthur "Artie" Wallace based only on the clues Gunnar had given her. She'd made it a point to tell him, in great detail, how she'd accomplished this feat, since it had taken her the better part of the morning and had quickly soured her mood. Impressive work, and he didn't mind telling her so—which perked her up a bit. Or at least her grumpy "harrumph!" had been belied by a semi-smile. He'd have to remember to give her a bonus for being a miracle worker.

Following her notes, he pulled onto the Georgetown University campus and searched for the Edward B. Bunn S.J. Intercultural Center. The ICC housed an auditorium, a language learning center, classrooms, and professors' offices. Artie's office was on the fourth floor.

Gunnar drove Sheila into the Leavey Center Garage, just down the street from the ICC. On the second level he found an opening where the vehicles on either side had gone over the lines marking the parking spots. No car would fit in the remaining space, so it was perfect for his bike. He parked Sheila between the cars, then made his way across the street to the ICC and took the stairs to Arthur Wallace's office.

The door bearing his nameplate stood ajar. Inside, a young man in his mid-twenties bent over a scarred wooden desk, a large stack of college blue-books on his left, a smaller stack on his right, and one opened in front of him.

Gunnar rapped a knuckle on the door, and the kid looked up. "May I help you?"

He stepped across the threshold. "I'm looking for Arthur Wallace."

"And you are …?"

"Gunnar Schofield. Old friend, high school buddy."

"Did you have an appointment?"

"I was hoping to surprise him."

"Well, he's not here." The young man twiddled his pen, drumming it on the desktop. "He only teaches a couple of classes. He's usually on campus just when he's teaching or during scheduled hours."

"What's his day job?"

"He does a lot of things. He writes for the Washington Post, mostly book reviews, but he also writes on the arts and sciences." He looked Gunnar over as if just noticing him, taking in his jeans and the white tee hidden under his leather jacket. Skepticism entered his eyes. "You're old friends and you two haven't kept up?"

"No, not really." He leaned against the door post. "Thought about him now and then over the years, but never did anything about it until his name came up in conversation with Wayne Oakford. Are you familiar with him?"

Skepticism gave way to wariness. "Of course. Dr. Wallace was working with him on a project over the last few months."

Gunnar shifted gears in case the suspicious kid planned to shut down the info mill. "So if he's not here, how do I reach him? We have a lot of catching up to do."

"His office hours are Wednesday from three to five."

"I'd rather not wait a week. Know where I could find him now?"

He wrote something on a pad of paper, ripped off the page, and raised it for Gunnar to retrieve. "He owns some property off campus. He's usually there during business hours."

Gunnar thanked him and headed out. The address was in a familiar neighborhood not far away.

*

Val's phone vibrated in his pocket, and he checked the screen. He held a finger up to interrupt Stark's story of his last sniper assignment and answered.

A young man's voice responded. "Yeah, uh … some guy just stopped by the office looking for Artie. Said he was a high school friend. He asked about Wayne Oakford and whether they knew each other."

"Get a name?"

"Yeah. Gunnar. Gunnar Schofield."

Val cursed. "What did you tell him?"

"Basically that Artie wasn't in, but I did give him his home address."

"Did he say whether he was going over there?"

"No, but I bet he's on his way now."

"Thanks, bro." Val disconnected and caught a glimpse of concern on Stark's face.

"What's going on?"

"Gunnar Schofield, Mary Dillard's dime-novel detective. He's alive." Which shouldn't have come as a surprise. If the woman had survived the blast, her PI would have too. "He stopped by Georgetown a few minutes ago looking for Arthur Wallace."

"Who's he?"

Val hesitated. How much did the major know? How much should Val tell him?

Very little.

"That doesn't matter," he said. "Turn around, we need to go back. We'll deliver the skull later."

He rattled off the address. Terry pulled a U and kicked up the speed.

The Headmaster was waiting for them, but Val decided not to call about their change of plans. He'd be in trouble either way because of the loose ends he'd left untied, and the Headmaster definitely wouldn't like that. Val had to remedy the situation, and not just to appease the Headmaster. Schofield and Dillard had survived two of his attempts to put them away. They'd made a fool of him.

Now it was personal.

CHAPTER TWENTY-FIVE

"NICE PLACE YOU have here," Gunnar looked around Dr. Artie Wallace's second-floor condominium. Although it was small, the main room sported polished hardwood floors, leather upholstered couches and easy chairs, high-end paintings, and large potted plants. Its nice, homey atmosphere had undoubtedly been staged by an interior designer. "This looks like one of those model homes."

Dr. Wallace beamed at Gunnar's compliment. "Thanks. It's a fixer-upper. My brother-in-law works in construction, a jack of all trades—as long as I provide the capital. We still need to finish the apartments on the lower level, but I believe it's coming along nicely. Once it's done, we'll be putting it back on the market. Interested?"

Gunnar held a hand up to fend off any further sales pitches. "No. I couldn't afford this place. Looks great though."

"Well, keep it in mind. Maybe you have a friend who'd be interested." He waved Gunnar to a chair. "Can I get you something? Beer? Something stronger?"

"No, I'm good, thanks."

"Okay, then. I'd offer something lighter, like tea, but I don't have any." Dr. Wallace crossed to the kitchen, divided from the den by an island/breakfast bar, and filled a long-spouted pitcher with water. He was a middle-aged man, long and lean—skinny would be a better term, similar to how Gunnar had pictured Ichabod Crane the first time he'd read *The Legend of Sleepy Hollow*.

He returned to the den and started watering his plants and glanced at Gunnar over his shoulder. "Now, what can I do for you?"

"I'm sure you're aware Dr. Wayne Oakford was murdered recently."

"Of course."

"Who you think would have a reason to kill him?"

He moved to the next plant. "According to the newspaper, a burglar—who has already been apprehended."

"My client doesn't think so."

"If his killer is on the loose, I certainly want to help in any way that I can." He stopped watering and gaped at Gunnar. "Your client doesn't believe the police?"

"She thinks the murder had something to do with Paluxy Man." He leaned forward, forearms settled on his knees, and studied the man's eyes. "You were helping Oakford write a book about it, weren't you?"

"Not write, research. And not really about Paluxy Man, although that was part of it." He drained the water in the last plant and put the pitcher on the kitchen island. "Wayne had approached Gary Babson about it, but Gary declined and recommended me."

"Babson. I've heard the name before. Is he a friend of yours?"

"We're both quantum physicists. I'd call him a colleague, but I suppose you could say we're friends. We've known each other for a while."

Gunnar sat back. "I'd heard Oakford was working with a quantum physicist in writing his book. I thought it strange. Why would he need the help of someone of your specialty to write a book about fossils? But then I read that you have a background as a science historian as well, and it all made sense. He wanted your help to place Paluxy Man in the context of history, right?"

"To a certain extent, yes." Dr. Wallace settled on one of the leather chairs across from Gunnar. "Wayne was formulating a new theory on the origin of human life, and he wanted to know the historical views of scientists and philosophers. In particular, he was interested in an old scientific theory known as 'spontaneous generation.' Are you familiar with it?"

"Vaguely. I remember the term from high school." Gunnar shifted his eyes to the right and tried to dig out the memory. "People witnessed flies crawling out of a slab of meat and believed the flies popped into existence out of nowhere."

"That's right. At first, even the scientists believed the flies appeared out of nowhere. Over time, as a result of experimentation, they realized the insects were actually hatched from eggs laid on the meat by adult flies. So life didn't appear spontaneously after all. Life came from life."

"And he thought this was relevant to Paluxy Man?"

"Wayne believed Paluxy Man was a homo sapien. And he believed that homo sapiens appeared suddenly, fully evolved, six thousand years ago. Now obviously I didn't agree with him, but that was his conclusion." *He propped his left ankle on his right knee.* "In his view, this highly complex form of life suddenly appeared six thousand years ago without having undergone any evolutionary process. Wayne intended to argue in his book that a sudden appearance of complex life is scientifically possible. Obviously, that's very similar to the old theory of spontaneous generation, so he wanted to understand why it was abandoned rather than modified."

"I'd bet resurrecting a rejected theory wouldn't make him very popular among his peers."

Dr. Wallace raised a brow and smirked. "You'd be right. It would have been highly controversial."

"Did anybody threaten him?"

"I don't think so." He interlaced his fingers around his knee, raising his thumbs as he spoke. "Honestly, I doubt very many people were even aware of what he was writing. But if he'd survived to finish and publish his book, it would have caused quite a stir within the scientific community. The idea that complex life can suddenly appear has been opposed by scientists for quite some time now. The theory of spontaneous generation in particular was targeted for extinction hundreds of years ago. It was opposed by some of the greatest scientists in history, including key members of the Invisible College."

Gunnar narrowed his eyes. "The what?"

"The Invisible College—a secret society of alchemists, scientists, magicians, and astrologers formed in the 1600s. It was organized as a Masonic lodge, but it doesn't appear they were focused on the religious aspects of Freemasonry. The members had different beliefs on many issues, including religion. Some of the world's most renowned scientists were members–Francis Bacon, Robert Hooke, Robert Boyle. Many others."

"And this Invisible College wanted to destroy the theory of spontaneous generation?"

"I wouldn't say they were out to destroy, but to defend," Wallace said. "I'm sure you've heard the theory that life on Earth originated in a pool of primordial slime?"

Gunnar snorted. "Who hasn't?"

Wallace grunted his agreement. "It's one of humankind's oldest creation myths. Not only is it older than science, but it predates the great Greek philosophers like Aristotle and Socrates. And that creation myth was fully embraced by the Invisible College. Today, it's taught as science under the name 'abiogenesis.'"

"Wait a second," Gunnar held up a hand to stop him. "What are you saying? That what they're teaching in classrooms as 'science' is actually a creation myth?"

"Yes, it's a creation myth. But you have to understand what I mean by that." He rested his elbows on his thighs and pressed his hands together. "The earliest living matter on Earth probably did originate in some kind of primordial soup. When something is called a 'myth,' it doesn't necessarily mean that it's false. When I say that life originating from primordial soup is a 'creation myth,' I simply mean it's a story told in Western civilization, arising out of Greek mythology, that helps explain how life first came into being."

"And this 'abiogenesis'–they teach it in public schools?"

"Yes," Wallace replied. "As I explained to Wayne, this cherished myth was threatened by the scientific theory of spontaneous generation. The members of the Invisible College continued to believe in the ancient teaching that life arose from non-life in the distant past. To defend that belief, they worked to discredit the upstart scientific theory of spontaneous generation. The members of the College publicly opposed the theory, and they ridiculed any scientist who dared to support it."

"And that worked?"

"Quite well. Those scientists who believed complex life could suddenly appear on Earth were ostracized. And today, the scientific community not only asserts that the theory of spontaneous generation is wrong, it now denies it's a scientific theory at all. And the ancient belief that life arose from non-life in a primordial slime? That's now accepted as science."

"Ironic." Gunnar shifted in his chair and tried to process what he was hearing. This stuff was unreal. It would be far easier to believe that some supreme being sneezed life into existence than it was to follow the convoluted trail left behind by centuries of so-called scientific experts.

"The Invisible College succeeded in killing the scientific theory of spontaneous generation, but the question remained—how did complex life appear on Earth?" The professor's eyes held the gleam of a challenge.

But Gunnar didn't know the answer. How could he? Everything seemed to be a colossal guess. He shook his head. "Okay, I'll bite. How?"

"We found the answer in the 1800s when Charles Darwin explained how simple life could become increasingly complex by evolving through a process of natural selection. And at that point, the College had everything it needed: abiogenesis to explain the origin of simple life in the distant past, and Darwinian evolution to explain how that simple life turned into the complex life we see today."

Gunnar rubbed the stiffness out of his right shoulder. "So does this Invisible College still exist?"

"Not in its original form, but it does have a successor. An institution known as the Royal Society was formed in 1660 as a scientific academy. Two years later, it was given a charter by the king of England. Once the Royal Society came on the scene, the Invisible College disappeared from the historical record, which strongly suggests that the College went out of existence at the time the Royal Society came into existence. Secondly, most of the scientists who formed the Royal Society were known members of the Invisible College." Dr. Wallace held up his index finger, his eyes gleaming. "And there's a third reason to believe that the Invisible

College transformed into the Royal Society—the motto of the Royal Society: *Nullius in verba*."

Gunnar knew this without having to strain his brain. "'Put nothing in writing.'"

"Right. It's the same Latin motto that was used by the Invisible College."

All this talk and digging out high school science lessons from his memory banks were giving Gunnar a monumental headache. More so than usual. Probably the weird hours he'd been keeping. He rose and paced to the window. "I don't get it."

"What is it you don't get?"

"Why would a scientific academy be opposed to putting anything in …"

Below, two burly men crossed the street toward the apartment building. Body-builder types. The first wore a jacket and had a noticeable bulge on his side. His companion had a buzz cut; his weapon protruded obviously from a shoulder holster.

"You were saying?" Dr. Wallace prompted, but Gunnar held up a hand to silence him.

Neither of the men below looked familiar, but he knew who the second one was just based on the haircut—and he'd be willing to bet the man sported a tattoo of a square and a compass on the nape of his neck. The guy who showed up at Jim Merrow's place looking for Eric. The guy who tried to kill them in Tennessee.

"Are you expecting company?"

"No." The professor joined him at the window. "What's wrong?"

"I think I may have just found Oakford's killers," he said. "Only one problem. They're coming for me, and I don't have my gun. How do I get out of here?"

Dr. Wallace paled. "The only way out is the way you came in."

"There has to be an emergency exit."

"The building has a fire escape, but it's unstable." He pointed out a window that overlooked an alleyway. "It's one of the things we need to fix before renting the apartments out. Besides, the window is painted shut."

Gunnar peered down at the fire escape. It was rusty and rickety, and held no visible evidence it was even attached to the building. But after surviving the explosion at the cave and the ladder-climb out of it, he could easily survive this. He delivered some well-placed blows to the windowsill with the heel of his hand, then tried to lift it.

"I can't believe this. You've brought killers to my home?" Dr. Wallace paced from the window to the door and back to the window, wringing his hands as he walked. "Oh, good Lord—they're coming! You brought killers to my home!"

Another blow to the window's right side. "They're not after you. You're safe." The window squealed and whined as it rose, but it did rise—at least far enough for Gunnar to climb out. "Call nine-one-one."

"Yes, yes—call the police." Dr. Wallace headed for his desk with a purposeful stride. "I'll call the police."

As Gunnar climbed onto the fire escape, one of the goons pounded on the door. The noise rattled Dr. Wallace. He turned from his task and again began wringing his hands.

"Nine-one-one," Gunnar hissed. "Call nine-one-one!"

He didn't wait to see if the professor regained his reason, but darted down several stairs as fast as he could before the entire thing came unbolted from the building and collapsed to the concrete below. He didn't make it quite far enough. A portion of the ladder yanked free from the wall, tossing him to the ground. He landed hard on his shoulder in a tangle of rusty metal. He scrambled free from the wreckage and took assessment of the damage to his body. Nothing seemed broken, but he'd be living on pain pills and bathing in Aspercreme for the next several days.

He yanked a Buck knife from his hip pocket and limped toward the white utility truck the goons had emerged from. Florida plates. Just like the truck in Tennessee. A solid shove of the blade in both tires on the driver's side should keep them occupied.

He hobbled to Sheila just as Buzz-Cut exited the building and shouted, "Hey, you!"

With sirens ringing out in the distance, Gunnar sped away in the opposite direction. He stole a glance behind him. Buzz-Cut angrily kicked a flat tire on the truck, and Hulk #2 waved his pistol toward the retreating motorcycle.

Gunnar urged Sheila to give him her all.

*

Val and Maj. Stark scrambled to hide their guns in the utility van before the police arrived, then strolled down the tree-lined street to a nearby coffee shop. Vital now to look like innocent pedestrians.

Two squad cars squealed to a stop at the condo. As bystanders would do, Val and Stark turned to watch the action and were soon joined by other morbidly curious gapers. When the crowd around them increased, they slipped away and continued to the cafe. They'd done everything right, but Val continued to grind his teeth.

They went inside, ordered coffee from a pimply kid with rings in both nostrils, then returned to one of the outside tables under a cabana-striped awning. The hubbub down the street settled, the crowd dispersed. Before long, the cops returned to their squad cars and drove away.

Stark swirled his swizzle stick around the brew in his paper cup. "This was your play. What's the game plan?"

"We call someone to help with the van tires. Then we wait."

Val's phone vibrated and he looked at the screen. James Darbyshire. The Chancellor was no doubt calling to let him know the Headmaster wasn't happy. Great. He grumbled a few choice words and let the call go to voice mail.

"Trouble?"

"More than you know." Val shifted to pull his wallet out of his hip pocket, then flipped through to find the roadside service contract that came with the van rental.

CHAPTER TWENTY-SIX

MARY SLAMMED INTO her office, startling Celeste from whatever held her concentration.

"Fun time at the Quigley estate?" Celeste's voice held a sarcastic tone to compliment her wry smile.

"Grand. Simply grand." Mary matched Celeste's tone, then let her anger take over. "That man is impossible! Do you know what he wanted me to do?"

"Don't know, don't care." Dr. Lodge rumbled from inside his office. "Did you get the check?"

Heat rose to Mary's cheeks. She mouthed to Celeste, "Why didn't you warn me he was here?"

Celeste shrugged.

Mary took a second to calm her nerves and smooth her clothes, then stepped to Dr. Lodge's open office door. "No sir, I didn't get it."

"Why not?" he thundered. "That was the whole point of you going out there this morning! You blew half a day and don't have a thing to show for it."

"He wanted me to do more than blow half a day. He wanted me to fly to Miami with him."

"So? Go! If that's what it takes to make him happy and bring a fat check to the Academy, why aren't you on the plane?" Dr. Lodge shooed her with his hands.

"He's a married man." She crossed her arms and smirked. "Besides, you can't require me to do what he was suggesting as part of my job description. That would be illegal on so many levels."

"No, no, of course not." He huffed a breath from his ruddy cheeks. "I'm not requiring it of you. Not at all. You know I wouldn't do that. I just overreacted is all. We could sure use that money."

"I know we could." With a sigh, she toned down her snarky attitude. She entered the office and sat in a leather chair across from him. "Maybe next time you should try the buddy system and send a guy to collect. No woman would be safe around that man."

Dr. Lodge snorted in agreement. "Good thing you didn't go to Florida. We have a meeting at the Strickland Dunn office in thirty minutes."

"Oh, that's right." Another thing Mary had completely forgotten as she traipsed all over the country in search of Wayne's killer. She vaulted from her seat. "Give me a few minutes to freshen up, and we can ride over together."

*

Mary and Dr. Lodge took seats at Strickland Dunn's glossy conference table. They were in the company of the Academy's largest contributors, less Robert Quigley of course, who was no doubt sunning on some Miami beach by now. At the far end of the table sat handful of people Mary didn't know. The attorneys, probably. She recognized Dean Purcell, the lead attorney for the Borden School Board.

In his mid-forties, Dean had the physique of a much younger man, belied by silver streaks in his rich dark hair. His suit was no doubt tailored, the tie probably silk, and there was no questioning the Italian background of his loafers. The wedding band on his finger meant very little. He was still a nice catch for any single woman, particularly since he was recycled into the market every five years.

He concentrated on his power-point presentation, fiddling until the words "*CARSON V. BORDEN SCHOOL BOARD*" finally glared from the white screen on the far wall.

He gave a satisfied nod, then turned to the others in the room. He flashed a smile, showing off too-white teeth, and introduced himself, then the others at the table. Each grave-faced professional nodded in turn, and Mary did the same with a professional coolness she didn't feel. Many of those in attendance were the same ones at the party, the contributors who'd witnessed her frantic escape from the Lodge home to race to Uncle Wayne's house. They greeted her with sympathetic smiles she was wary of—what did these people really think of Uncle Wayne? Were they aware of the controversy surrounding his name?

If not now, they soon would be.

Dean introduced Dr. Steven Frampton, a noted professor of paleontology from Georgetown University and an expert witness for the respondents, the Borden School Board. Dr. Frampton was Dean's opposite. Short and dumpy, with mousy brown hair apparently styled by a Byzantine monk, Dr. Frampton still seemed to command the panel's attention with an inexplicable, yet undeniable charisma. His dark brown eyes were sharp, intelligent, and lively, as if devouring everything they saw. His head tilted when he caught her eye, as if he was trying to figure something out.

She shuddered and turned her attention to Dean.

He said, "I'll be turning the podium over to Dr. Frampton in a few minutes to help explain the science involved, but I want to quickly review the law."

At his cue, the lights dimmed and he dove into his presentation. "Thomas Carson has sued the school board for reinstatement into his teaching position and compensatory and punitive damages on the basis he was unlawfully terminated. According to Carson, he was not teaching creationism—that is, not teaching religion."

Dean clicked the gadget in his hand and the slide changed to "CASE LAW," followed by a number of bullet points. He went through a litany of court cases about creationism and the classroom, starting with the 1982 case of *McLean v. Arkansas Board of Education* and ending with *Kitzmiller v. Dover Area School District* in 2005.

"So, how does this all this apply to Thomas Carson and the Borden School Board?" Dean verbalized the question that was undoubtedly on everyone's mind. "Carson was teaching scientific criticisms of the theory of evolution, which the Supreme Court has said is permissible. He went outside the classroom texts, but he didn't pull his arguments from creationist sources–he relied solely upon respected science journals. He relied on two primary discoveries: the Cambrian Explosion and the fossil found in Texas, which was dubbed 'Paluxy Man.'"

The slide changed to a picture of Darwin's Tree of Life. It showed a single organism at the bottom, from which a tree branched out to a large number of species of increasing complexity.

"From here, I'm going to let Dr. Frampton take over." Dean waved a hand to the scientist, who stood and retrieved the device from him.

"When Darwin came up with his theory," Dr. Frampton began in an authoritative voice, "the oldest known fossils were from the Cambrian period, which already had a wide variety of complex life forms, including different classes and phyla. Darwin believed future exploration of the Precambrian beds would show a long history of gradual divergence, going all the way back to a single common ancestor. But he was wrong. Precambrian beds hold mostly single-celled organisms. Then, in what is called the Cambrian Explosion, a wide variety of complex life appears from out of nowhere in the Cambrian strata. Some scientists refer to this sudden appearance of complex life as 'the biological Big Bang.'

"Did the lack of transitional fossils in the Precambrian record disprove Darwin's theory?" He shook his head to answer his own question. "Not at all. Scientists came up with an explanation known as the Artifact Hypothesis. According to the hypothesis, transitional fossils are missing from the oldest strata because the earliest life forms must have been too small and soft-bodied to become fossilized.

"However, in recent years, scientists were able to examine the Precambrian beds in China. What do you suppose they found? Sponge embryos!" He clicked to a new slide showing a black-and-white image of a single-celled organism. "They found sponge embryos in the Chinese Precambrian strata, demonstrating that even the smallest and softest life forms would have been preserved if they existed."

He aimed those piercing brown eyes at each person in turn as he let them soak this in.

Mary drew her brows and nodded, hoping to appear intelligent. Truth be told, it would take far more than the instant allowed for much of this to click with her brain. If the sponge embryos disproved the Artifact Hypothesis, then Darwinian evolution was discredited. Wasn't it?

Certainly not. Evolution was established science ... wasn't it?

She studied her fingernails to hide her confusion.

None of this made sense. The fossil record wasn't perfect, there were some gaps and certain unanswered questions, but it supported Darwin's theory of evolution. If anything fully discredited the theory, this meeting would be moot. Surely the professor would present evidence supporting evolution. Maybe he was just building up to it.

That was it. He had to present Carson's case first, then he'd show how he would tear it apart.

Dr. Frampton's voice demanded her attention. He raised his finger to the air. "If sponge embryo fossils exist, anything can be fossilized. Including transitional creatures. That was one of Carson's strongest points. He taught his students that the lack of transitional fossils in the Precambrian record is simply inconsistent with evolution by natural selection.

"But Carson didn't stop there." The slide of Darwin's Tree of Life reappeared on the white board, and Dr. Frampton continued. "Darwin's theory predicted that the number of species would expand from the Cambrian period to the present, like branches on a tree. Carson pointed out that the fossil record shows the exact opposite: the number of species was highest during the Cambrian era, and it slowly decreased over time due to extinctions."

The professor tapped the remote, and the next slide appeared, showing a series of primates walking from the left to the right, beginning with a knuckle-dragging monkey on the left and ending with a modern human on the right. The slide was titled "THE MARCH OF PROGRESS."

"Carson's second criticism of Darwinian evolution was based on Paluxy Man." Dr. Frampton recounted the discovery of the hominid fossil, followed by the discovery of the fossilized dinosaur, and Wayne's carbon dating of both. "It's an old creationist trick."

He focused on Mary, his stare branding her as if she had collaborated in her uncle's actions. His attention made her feel like a soldier in enemy camp. But she'd had nothing to do with Uncle Wayne's research and theories. She couldn't decide whether to squirm in her seat or glare back at the sharp-eyed little gnome.

Finally, he shifted his gaze to the others. "Carbon dating test results show the fossil is only thousands of years old, when we known that the fossils are in fact millions of years old. The creationists use the results to claim that science supports a literal reading of the Book of Genesis. Scientists agree you can't carbon date a dinosaur fossil, but the public doesn't understand this. When carbon dating indicated both fossils to be roughly 6,000 years old, Dr. Oakford claimed the results were accurate. Thomas Carson quoted extensively from Dr. Oakford, leading his students to believe humans and dinosaurs may have co-existed."

Every time Frampton had mentioned her uncle's name—with obvious contempt in his voice—her cheeks burned.

At last, he resumed his seat and someone switched on the lights.

Mary unclenched her teeth and released a sigh of relief. She cast furtive glances at the others in the room, half expecting everyone to be glaring their accusations at her. Apparently most of them hadn't made the connection; those who had studiously avoided her eyes.

Dean rose from his chair near the head of the table. "Our challenge is to keep this case from getting to a jury. Carson never directly taught creationism. He simply presented scientific information that raised questions about evolution, and the Supreme Court has ruled such teaching techniques permissible. In order to prevail in court, we have to satisfy the *Lemon* test. We have to show that teaching students about the Cambrian Explosion and Paluxy Man has a prima facie religious purpose or the primary effect of advancing religion. And that won't be easy before a judge, let alone a jury. If this case goes before a jury, evolution will be placed on trial, and we will probably lose." He looked around the room with a brow raised to make sure everyone got his point. "Questions?"

Dr. Lodge settled back with a confident air, as if dismissing the attorney's entire argument. "It seems to me this case is just like the *Kitzmiller* case. It involved a public school presenting information critical of evolution, just like Carson. The court ruled their activities unconstitutional because they advanced religion. If that was unconstitutional, Carson's case should be too."

"No, there's a big difference. In *Kitzmiller*, the school was promoting creationism under the name of 'Intelligent Design.' In our case, Mr. Carson only provided scientific information that would tend to raise doubts about evolution. He never promoted any alternative."

"The proponents of Intelligent Design don't promote an alternative, either," Dr. Lodge replied. "They criticize evolution, but they never identify the designer. Why? Because everybody knows if there's a designer, that designer is God." He flipped up a couple of fingers. "There are only two salient explanations for the existence of life on Earth: evolution or creation. So, if you attack evolution, you are, de facto, advancing creationism, which is religion. Carson was advancing religion, and that's unconstitutional."

"I agree with you," Dean said. "And that's probably our strongest argument. But the law isn't clear on this. If the judge rules against us and the case goes to trial, we could lose. The last thing we want is twelve people off the street deciding the case based on whether they believe evolution is true."

Mary asked, "Why can't you just explain the truth of evolution to the jury?"

"The science of evolution is too complex," Dean said. "It would confuse them."

She started to protest, but Dr. Lodge gave a slight shake of his head. He leaned toward her and whispered, "He's right."

CHAPTER TWENTY-SEVEN

THAT DR. LODGE'S fat fingers could nimbly work a Blackberry never failed to amaze Mary, almost as much as the fact that he would send text messages at all. His chubby paws seemed more apt for his golf clubs than a delicate piece of modern technology. Appearances could indeed be deceiving.

Shaking her head, she returned her attention to her driving, which she'd agreed to do so he could send his text messages. Traffic was moderate for the drive back to the Academy, but this close to quitting time, that blessing could change instantly. Five o'clock traffic could be a bear in the city.

After a few moments, Dr. Lodge returned the phone to his inside coat pocket. "I apologize if it was uncomfortable for you at the meeting. I should've thought of your connection to Wayne before subjecting you to that discussion."

She waved off his concerns. "It wasn't that bad. I couldn't consider myself a professional if I couldn't survive a few concealed sneers."

He gave her a distracted nod, and she took the hint that his mind was elsewhere and concentrated on traffic.

After a few moments, he said, "It's not really as easy as that, you know."

"What isn't?"

"Explaining the science of life origins to lay people."

"That's what you and Dean were saying, but I don't see why not."

She squeezed Dr. Lodge's Lincoln MKS into the left lane to pass a slow driver, then maneuvered back to the right. "Just put the theory in non-scientific language."

"I'm not talking about the language." He shifted in his seat. "Let me give you an example. The age of the geologic column is critical to dating fossils. Scientists say there are twelve major rock layers in the column, the oldest being the Precambrian, like Dr. Frampton said earlier. Because the layers of sediment were laid down over time, one would think the layers would go in order. The oldest layers on the bottom, the most recent on top, right?"

"Of course. Eric Merrow uses biostratigraphy to argue that Paluxy Man is a one hundred million-year-old monkey. He says the deeper you go in the strata, the older the things you find. Paluxy Man was found in the lower Cretaceous strata." But there was no doubt Paluxy Man was human. And she had more than her uncle's word for it—she had the skull. So didn't that disprove biostratigraphy as a fossil dating method?

She was about to ask, but Dr. Lodge held up a hand to stop her.

"It would make sense if the theory were true, but in practice, it's very rare for a location to have all twelve strata, much less have them in the proper order. Often there are missing layers. For example, even the Grand Canyon shows only five of the twelve major strata."

"Okay, so there are missing strata–"

"But like I said, it's not just missing strata," he continued. "There's also the order of the strata. What we believe are older layers are often found closer to the surface, on top of newer layers. For example, Heart Mountain in Wyoming is capped with ancient limestone. Below the limestone cap are much younger strata."

Mary scowled at the windshield. "That doesn't make sense. How could that have happened?"

Dr. Lodge settled back with his arms crossed over his chest, as if enjoying her confusion. "Scientists believe the limestone came from a similar formation in Yellowstone National Park, about sixty miles away."

"You have got to be kidding me. That implies that a layer of limestone moved sixty miles sideways."

He grinned. "That's the scientific consensus."

"And then the limestone moved up onto the top of the mountain?" Mary didn't even try to keep the skepticism out of her voice. The entire concept seemed ludicrous. "That's too farfetched for words. No logical person could possibly believe it!"

Dr. Lodge smacked his knee. "Now you can see the problem. If a scientific principle is difficult to understand or some unanswered questions remain, everyone is quick to blame the science. It must be faulty, right?"

"In this case, I believe it is."

"No, it doesn't mean there's a problem with the science. We have faith that science can and eventually will answer every question. But your average person on a jury may look at these difficulties and think just like you did—that there's something wrong with the science. The age of Earth, the fossils, the theory of evolution–all of it."

"Quite frankly, I still think there's something wrong with it. I certainly hope scientists can come up with a better theory than levitating limestone."

"And there you have it. Can you imagine how a layman would view it?" He shifted again, and his leather seat squeaked softly under his weight. "We've looked into the issues extensively and spent a lot of time consulting with experts. I can assure you, there's really no easy way to convince people outside the realm of science of the truth of evolution."

"I can see that some of the issues can be confusing, but aren't there clear, simple ways to show that life started from natural processes and evolved from there?" She remembered something she'd read recently from a book in her own library, and snapped her fingers. "Like the Miller-Urey experiment. Scientists simulated the chemical conditions of early Earth in a laboratory, added a spark, and created a primal form of life."

"That test was performed back in the 1950s," Dr. Lodge said. "Scientists now know that Earth's early atmosphere was nothing like the one used in that experiment. It was oxygen-rich, just like our atmosphere today. When the Miller-Urey test is performed using realistic atmospheric conditions, the test fails. And besides, the experiment never created life, not even the simplest kind. All it actually created were some amino acids."

"Okay, what about Haeckel's Embryos? Embryos change shape as they grow, following the same sequence of evolutionary change as their ancestors. Early embryos of different vertebrate species all look the same, but as they grow they retrace the evolutionary path of their species. For example, you can see a human embryo growing gills and a tail on the way to becoming a baby–"

Dr. Lodge waved a hand to cut her off. "Urban legend. Human embryos never have gills or tails. Not at any time during development. Ernst Haeckel was a fraud. That's been known for decades. It's an embarrassment that those drawings are still used in American biology textbooks."

"Fine then." Mary grew flustered. Surely something she'd learned– some theory supporting evolution–would suffice to illustrate its voracity … oh, there was! She gave the steering wheel a triumphant slap. "The peppered moth. It comes in two shades, white and brown. Originally, the white version was common and the brown version was rare. That's because the tree trunks were covered with white lichen, so the white moths were better camouflaged against birds. But then Britain became polluted in the 1800s and the lichen died, leaving dark tree trunks. The brown moth now had the better camouflage, and birds devoured the white moths off the tree trunks, so the dark moth became common and the light moth became rare. Then, in the 1950s, anti-pollution laws were passed. Sure enough, the white lichen returned to the trees and the white moth again became common. It's a clear, simple example of survival of the fittest that any jury could easily understand."

"That does indeed sound like a beautiful and elegant example of evolution, but unfortunately it's another canard." Dr. Lodge gave her a smug look. He really did seem to be enjoying toppling all her ideas. "Since the 1980s, there have been a number of published articles debunking that claim. In twenty-five years of research, only one peppered moth was ever found resting on a tree trunk in the wild. The moth is active at night and when it rests, it typically chooses a place where it'll be hidden during the day–the underside of tree branches far up in the canopy where birds can't see them, regardless of their coloration. Despite what you've heard, peppered moths seldom rest on tree trunks in the wild. And those rare exceptions are insufficient to explain the rapid change in the moth's coloration."

Had all the evidences she'd been taught to prove the validity of evolution been debunked? It couldn't be possible. She tried again. "Look, this isn't something I read on the internet. I was taught about the peppered moth in college biology. I distinctly remember seeing pictures of the moths resting on tree trunks. I'm not talking about drawings, either. I'm talking actual photographs of peppered moths on tree trunks. Photographs."

"You're right. There are pictures of peppered moths resting on tree trunks, and you can find them in most biology textbooks across the country. But those photographs aren't real. Do you know how they make them? With glue. They add a drop of glue to a dead moth's underside and attach it to the tree, then they snap a photo. That's how they made the pictures you saw in your science textbooks."

Mary slipped lower in the driver's seat. He'd just shot down every ounce of proof she'd been taught about evolution. And he believed in it! A creationist would have a field day with all the fabricated evidence. Based on her experience with him, she knew Gunnar would have a blast with it. And she would be defenseless against his derisive witticisms. Every thread of evidence supporting her stance had just been expertly snipped away.

"I'm relieved no one in the meeting mentioned the article in the *Proceedings* this afternoon," Dr. Lodge said. "Having Paluxy Man discredited like that could scare away some of our contributors."

"Oh, the only thing that's going to be discredited is that article. I'm sorry to have to take Eric down, but his conclusions are wrong. You said yourself the dating technique he used was in error. Paluxy Man was undoubtedly homo sapien."

He frowned. "You never got back to me with proof of that claim. I thought we'd established that the skeleton is that of an ape."

"Nope." Mary tossed him a grin. "It was human, and I can prove it. I have the skull–the real skull."

"What do you mean, 'the real skull'? The entire fossil is locked in the Smithsonian vault."

"I'm sure the rest of the skeleton may be there, but I have the skull. And the plaster cast of Paluxy Man on display at the Smithsonian doesn't match the original. Uncle Wayne kept the skull. He never sent it."

"Never sent it," Dr. Lodge repeated. He seemed dazed, as if she'd hit him between the eyes with a two-by-four.

"That's right. He kept it."

His mouth gaped like a guppy's, then he seemed to gather his senses.

As she pulled into the parking lot, she cast a quick glance at him. He'd burrowed down in his seat, and seemed lost in thought. Probably not a good time to tell him all she'd learned the past few days.

CHAPTER TWENTY-EIGHT

JAMES DARBYSHIRE STRODE into the laboratory at Hadley Scientific in a cloud of self-importance and impatience. A young man in a white coat greeted him, but the Chancellor waved him off. "Where is Val Gordon?"

"He's probably in the loading bay assisting with the crates."

"No, I just came from there. Nobody has seen him all day."

"I don't know then. He should be here by now. Let me check the calendar." The lab tech clicked the keys on his computer and began tapping. "If he had somewhere else to be, it should be noted here."

"This is shipment day!" Darbyshire waved his hands. "There's nowhere else he should be. He didn't call?"

The tech shook his head.

Darbyshire emitted a stream of choice words as he barreled out of the lab. As he marched down the hall to his office, he hit the redial for Val's cell number—again—and checked his watch. Just after three p.m. He'd called an hour ago and an hour before that, but Val hadn't answered. He knew better. The only excuses for not answering his phone were unconsciousness or death.

His blood sped through his body. With every ring on Val's phone, Darbyshire's pulse rocketed.

The trucks needed to leave at nightfall, and the man was nowhere to be found.

Finally, Val answered.

"Where are you?" the Chancellor demanded. He shoved open his office door so hard it slammed against the adjacent wall.

"In my truck."

"In your truck? You were supposed to be here hours ago!" His left eye twitched. He pressed his free hand to it and tried to calm down. "Why aren't you at work?"

"I am working. I have Paluxy Man's skull."

His breath caught, and he glowered out the window. "What are you talking about?"

Val brought him up to date, finishing with how Gunnar had escaped from Professor Wallace's condo. "But we have a hunch where he's going."

"Leave him alone. Don't worry about that stupid detective. Get over here!"

There was a pause. "But he's alive, and Mary Dillard is alive—"

"I don't care. Let them go. I want Paluxy Man—the entire skeleton, including that skull—shipped to Wright-Patterson tonight. Get your butt over here!"

"But I thought the Headmaster wanted them dead."

"Are you arguing with me? Are you seriously arguing with me?" His blood pressure soared high enough to heat his face. "Listen up. I don't care if they're alive, and I don't care what they know. They can say anything they want, but nobody will believe them without the fossil. If they don't have proof, they have nothing. Nothing." He took a breath and brought his voice back to its normal tone. "If the Headmaster still wants them dead once that fossil's secured, fine. But get that skull here immediately. Do you understand me?"

Val assured him they'd reversed course and were headed his way.

Darbyshire clapped his phone on his desk with enough force he had to check it to make sure it didn't break. With a deep sigh, he closed his eyes and rubbed his temples.

So, there really was a skull. A human skull. Who all knew about it? Cranston, for certain, and his crew from the Paluxy dig. Mary Dillard and her P.I. And whoever they'd told.

Clearing the world of witnesses wasn't feasible—but it also wasn't necessary. Tell a lie long enough, it becomes the truth, and with the fossil in their hands, no one could successfully dispute the authenticity of the skeleton on display in the Smithsonian.

As far as the world was concerned, "Paluxy Man" was a misnomer.

CHAPTER TWENTY-NINE

MARY FOLLOWED DR. Lodge through the bronze doors of the National Academy of Sciences building. He pulled out his cell again, and she punched the button on the elevator. With him occupied and the elevator slower than a snail on ice, she took the time to study the building that housed her office. More often than not, she'd been distracted as she stormed through on her way to the third floor. Now, it was as if she was seeing it for the first time.

She'd always considered it beautiful and ornate, but now it seemed so … religious. The entrance doors themselves bore the medallions of philosophers, pagan gods, and scientists. The foyer held stained glass grilles decorated with the signs of the zodiac. Towering over the Great Hall was the magnificent Byzantine dome, its supportive arches adorned with the ancient mystical elements of earth, air, water, and fire; and below the dome was a pendulum with the images of pagan sun gods.

The place reminded her of the Roman Catholic Church her mother had taken her to as a child. Sure, there were some differences. The cathedral had marble statues of saints, stained glass images of the stations of the cross, while the Academy's windows were shuttered with the bronze icons of scientists. And the gods adorning this building were pagan, not Christian. But there were more similarities than differences.

As the elevator dinged its arrival, she shook her head. No wonder the Academy building was known as a temple of science.

Dr. Lodge scowled at his phone and slipped it back into his pocket.

They entered the elevator together, and he pushed the button for the third floor. "Let's talk in my office."

Once they'd settled in, him at his desk, her across from him, he said, "I just got news about Howard Sheldon's condition. He's declining rapidly, and the doctors say he probably won't make it through the weekend."

"That's terrible!" Mary's heart clutched. The former director of development wasn't expected to improve from his fast-spreading cancer, but hearing the update was still upsetting. "I haven't spoken with him personally, but Celeste has been visiting him every day at the hospital and praying for him. Apparently her church is praying for him, too."

Dr. Lodge grunted.

"It can't hurt." Mary said.

"You sure about that?"

His question—or maybe his cynical expression—stunned her. "Well, yeah. I believe in God. Don't you?"

"So you believe the Bible is the 'infallible word' of God?" He held his arms up, shaking his hands like a TV preacher, using the tone of voice of a slick-haired, smooth-talking evangelist.

He had never behaved this way before, and it made her uncomfortable. She wrapped her arms around her middle. "Not the infallible word, no. It's been translated and tampered with so many times, it has too many human mistakes in it to take too seriously. But I do believe in its message. There is a God. He loves us. He wants everyone to love each other and take care of his creation."

"And do you believe it's his creation?"

"Of course—but not like it's presented in Genesis. Much of the Bible is poetry and symbolism. I believe in science, but who's to say evolution isn't God's plan?" She squinted at him. His reaction to Celeste's Christianity—to her own admission of belief—seemed downright venomous.

Even now, he glowered at her as if she were an evil enemy.

She tightened the hold around her waist and clenched the fabric of her blouse. "I don't know why I thought you believed the same way. I didn't realize you were such a hardcore atheist."

"There is no god—and only a fool would believe otherwise." His chest, which an instant ago seemed puffed in fury, now seemed to cave in upon itself. He sighed and shifted his gaze. "When I was eight years old, my mother was diagnosed with leukemia. The doctors gave her only a couple of months to live. But she didn't believe them. She was a fundamentalist Christian, and she believed God would heal her." He smirked. "It's funny. Even after all the years, I can still see that confidence in her face. 'You pray with me,' she'd say. 'If you ask anything in Jesus's name, he'll do it. If you ask him for bread, he won't give you a stone.'"

He rose, headed to the portable bar in the corner, and poured a couple fingers of scotch into a glass of ice. "Want one?"

Mary shook her head, and he replaced the lid on the bottle.

Rattling the ice in the glass, he said, "I believed it then. That God would heal her cancer. Two months later she died, just as the doctors had predicted."

"I'm sorry," Mary said softly. And she was sorry, for the little boy of eight, and for the grown man who still grieved.

"It was a long time ago." He toasted her with his glass, then drained the scotch in a single shot. "I'm thinking about recommending you to be the new director of development."

She blinked. The sudden change of topic spun her mind like a top. But once his words sunk in, she mentally pumped her fist in victory. Her hands relaxed, and she tried to conceal her elation with a professional demeanor. At least she hoped she appeared professional. "Thank you. I'm honored."

"But I need you to understand something." He poured himself another, then returned to his desk. "The next director must be somebody I can trust. Somebody who's realistic, and who understands the importance of being a team player."

"Okay." The word came out in four syllables as she tried to understand his point. She put her celebration on hold and eyed him warily.

Was this because she said she believed in God? It wasn't like she actually went to church or anything.

Maybe it was something else. He said he wanted a team player.

She tilted her head. "What are you getting at? Are you still upset I'm not in Miami working a check out of Quigley?"

"No, no, of course not." He waved her concerns aside. "I'm talking about Paluxy Man's skull. You really have it?"

"Yes. I locked it away just last night."

He nodded, regarding her with an expression she couldn't read. "You know how important the Borden School Board lawsuit is, don't you?—of course you do." His lips turned up in a smile that didn't brighten his face. "When the case goes to trial, I want there to be a scientific consensus that Paluxy Man was a monkey."

"But he wasn't a monkey."

"Doesn't matter. If people believe it was human, the odds of us winning the lawsuit decline dramatically."

A sense of injustice began to coil in Mary's gut, along with a healthy dose of suspicion. "What are you asking me to do?"

He shrugged a shoulder. "Just keep quiet about the skull."

She shook her head sharply enough to toss her hair. "I can't do that. If Eric Merrow's article goes unchallenged, people will believe my uncle was a fraud. He worked his entire career to establish his reputation. I won't allow his memory to be destroyed by a lie."

"I've known your uncle since grad school at Harvard. We went on different paths, but we stayed in touch over the years. And I can tell you that the Wayne Oakford I knew wasn't too concerned about his reputation. Yes, he had tremendous respect and admiration from his colleagues and the public, but that wasn't what motivated him. Wayne cared about the truth—"

"Exactly. And the truth is that Paluxy Man was a homo sapien. Uncle Wayne kept the skull for a reason. He wanted the public to know the truth."

Dr. Lodge rubbed his brow. "Look, Thomas Carson and his kind are trying to destroy science. They want to use Paluxy Man, perhaps the most significant find of our century, to damage the public's trust in science. Do you understand? They're trying to destroy everything your uncle believed in, everything he lived for." He jabbed his index finger on his desk in cadence with his words. "If they win that lawsuit, they'll teach creationism in public schools all across the country."

Mary narrowed her eyes. "You want me to distort the scientific record to save the public from creationism? Destroy science in order to save it? Darwinian evolution will always be challenged—has always been challenged. My hiding the truth of this one skeleton isn't going to change that."

"Of course not." He raised his hands, his tone rational and appeasing. "I'm not asking you to be quiet forever. When the lawsuit is over and everything has calmed down, you can show the skull to the public, correct the record, and everybody will know that Wayne just made an honest mistake."

"Wayne made an honest mistake?"

"Sorry, I meant Eric. Eric Merrow made an honest mistake in his article by relying on photographs of the fabricated skull." He circled his desk to stand beside her chair, then rested a hand on her shoulder. "Look, until the Borden School Board lawsuit is finished, I'm asking you not to show the skull to anybody. Is that asking too much? Just until the case is over."

She hesitated. It was a reasonable request. He wasn't telling her to deceive anybody, just to keep the fossil on hold awhile. The public would learn the truth in time, and her uncle's reputation would be exonerated.

Dr. Lodge returned to his side of the desk. He scribbled on a scrap of paper and handed it to her. "That's how much you'll be earning as director of development."

She looked at the number and gulped. Thanks to her parents' estate, she was in comfortable financial shape—but she was mostly living on family money. With this, she could support herself as never before without ever touching her trust fund again.

But was it worth sacrificing Uncle Wayne's good name?

She raised her eyes to meet his. "I don't know what to say. Can I take some time?"

"Sure, think it over. Sleep on it, then call me tomorrow and let me know."

"About the position or the skull?"

"The skull. Make the right decision on that, and the position is yours." He tightened his lips as he regarded her. "As I said, I need someone I can trust in this position."

*

Mary left the office, still clutching the slip of paper with her potential salary scrawled on it. Her mind reeled from the figure, the conversation, the insinuations—not to mention the hours of having her beliefs crumble like dry cookies preceded by a wasted morning of getting hit on by a lech—all on a few hours sleep.

She should be ready to drop, fully-clothed, on her queen sized bed, but she felt hyped as if all the coffee she'd consumed had finally kicked in. She wanted to do something, and although she had plenty of work, hanging around the office didn't sound appealing. Her watch read three-thirty, plenty of time to make a run to the hospital and visit with Howard Sheldon, but first she'd head home for a quick shower to freshen up.

How would Howard feel about her taking his place? What would he think about the terms? Did she dare ask? She'd have to tip-toe around several topics she wanted to discuss with him until she determined his ability and willingness to talk to her.

The money was so very tempting. Could she put off clearing her uncle's name? Should she? Forget what Howard thought—what would Uncle Wayne think?

She pulled into a florist shop en route to her condo and took a moment to call the hospital to verify Howard's visiting hours. With the phone parked at her ear, she exited her car and entered the shop. The sweet scent of gardenia overrode the fragrance of the roses and carnations. A smell that strong would be overpowering in a space as small as a hospital room. A bouquet of yellow, orange, and white carnations would be cherry, but should she choose something more subdued? Maroon, perhaps? Deep red?

Someone at the hospital finally answered the phone, and her question. Howard's visiting hours would end at five.

"I thought they weren't over until eight?"

"Those are the regular hours," the nurse said. "He's under special orders."

"Oh, okay. Thanks." That didn't give her much time. She requested a bouquet of deep red carnations and headed out the door with them.

No way she had enough time for a shower, but she did have enough for a quick change of clothes before going to the hospital.

As she drove, Dr. Lodge's proposal danced through her mind. The more she thought about it, the more she realized he was right. She didn't want to do anything that might help the creationists win the lawsuit. Uncle Wayne had dedicated his life to paleontology. It was everything to him. He would roll over in his grave if she helped the creationists teach religion in the public schools. What harm would there be if the world believed the skeleton they found in Paluxy was a monkey for another year or so?

No harm, really, yet somehow it just seemed wrong. She needed to think more about it, but she also needed to hurry if she was going to get to the hospital in time. She parked in front of her condo and flipped through her key ring for the one to the house as she walked to the front door.

The door was ajar.

Her heart began to hammer in her ears. She gently pushed it open with one finger, afraid to touch it with any more force, and peeked inside. Everything seemed to be where it should be. Nothing out of place.

"Who's in here?" she asked with as much authority as she could muster, but she couldn't keep the tremor from her voice. She fisted her key ring, leaving one key protruding between her index and middle fingers, then cautiously crossed the threshold. "I know you're in here!"

Silence.

She tiptoed into the kitchen and softly set her keyring on the counter. The clinking of the metal keys seemed to echo. She smothered the ring with both hands and darted a glance around her. No bogey-man appeared at the door, but that didn't mean there wasn't one somewhere in the condo.

She pulled out a butcher knife from its wooden block and clamped her fingers around the handle like a murderous maniac in a bad horror flick. Then she sneaked up stairs. When she reached the landing on the second floor, she stopped and listened with her breath trapped in her lungs.

Silence.

The door to her bedroom was open. She peeked inside. Nobody there. She turned around and walked into the spare room. It seemed undisturbed too. The only evidence anyone had been in the house was the door she'd probably left ajar when she rushed to work in her sleep-deprived stupor this morning. Chuckling at herself, she carried the knife back to the kitchen. After the week she'd had, it was a wonder she hadn't lost her mind.

She jogged back up the stairs to her bedroom and opened her closet for a change of clothes. Then stopped short.

The closet floor was littered with metal scraps, and the door to the safe lay on the floor. She knelt in front of the safe to peer inside.

It was empty. The skull was gone.

A noise from the first floor made her jerk around. The front door had opened and shut. Had whoever was in the condo left, or had some-one else come in?

Her knife would really come in handy right now, but without it, the closest thing she had to a weapon was a six-inch spike heel. She grabbed her shoe and slipped over to her bedroom door.

Footfalls. Someone was definitely inside.

Fear-chills scampered down her back. She tiptoed to the landing and peered over the railing to the living room below. She couldn't see anyone. She held the shoe up like a club and crept down the steps, her muscles tight and ready to spring at the first sign of danger.

"Mary, you up there?" Gunnar came around the corner from the kitchen then and looked up at her.

Her breath rushed out in a huff. "What are you doing here?"

"I need to talk to you." He smirked and pointed at her shoe. "You got a license to carry that thing?"

Heat climbed to her cheeks, and she whipped the shoe behind her back. "You could have called me first."

"Yeah, a cell phone would've come in handy." He stood at the foot of the stairs with his arms over his chest.

"Yes. It would." She leaned against the rail with her arms crossed, too. "You should step into the twenty-first century sometime. You may like it."

"So you've told me."

"You could've at least knocked."

"I did."

She released a tired sigh and sat on the step. "What are you doing here?"

Gunnar sat a few steps below her. A bruise was developing on his cheek, a knot had popped up on his right temple.

She frowned. "What happened to you? You look awful!"

"You remember Eric Merrow's grandfather told us about the guy with the buzz-cut who came just after we left? Before the mine exploded? Same guy showed up when I was speaking with Arthur Wallace. Armed and paired with an equally dangerous-looking goon. Also armed."

Mary raised her hand to her throat. "Oh no! Are you okay? How did you get away?"

"Crashed down a fire escape. Literally." He fingered his lump and winced. "But that guy's definitely after us, not Eric. Probably the same one who shot at us in Texas."

"I wonder if that's who broke in to my apartment."

Gunnar's brows drew together. "Someone broke in here?"

"Yeah. The door was ajar when I got home a few minutes ago. I just finished going through the place."

"Alone?" Gunnar shot to his feet. "Why didn't you call me? Or the police? What if he had still been in here? What were you going to do—impale him on your heel?"

Mary shot him an exasperated look. "He wasn't here. The place was empty when I got home. It looks like the only thing they took was the skull."

"The skull is gone?"

"Yes. They cut through the steel door on my safe." She released her breath in a frustrated huff. "It's gone."

He lowered himself back to his seat on the stairs. "Oh, wow. I'm sorry."

"Yeah. Me too. I just put it in there last night. How could anyone know about it?"

"You didn't tell anyone about it last night?"

"Of course not. Who would I tell?"

Gunnar rubbed his chin. "You told me several file boxes and stuff were missing from your uncle's home office. Maybe whoever did that was looking for the skull. Could be they figured you had it long before you did."

"Then why didn't they break in earlier? We've been gone all week. They would've had plenty of time."

His lips tightened. "We just don't have all the players on the field yet. So far we're no closer to figuring this out than when we started."

"No, it doesn't seem like it." Mary glanced at her watch and jumped up. "I don't have time for this. My old boss is in the hospital and probably won't make it through the weekend. I need to get there before visiting hours are over."

"But we need to talk. Can you give me ten minutes?"

"No, I really can't."

"Then I'll go with you."

She sent him into the kitchen while she ran upstairs for a quick change of clothes and a chance to freshen her make-up.

He was right. She shouldn't have entered her house if she suspected someone was in it. What if Mr. Buzz-Cut had been there? No way could she have fought him off.

CHAPTER THIRTY

THE TRAFFIC FINALLY let up. Val, who'd switched seats with Maj. Stark thirty minutes ago, steered the utility van toward Hadley Scientific. The Chancellor had made it clear he wasn't pleased. At the moment, Val wasn't pleased either. Being called off the scent of his prey before he could catch them didn't sit well with him. But it wasn't like Gunnar Schofield and Mary Dillard were safe. He may not be on their trail now, but he would be just as soon as he dropped off the skull.

Stark spoke into his phone. "We have it. This completes the order. I'll personally make sure that it ships and arrives on time." He listened for a few moments, then ended his call with a sharp, "Yes, sir!"

His face looked grim as he slid his phone back into his pocket.

"Something wrong?" Val asked.

"Not as long as the skull arrives on time. Otherwise my neck will be relieved of my head." He snorted. "I honestly think General Hayden meant it."

"It'll be there on time. Don't worry." In spite of the loose ends, Val felt confident. This would have to go down as one of the greatest successes in the history of the Invisible College. "This is huge, do you realize that? Tonight, Paluxy Man will be secure inside Wright-Patterson Air Force Base. The only other mission that could rival this is Piltdown Man."

"What's that?"

"A skull found in 1908 in a gravel pit at Piltdown, England. Long story."

"We've got a long ride." Stark propped a boot on the dashboard. "Entertain me."

Val shrugged, took a swig from his water bottle. "The workers who found it handed it over to a wealthy collector named Charles Dawson. Even though it wasn't a complete skull, what Dawson had of it was enough to let him know it was the skull of an early human. He showed it to Arthur Smith Woodward, the keeper of the geological department at the British Museum. In 1912, Woodward and Dawson went to the gravel pit and found additional pieces. When they started reconstructing it, they realized the skull was very similar to that of a modern human but with a smaller cranial capacity and a chimpanzee-like jaw.

"Aside from being only six thousand years old, Piltdown Man was not a challenge to evolution. Actually, a human with some monkey-like features was exactly what the evolutionists had hoped to find. Scientists had long been perplexed by the lack of transitional fossils between apes and humans, and Piltdown Man could potentially have served as the 'missing link' between the species. There was only one problem. If it was the missing link, it would mean that the evolution from apes to humans occurred in Europe, and that belief had become strongly disfavored among scientists." Particularly within the Invisible College. Not wise to go against the College, but Val didn't want to delve into the secret society with Stark. "In the interest of diversity, certain scientists voted that human evolution occurred in sub-Saharan Africa. So, while the Piltdown Man find did not threaten evolution itself, it conflicted with the current vision of evolution. It had to be destroyed.

"In May 1916, a high-ranking scientist, Francis Edmund Faraday, replaced the original fossils with clear fakes. Pieces of a human skull just hundreds of years old, together with the lower jaw of an orangutan and fossilized teeth from a chimp, were filed down and stained to approximate the original fossil. Faraday switched out the fossil fragments for his fakes, and the real Piltdown Man was then ground into powder. A few months later, Charles Dawson suffered a suspicious and premature death, allegedly from blood poisoning."

"Anybody ever figure it out?"

"Nope. If Dawson had actually presented Faraday's orangutan and chimp bones as human, Arthur Smith Woodward would have immediately recognized the forgery. Woodward was not only an expert, but one of the most brilliant and accomplished paleontologists to have ever lived. And it wasn't just Woodward–many of the best and brightest scientific minds in all of history had examined the original Piltdown Man and confirmed that it was genuine. Only years later–after it had been replaced with the Faraday forgery–did anybody notice the patently obvious indications that Piltdown Man was a fake."

"You'd think the scientists who examined the Faraday forgery would have known better." Stark shifted in his seat. "They should have realized that the world's foremost experts couldn't possibly have been fooled by a collection of stained and filed-down animal bones."

"Yeah. And they should have suspected that the Piltdown Man of 1916 was not the same as the one found by Dawson and Woodward. They should have known such a patently obvious fraud could never have succeeded, and the fossil must have been altered after it was found." Val took another swig of his water. "But they never questioned it. They believed what they wanted to believe. About Piltdown Man, about Darwinian evolution, and everything else."

Good thing technology had progressed from that time. Val didn't have to cobble together fossil bones from animals when confronted with an inconvenient human fossil. The United Nations had the tools to create replicas from limestone and other materials that could fool most experts. And with his manufactured "fossils" securely locked in museum vaults and scientists relying on inexact plaster casts based on those fossils, the odds of his handiwork ever being discovered were slim to none.

The sign for Hadley Scientific stood among the trimmed hedges up ahead. Val slowed and flipped on his blinker for a left turn.

Stark grabbed his cell phone. "Got to check in with the general, let him know we're here."

Val drove across the public parking lot and up to the gate at the far end. He slid his keycard through the computer and the gate rolled opened. After parking in the back lot, they carried the box holding the skull into Hadley's storage unit. The large room held more than a dozen gray storage containers, each eight feet long, six feet across, and six feet deep.

The hallway door opened, and the Chancellor stepped in, eying them. He shoved his hand out to the major. "I assume you are Terry Stark?"

"Yes, sir. Good to meet you." He shook the Chancellor's hand.

Val pulled the lid off the box. "Here it is."

The Chancellor grinned as he looked inside. "Excellent." He pointed at a container against the wall. "Let's put it with the rest of the fossil."

The three walked over and lifted the lid on the container. The fossilized human skeleton rested on a layer of yellow foam. An indentation for the skull lay just above the skeleton. Val carefully removed the skull from Mary's box and placed it inside the gray container, completing the skeleton.

"When does it ship?" Stark asked.

"Tonight," the Chancellor said. "The trucks will leave just after dark. And you two will be with them."

CHAPTER THIRTY-ONE

THE CROWDED HOSPITAL lobby didn't offer too many places to sit quietly, so when the elevator doors closed Mary inside, Gunnar searched for the cafeteria or at the very least a coffee shop. A bistro just beyond the bank of elevators filled the bill perfectly. The room was bright, but quiet, the coffee was self-serve and another minute away from becoming syrup, and an abandoned newspaper lay on every available surface. Gunnar chose a corner table and sat with his back to the wall. He had a full view of the coffee shop.

He'd begged Mary's phone off her before she entered the elevator, and felt sheepish doing it. Back in the day, public phones were everywhere. Now if they could be found at all, they were broken—lines clipped, trash jammed in the slots. He might have no choice but to buy another cell phone. They'd come a long way since the last time he'd owned one.

His thumb hovered over Mary's phone. Two years had passed since he last talked to Becky's father. Since Gunnar had been unconscious for a couple of weeks after the crash, Dan found out about Becky's death from someone neither of them knew. He'd arranged the funeral, and Becky had been buried long before Gunnar was released from the hospital. He still didn't know how he felt about that.

Afterward, Dan never answered when Gunnar had tried to call, so he just quit calling. But the number came to his mind as easily as if he'd just used it yesterday. After a deep breath, he entered it and pressed send.

His breath caught when Dan answered. He sounded older and … sicker. "Dan? It's me, Gunnar."

"I'm not supposed to talk to you. I have a lawyer now." But he was talking to him—he did answer his phone this time. That was something. "Yeah, I know you have a lawyer, but I don't understand why. Why now?"

Dan's phone rustled, a sound Gunnar associated with his hand shaking because of the Parkinson's.

"Dan?" Gunnar kept his voice gentle, non-accusatory, non-judgmental. No anger, no emotion. Just reconnect. "Why now?"

"You need to talk to my lawyer."

"I'd like to settle this between us. A lawsuit would wear you out, and I don't have time for it."

A croaky laugh spouted through the line. "You don't have time is more the reason than any concerns for my health. I haven't heard from you in—"

"You never answered my calls back then." Gunnar's voice held an edge, and he took a moment to calm down. "I don't know why you didn't take my calls, but I did try."

Dan stayed quiet.

"Look, let's meet. Let me come out to the house and we'll have a talk. Whatever's on your mind, I'm sure we can settle it between ourselves."

"Talk to my lawyer."

He disconnected.

Gunnar huffed out his breath and dropped the phone into his shirt pocket. No way would he carry a conversation with his father-in-law through a snail-slime lawyer. And the guy must've been snail slime—no one else would've taken a case he couldn't win. How much had Dan already paid him? Not Gunnar's business, of course. Dan could afford whatever the amount. Funny how he'd never flaunted his wealth or held Gunnar's poverty against him. Dan had worked for his money and handled it wisely. As long as Gunnar followed his example, Dan had treated him with a respect he'd never received from the senior Schofield.

For that alone, Dan deserved another chance to settle this without lawyers.

*

Holding the bouquet behind her back, Mary poked her head in to see if Howard Sheldon was awake. The room smelled of medicine and antiseptic and human frailty. Piggy-back IVs dripped impotent drugs into his arm with the aid of a pump that wheezed off-beat to the heart monitor. To the side sat a contraption that allowed him to give himself morphine in premeasured doses. A few cards, flowers, and balloons littered the room in a futile attempt at merriment.

Howard was going to die, and the thought made Mary choke on a sob.

She composed herself and approached the bed. "Howard? Are you awake?"

"Come in, Mary," he rasped. He had wasted away even more than when she'd last seen him. Watching him move his boney finger to adjust the bed to a sitting position made her wince.

"I brought you something."

"Thank you." In his morphine-drugged state, he barely acknowledged the carnations she held. He waved a withered hand toward the shelf to his left. "Put them with the others."

She busied herself arranging her flowers with others on the shelf. What could she say to him? How could she cheer someone so close to death's door?

"Is it true what I heard?" he asked. "Are you the new director of development?"

"Interim." She turned and gave him a weak smile. "I understand I'm in the running for the position permanently."

"Congratulations."

"Thanks, I think. I'm under strict orders to be a 'team player.'" She bit her lip. She shouldn't have hinted at any misconduct on Dr. Lodge's part. Who knew whether her doubts would make it back to his ears? She turned from the flowers and perched on the uncomfortable straight-back chair near the bed. "Did you hear about Uncle Wayne?"

He nodded.

She studied him a moment, gauging whether she should continue. With his eyes half-closed, he didn't look up to the conversation, but she may never have another chance. "I've been trying to figure out what really happened to him. The police say it was a random killing, but I'm not so sure. I have reason to believe that a scientist may have been behind it."

His eyes opened wide. He seemed more awake and aware than he had when she first came in, as if he were eager to have this conversation. "You're right. But the scientist was Oakford himself. His own stubbornness did him in."

"What are you talking about?"

"Do you know Gary Babson?"

"I've heard of him. From what I've been told, he was the person who warned Uncle Wayne that his fossil would be altered."

"Yes, exactly. He's the one who caused this whole tragedy." He squirmed up on his elbows, trying to raise his frail body higher on the pillows. Mary helped him until he seemed settled and comfortable. He thanked her and offered a feeble smile. "I'm not sure where to start. There's a United Nations operation—"

"Operation Remnant," she said. "I know."

"Right. Babson warned Wayne not to let Paluxy Man out of his sight or the scientists from Operation Remnant would change it into an ape. Wayne wasn't sure what to believe, until he saw the plaster replica on display in the Smithsonian. It didn't match the real fossil—it resembled a monkey, just as Babson warned. Wayne went straight to James Darbyshire in a rage, furious about what Operation Remnant had done to his find. He ranted about a book he was writing and how he was going to expose the operation to the world. He carried on about his new theory he was going to present at the paleo-anthropology conference this summer, and how it would bring an end to Darwinian evolution." He grimaced, obviously in pain again. After a moment, he continued. "Telling James was the worst thing he could have done. Wayne didn't know he's an insider."

"An insider? You mean James Darbyshire–the president of the Smithsonian–is part of Operation Remnant?"

"No, not Operation Remnant." He put a paper-dry hand on Mary's. "The Invisible College."

"The secret society of scientists?" Mary tried to wrap her brain around the new information. How did the president of the world's largest museum fit into all this?

"The College has used its influence to put its members in key positions. Many of the people involved in Operation Remnant are members of the College."

"Operation Remnant is part of the United Nations. Why would the UN want to change fossils?"

"It doesn't, it just wants to preserve them," he answered. His voice was still raspy. He coughed, and the action seemed to rack his body. Mary gave him a sip of water, and he seemed to settle down. After a moment and a rattling breath, he continued. "The United Nations is creating stone replicas so realistic, they're indistinguishable from the real fossils. But with the help of Operation Remnant and Hollister Baird, the replicas are changed–size, shape, age–so that the supposed 'fossil' supports the theory of evolution." He raised his index finger. "That's the point. Protecting the theory of evolution. It's a religion to them."

"So why was Wayne wrong to confide in Dr. Darbyshire?"

"He is the Chancellor of the Invisible College, the highest ranking member, second only to the Headmaster. He, more than any of us, dedicated his life to preserving the theory. He took any threat to Darwinian evolution personally."

A knot formed in her belly. Had Darbyshire ordered a hit on her uncle? "Uncle Wayne posed a threat, didn't he?"

"A dangerous threat. Darbyshire asked him if he could prove his allegations, if he had evidence for his new theory—"

"And Uncle Wayne told him about the skull."

"What skull?"

"What skull? Paluxy Man's skull! You don't know?" That didn't make sense. Without the skull, how had her uncle posed a threat? "Uncle

Wayne kept it. He must've taken Babson's word seriously enough to protect himself. Didn't you know about it? Didn't Darbyshire?"

Howard shook his head. The effort made him wince, but he kept his attention on her. "No, we never knew about a skull. Where is it now?"

"I don't know. I had it for a while, but someone stole it. Nothing else in my apartment was touched, just that. How they discovered I had it, I'll never know." A worm of suspicion slithered into her thoughts. "Wait a minute. You said 'we.' 'We never knew about a skull.' Who are you talking about?"

"The Invisible College. I was a member, too."

"You?" Her mind reeled. Was Howard part of murdering her uncle? Bile rose in her throat. "You are a member of the college?"

"Of course. Some of the biggest names in science are members. Deans of prestigious universities. Publishers of science journals. Presidents of museums. The president of Hollister Baird is a member too. I know all the names. I was a member of the High Council." He shifted his focus to the wall in front of his bed. "When your uncle told the Chancellor—Darbyshire—about his new theory of human origins, he called an emergency meeting of the High Council. I was there. Darbyshire wanted to put out a hit on Wayne. The Councilors approved it. The Headmaster had the authority to override the High Council, but he accepted the vote."

Tears formed in Mary's eyes. She shook her head. "Howard, you? You voted to have my uncle killed?"

"No!" Pain overcame him, twisting his features. He fumbled for the morphine button and clicked it, then returned his gaze to her. "I was outraged—gave them my resignation. When I got home, I called Kevin and Wayne and warned them that their lives were in danger if they didn't retract their statements. I begged them to publicly state that Paluxy Man isn't human and that they'd never mention their theory again. Kevin agreed, he did what I asked. But your uncle ..." The morphine began kicking in, and Howard's words became slurred, his eyes less focused. "Wayne was so stubborn, he wouldn't back down. I wasn't surprised a few days later when I heard that he'd been killed ..."

"You said the Headmaster could've stopped the hit," Mary said. "Who is he? Who is the Headmaster?"

Howard's eyelids fluttered. "So tired."

"Howard, who is he?" Mary stood over him, gently shook his shoulder, willed him awake. "Who? Who is he?"

But he was beyond reaching now.

He'd at least tried to save Uncle Wayne. That was something.

She pressed the controls and set the bed to approximately where it had been when she entered, then smoothed the covers around him. She sniffed back her tears. He'd at least tried.

A haggard woman entered the room with a large cup of coffee. She started at the sight of Mary. "Who are you?"

Mary rushed over to shake Mrs. Sheldon's hand and introduce herself. She'd never met the woman, but her picture had held a predominant place on Howard's desk.

"Well, thank you for coming by, Mary." She moved to the chair beside her husband's bed and dropped into it wearily, placing her coffee on the service table. "I'm sorry if he wasn't much company. He stays drugged these days."

"Actually, we had a good talk, and he helped me understand some things about my uncle Wayne."

Mrs. Sheldon narrowed her eyes. "Wayne Oakford?"

"Yes, did you know him?"

"You're one of them, aren't you?" The woman shot from her chair and pointed to the door. "Get out. Get out now!"

"But—"

"Go! And don't come back!" Mrs. Sheldon's finger shook, her face turned crimson. "Stay away from us!"

*

Mary exited the elevator on the first floor and found Gunnar sitting on one of the orange plastic benches lining the hospital's tinted windows. When he saw her, he stood. His brows drew together in a look of concern. "What's wrong?"

"Howard said James Darbyshire ordered the hit on Uncle Wayne.

Do you know who he is? The president of the Smithsonian! And he's the Chancellor of the Invisible College—can you imagine? And some other guy, the Headmaster, could've stopped the hit, but he didn't." She lowered herself onto the bench and slumped, elbows on knees, head in hands. Everything seemed so surreal, so hopeless. "How can we fight the Invisible College?"

"Did Howard tell you who the Headmaster is?"

"No, and I doubt I'll ever get to find out—at least not from him." She rubbed her temples and straightened on the bench. "Mrs. Sheldon kicked me out of his room with strict instructions not to come back. She accused me of being one of 'them.'"

Gunnar sat beside her. "Who?"

She shook her head. "I don't know unless she thinks I'm a member of the Invisible College out to kill him. Howard was in it, too. On the high council. He told me what they've been doing to science and what they did to my uncle. And he told me why. They didn't kill him because of Paluxy Man—they don't even know about the skull. They killed him because of the book he was writing. Because of his new theory. They were afraid it would destroy Darwin's theory of evolution."

"So, if they don't know about the skull, who stole it?"

Mary flipped her hands up. "I don't know. I don't know anything anymore. Nothing makes sense. Just that some huge secret society ordered a hit on my uncle. And why? Because he had a different theory? This wouldn't have been the first time Darwinian evolution has been attacked. What made him such a threat?"

"Maybe his position as a predominant scientist. Or maybe because his theory would make better sense. Be more widely accepted."

"We'll never know, will we?" Tears blurred her vision. She tried unsuccessfully to blink them away. "He never got to write his book. We'll never know whether his idea held any validity."

"Maybe we can find out." Gunnar said. "Remember the name Gary Babson?"

"Yeah, it came up again here." Mary ran a knuckle under each eye. Concentration mattered more than tears now. She'd have her crying jag later. "Howard confirmed what Dr. Freed said. Babson was definitely the person who warned them about the fossil being altered, but it was Howard himself who warned them how dangerous their plan was."

"Arthur Wallace said Babson may know more about the book and your uncle's theory. Wallace himself just did some research, but he seemed to think Babson was more deeply involved." Gunnar flipped through his notepad. "He works for the Institute of Science Research. I have the address and number right here."

She smirked when he pulled her cell phone from his pocket. Surely by now he'd realized the value of having one of his own.

He dialed the number, looked at his watch, and winced. "Hopefully somebody's still there."

After a few moments, he spoke into the phone. "Hi, I'm trying to reach Gary Babson … I really need to talk with him. It's urgent." He shot a glance at Mary. "What's the flight number? When does it leave?"

Gunnar scribbled on his notepad, then disconnected. "Let's go!"

Mary's pulse raced as scrambled to her feet. "Where are we going?"

"To the airport. Babson's on his way to Australia."

CHAPTER THIRTY-TWO

"**D**R. BABSON! DR. Gary Babson!" Mary called over the din of the crowd at the security gate for the United flight to Sydney. Weary business people and excited vacationers barely gave her a glance, so she and Gunnar moved farther ahead, closer to the TSA security scanner. "Gary Babson! Is Dr. Gary Babson here?"

A few feet from the scanner, a short, stocky man with a thatch of salt-and-pepper hair turned to her. He bore the shoulder stoop of fatigue and dark circles under his eyes to match. His clothes held the wrinkles of what must've been a long, tiring day. He looked her over. Curiosity vied with the irritability in his eyes. "Have we met?"

She hustled toward him. "No, we haven't, but I need to speak with you."

"I'm busy."

"It's important."

He turned his back to her and advanced closer to the security scanner.

"It's about the Invisible College!"

He stopped and twisted to stare at her. His lips were tight; a vein pulsed in his right temple.

She had his attention. "It's about the college and Wayne Oakford."

"You know Dr. Oakford?"

"He was my uncle."

By now, the short line ahead of him was gone, and the people in the longer line behind him grumbled about being held up.

He raised a hand in acknowledgment of their frustration and stepped out of place. He focused on Mary. "Your uncle, you say?"

"Yes. I'm Mary Dawson. This is Gunnar Schofield. I hired him to find out who killed Uncle Wayne." She took Dr. Babson's arm and drew him aside. "I'm sorry to bother you, but I must know what's going on, and right now, you seem to be the only one who can provide answers. Can we find someplace to talk?"

Babson allowed her to lead him away. They stood near a wall in the busy corridor leading to the United terminal. Mary filled him in about everything, from the day her uncle died to today's discovery that the skull had been stolen and her visit to the hospital. "Howard Sheldon told me the Invisible College ordered the hit on Uncle Wayne."

"It wouldn't be the first time they've killed to protect their science. Did he say why?"

"I thought it was because Uncle Wayne had hidden the skull when he sent Paluxy Man's fossils to the Smithsonian, but Howard said nobody knew about the skull. He said the threat Wayne posed was his theory and the book he was writing about it."

Rubbing his tired eyes, Dr. Babson nodded. "He called it 'panhominism' or 'the theory of spontaneous origins.'"

"And you were to help him write it?"

"He approached me about it, yes. He knew about my background in quantum physics and wanted me to verify his understanding of the science as it applies to human origins."

Gunnar raised his brows. "What on Earth does quantum physics have to do with human origins?"

Dr. Babson regarded them for a moment as if trying to reach a decision. Finally, with a weary sigh, he said, "This is going to take awhile." He nodded toward a nearby Max and Erma's. "Let's grab a table."

"What about your flight?" Mary asked.

"I'll make other arrangements."

"I hate to make you miss your plane." But she didn't mean it. She needed to know what he could tell her. It was a shame he'd miss his flight—but like he said, he could make other arrangements.

He dismissed her concerns with a wave of his hand. "I think we need to talk."

The savory scent of onions frying and hamburger meat sizzling on a hot grill reminded Mary she hadn't eaten all day. She ordered a burger with avocado and a side of rings to go with her soda, and waited while the men placed their orders.

They found a table in the back, and as soon as they'd settled in, Gunnar asked again, "What does quantum physics have to do with evolution?"

"Evolution? Nothing. But it had everything to do with Wayne's theory." Dr. Babson tore open a packet of artificial sweetener and stirred it into his iced tea. "In 1997, a physicist named Nicolas Gisin performed an experiment. He sent a pair of entangled photons through optical fibers. At the end of the fibers, roughly seven miles apart, the photons were forced to make a choice between alternate pathways. The choice of path for each photon should have been random, but guess what? Whatever choice one photon made, the other photon–seven miles away–also made. The exact same decision. If you place a mirror in front of one photon and it bounces off of it, the other photon will move in the same manner, even in absence of a mirror. In essence, the second photon that's seven miles away 'bounces' in the same manner, even though it's not bouncing off of anything at all."

Mary glanced at Gunnar. The confusion plain on his face matched what she felt.

Dr. Babson apparently understood their response. "In a nutshell, quantum physics has proven that you can have causation in one location and an effect miles away, with no apparent, explainable connection between the two. And it's believed that this phenomenon could occur at literally any distance–even the entire distance of the universe."

The waitress brought their orders, checked if they needed anything, and left.

While the men dug into their burgers, Mary tried to digest the implication of what Dr. Babson said. And couldn't. "I'm still confused."

Dr. Babson swallowed and wiped his lips with a paper napkin. "Okay. Let me ask you something. For the sake of argument, let's assume that human life did not appear on Earth through a process of evolution over a period of millions of years. Let's assume, instead, that human life appeared on our planet suddenly and fully formed 6,000 years ago. How could it have happened? How could complex life appear instantaneously?"

"I don't believe that happened," Mary said. "But for the sake of argument, I would have to believe it was a miracle."

Dr. Babson held up a finger. "Ah, but Wayne was a scientist. He didn't believe in miracles. He wanted a natural explanation for the sudden appearance of human life. How could it appear without the aid of the supernatural?"

Mary shrugged. "I have no idea."

"Wayne thought he found the answer in quantum physics. You can't have an effect without a cause, but what if the cause is undetectable because it's happening seven miles away? What if the cause cannot be detected because it's on the other side of our universe, or in another universe far across the multiverse?" Babson's eyes twinkled. "What if the effect–the sudden appearance of human life–happened on Earth six thousand years ago, but the cause occurred in a parallel universe somewhere across the multiverse?"

Gunnar squirted ketchup on his fries, then raised serious eyes to Dr. Babson. "Do you think he's right?"

"Well, of course not," he replied. "I'm a Christian and a Creationist. I believe the evidence is best explained with reference to the Judeo-Christian God. But if I were an atheist and looking at the same data, who knows? I might agree with him. It's certainly the most plausible *secular* explanation I've ever heard."

"It doesn't sound plausible at all to me." Mary scowled. "Parallel universes are science fiction."

"Actually, it's not science fiction. In fact, the existence of parallel universes is rapidly becoming the mainstream scientific view. It's called the 'multiverse.' Our universe is just one universe within a collection of parallel universes."

"But complex life suddenly appearing on Earth due to something happening in a parallel universe? I honestly can't understand why scientists would care whether my uncle published something so preposterous!"

"Wayne's theory might have been hard for the layman to believe, but so is nearly every truth in quantum physics. And it was purely natural, scientific, and secular. That's what made it such a threat." He rested his burger on its plate and wiped his hands clean. "Darwinism can't succeed by convincing skeptical minds of its validity. It survives because it's the only available explanation for the appearance of complex life on Earth–the only *secular* explanation."

He took a sip of his soda, then put the glass back on the table. "The courts prohibit creationism from being taught in the public schools. They say Intelligent Design is creationism—a theory derived from the Bible and therefore derived from 'religion'—and you cannot teach religion in the classroom. With no other theory to compete against it, Darwinism goes unchallenged. Not even secular evidence against it is allowed. It wins by default. And that's how the scientists like it. They're afraid of an honest debate." He smirked. "When they were children, they hid behind their mothers' skirts. As adults, they hide behind judges' robes. And that's why Wayne's theory was so dangerous—he was a scientist and his theory of spontaneous origins was entirely secular."

"It sounds like creationism with a different name." And no way was her uncle a creationist. The idea he'd come up with this theory didn't make sense.

"No, you don't understand. Creationism is the belief that God miraculously created life out of nothing. God, being God, can do that. By definition, He's capable of doing the impossible. But that's not what Wayne was going for. In his book, he intended to present a new theory, a purely scientific explanation of how complex life appeared on Earth six thousand years ago." He popped his hand on the table. "And that's why they killed him."

He leaned back and stared at them as if they should understand the implications. But Mary didn't, and apparently he realized that. "Don't you get it? It could be taught in the public schools as an alternative to Darwinism."

A slow grin spread across Gunnar's face. "Life appeared spontaneously—just like the Bible teaches, but with a scientific explanation."

"Exactly. And that's why Wayne's theory was so dangerous to the entrenched establishment. They know that if Darwinism were subjected to a fair and honest debate, it couldn't win." His eyes gleamed. "Darwinism wouldn't be selected. It simply isn't fit enough to survive."

Mary offered a light laugh at the man's jokes, then asked, "Did you see the book he was writing?"

He shook his head. "When he told me about it and asked if I'd help him with the research, I told him no. It didn't take me long to recognize the significance of what he was proposing. Not that I didn't want to help, but I'm a creationist and I didn't want any involvement with his book—the scientists and lawyers will grasp any slender reed to preclude children from hearing both sides. So I referred him to Arthur Wallace, an atheist who is also a quantum physicist and a science historian to boot."

Gunnar shrugged a shoulder. "Arthur wasn't much help, except for bringing us to you. Why'd you choose him?"

"Wayne wanted the scientific community to take a progressive approach to the issue of life origins. I thought Arthur would be a good match for him."

A family of vacationers took a table not far away, and the toddler squalled as his mother tried to settle him in his booster chair. The high-pitched wail made Mary wince, but she couldn't help but to feel sorry for the parents. They both looked worn to a frazzle.

Finally the child settled, and Mary shifted her attention to the professor. "You mentioned the 'progressive approach.' What is that?"

"It's just a matter of coming at the same material from a different direction. We've seen it happen in other areas of study, and there's no reason why biologists and paleontologists couldn't do the same. For example, consider the ancient city of Troy. You know the story of the Trojan horse?"

Mary rolled her eyes. "Of course. Everybody does."

"So, tell me. Was the city historical or just a myth?"

"Myth," Gunnar answered. "From Greek mythology."

"Nope, historical." Dr. Babson gave him a *gotcha*! grin. "For the longest time, there was a consensus among historians that the city of Troy never existed. The world's foremost experts said it was simply a legend that originated in Virgil's *Aeneid* and was alluded to in Homer's *Odyssey*. But in the late 1800s, an archeologist named Frank Calvert discovered the remains of the city in what's currently known as Turkey. In light of the new evidence, it's now generally agreed that Troy did exist."

He directed his focus to Mary. "And that's what I'm referring to when I say a 'progressive approach.' We simply cannot make progress in our understanding of history unless we are willing to accept at least the possibility that humanity's recorded history might be correct. Our hope is that scientists will take the same approach to the early history recorded in the Bible, including the sudden, historical appearance of complex life."

"I understand what you're saying about the city of Troy and the Trojan horse, but the Aeneid and the Odyssey are not religious texts," Mary pointed out. "Don't you believe a religious work like the Bible should be held to a higher standard of proof?"

"There's no reason why it should. Besides, the same thing has happened repeatedly with persons and cities mentioned in the Bible. At first, the experts assumed they were legendary but archeology later proved them to be historical."

"That's fine for archeology," she said. "But surely you'd agree there's a difference between the Bible mentioning the existence of a city and the Bible claiming a miracle occurred."

The waitress came to the table with two fresh sodas and a tea refill for Dr. Babson. She cleared the dishes and left again.

Dr. Babson sweetened his fresh tea and raised a brow at Mary. "Of course there's a difference. But I believe the same progressive scientific approach would apply to miracles. You've heard the story of God speaking to Moses through a burning bush, right?"

"Of course."

"If you believe the Bible, the bush suddenly caught on fire but it wasn't consumed by the flame. The original approach of scholars–rather medieval and bigoted, in my view–was simply to deny that the event ever happened, to relegate the story of the burning bush to mere legend. The more progressive, modern, and–if I may be blunt–more honest approach is to accept the possibility that the historical events recorded in the Bible could be correct and to ask how they might have happened."

He rested his forearms on the table and leaned forward. "Guess what? It turns out there's a plant known as Fraxinella that's found in Israel and in the surrounding areas, and this plant is commonly called the 'burning bush.' During the summer, Fraxinella is covered with a highly flammable oil, and on a very hot day it can spontaneously combust. When it does, the fire burns but it does not consume the bush. And that's very likely the origin of Moses's burning bush.

"See?" He held his hands out. "There was a perfectly rational explanation for how the miracle of the burning bush occurred. All that was necessary was for historians to remove their blinders and examine the facts with an open mind."

"Okay." Mary shrugged. "Maybe the burning bush really happened. But how many of the so-called miracles can be explained away that easily?"

"Well, there is the story of Moses parting the Red Sea – or possibly the Reed Sea, depending on how the Hebrew word is translated. According to the Bible, there was a strong east wind that blew all night, creating a path through the sea that allowed the Israelites to escape the Pharaoh. Again, the standard approach of historians was to scoff and scowl, throw their hands in the air and deny the event ever took place. But science has now explained how this historical event occurred. There is a phenomenon known as a 'wind setdown.' The National Center for Atmospheric Research has used a computer model to show that a sixty-three mile-per-hour east wind would have created a mud flat roughly two-and-a-half miles long and three miles wide across the Red Sea. This path would have been clear for up to four hours, giving the Israelites more than enough time to cross the sea. And if the Egyptians were chasing them when the wind died down, they would have drowned as the water rushed back and covered up the pathway."

"So you're saying there could be a scientific explanation for the miracles in the Bible?" Gunnar asked.

"Or what they thought were miracles," Mary said.

"Just because there were scientific explanations, doesn't mean they weren't miracles to the people involved—or for that matter, to us. Yes, there's a plant that 'burns' and can explain the burning bush, but there is no other way to explain the voice Moses heard coming from the bush. The 'wind set-down' may have blown the sea dry, but it's no less a miracle that the Jews made it across just in time, and the Egyptians didn't."

The look Gunnar gave him held all the skepticism Mary felt. "So because you can prove one aspect of a Biblical story, you believe the entire story to be true?"

"Why not? Why is so hard to believe that God used His creation to perform miracles?" Babson asked, then waved his hands as if to erase his comments. "We're off the subject. We were talking about the veracity of the progressive approach in modern science, and the point is that my colleagues and I believe this approach will prevail in the coming years on the issue of life origins. Instead of giving the standard, knee-jerk denial to creation, some scientists are beginning to ask the tough questions and to study *how* complex life suddenly appeared thousands of years ago instead of *whether* it appeared suddenly. It's the future of the life sciences. And it's exactly the progressive approach Wayne Oakford was taking before his death."

Mary swirled her straw in her glass and watched the ice float in circles. Uncle Wayne was still taking a scientific approach, just from a different angle. A sensible angle.

Who knew what his conclusions would've been?

Dr. Babson sipped from his tea and sat quietly for a few moments. His weariness showed in the lines on his face, the slump of his shoulders, but judging from his squint, he seemed to be mulling something over. Soon he said, "Tell me about the skull."

"There isn't much to tell. Uncle Wayne apparently took your word that Operation Remnant would alter his find. I don't know what his plan was or how he intended to prove the skull was originally part of the skeleton."

Gunnar pushed aside his soda glass. "So how did you know it would be Operation Remnant instead of the Invisible College? The Invisible College was the one that ordered Wayne's death."

"I didn't know. And I didn't specify which would order the alterations—it could've been either organization. This has been going on for generations, far longer than the average person realizes. Alterations to the fossil record predate the formation of the United Nations and Operation Remnant, but not the Invisible College.

"Take Nebraska Man as an example. In 1917, a geologist found what appeared to be a human tooth in North America. Paleontologist Henry Fairfield Osborn inspected the tooth and determined that it was, in fact, the tooth of a modern human. According to conventional dating techniques, the tooth would have come from the Miocene Epoch, tens of millions of years ago. Now, this posed a serious problem for the evolutionists. They claim modern humans have only existed for the last two hundred thousand years. The Nebraska Man tooth was a dagger into the heart of evolution–a Precambrian rabbit, if you will. Did the evolutionists reconsider their dating methods or their faith in the theory of evolution? Of course they didn't. Instead, something very strange happened. The tooth was provided to other scientists for peer review. But when they received the tooth, they were shocked to find it wasn't a human tooth at all. It was a pig's tooth."

"A pig's tooth?" Gunnar asked. "Wouldn't Osborn know the difference between a human tooth and a pig's tooth?"

"You would think. Yet we are asked to believe that a seasoned paleontologist had somehow gotten confused. And there's nothing new here. It's been the pattern. An inconvenient human fossil is discovered, and later it's replaced with an animal fossil during peer review. It's been going on since Darwin's time, long before the UN was formed."

It all sounded so underhanded, so deceitful—a deliberate perpetuation of lies to protect a theory Mary was becoming less and less convinced of.

"I started looking closely at the chain of custody for the fossils," he continued. "That's how I was able to pinpoint when and where the modern alterations are occurring. When a human fossil is found, they send it to a company to prepare a plaster cast. A human fossil goes in, an animal fossil comes out. The company that prepares those plaster casts is Hollister Baird, owned by the United Nations. It has various subsidiaries across the globe, even in the United States. Right here in DC."

Hadley Scientific, Hollister Baird—the names were coming up frequently. Robert Quigley was president of Hadley Scientific. Was he part of the Invisible College too? Had he ordered her uncle's death? Her stomach turned. She'd been in his home. He'd flirted with her, knowing her uncle died because of his vote … if he was with the Invisible College. She had no way of knowing.

Babson said, "I didn't think Wayne believed me about the alterations, but months later he showed up at my office to thank me for warning him. He said everything had happened just as I'd feared. He knew the implications. A human fossil found with a dinosaur would not only shatter the conventional wisdom on dating fossils, it would completely upend Darwin's theory of evolution."

"I still don't see how that would be the case," Mary said. "His theory would've posed the greater threat. I mean, a human fossil discovered with a dinosaur fossil is significant, but it's just one piece of evidence."

"One piece of solid evidence is all you need. Look, let's say there was a murder in Florida. The victim was killed at three p.m. on a Wednesday. A gun belonging to your neighbor Johnnie is found at the crime scene. His fingerprints are on the gun. Not only that, but fibers from his coat and specks of his blood are found at the scene. He tells you he's innocent. What would you think?"

Gunnar snorted. "I'd think he was the king of all liars."

"Okay, but now let's assume you were hanging out with him in Washington, DC, the entire week. He never left your side. You were with him every minute the day of the murder. Now what would you think?"

"That's kind of hard to imagine, but if that's what happened I'd have to believe he's innocent."

"What about the gun, the fingerprints, the blood, the fibers? Doesn't that prove he was in Florida?"

"If he was with me the entire day, that fact would trump everything else. I wouldn't know how to explain the evidence down in Florida, but I'd know he wasn't there at the time of the murder."

"Exactly," Babson said. "That one additional fact completely changed your analysis. The fact that Paluxy Man was found with a dinosaur proved that the conventional dating methods are incorrect. That single piece of evidence is enough to trump everything else in Darwin's theory of evolution. And if you then add Wayne's theory into the equation, everything could crumble. Evolutionary sciences as we know them would fall apart."

"So they had to kill him," Gunnar said.

Babson tightened his lips and nodded. "I'm afraid so. They're very protective of their science."

"They can't get away with this." Mary sat up straighter. "Uncle Wayne gave his life trying to present that theory, and I'm not going to let him die in vain. Somebody else could recreate and publish his theory."

"Like who?" Gunnar asked.

"I could probably do it, with some help."

"Not without Paluxy Man," Babson said. "There's no point in writing a book to explain the mystery of a dinosaur living at the same time as a human being unless you can prove Paluxy Man was, in fact, a human being."

"You need that skull," Gunnar said. "And you don't have it. Not anymore."

Mary raised her finger. "But we know where to find Paluxy Man! Hadley Scientific!"

"If it hasn't already been shipped. Let me show you something."

Babson reached inside his carry-on and pulled out a notebook. "I've been watching how things operate at the Hadley Scientific building. It follows the same pattern as the other Hallister Baird subsidiaries around the world. On the last Friday of every quarter, just after sundown, they load large gray crates into trucks and they leave the Hadley Scientific building. I've followed some of the trucks. They drive straight to Ohio and into Wright-Patterson Air Force Base. And that, I believe, is where the United States is holding the fossils."

"The last Friday of the quarter. That would be the last Friday in March ..." Gunnar turned to Mary. "That's tonight!"

"We have to get inside tonight, before it ships," Mary said.

Babson shook his head. "The building's heavily fortified. It's surrounded by an eight-foot-high fence with barbed wire on the top. There's a secured door at the front of the building. No way you're getting inside without an ID badge."

"I know where to get one," Mary said. They stared at her, skepticism plain on both their faces. "Seriously, I know somebody who works in the building."

"Who?" Gunnar asked.

"Don't worry about it." She rose from her chair and threw on her coat. "I'll take care of it. Give me an hour. I'll meet you at Hadley Scientific."

CHAPTER THIRTY-THREE

MARY TYPED THE password on the keypad at the mansion Robert Quigley called his "summer home." The gate swung open. She mentally checked off part one of Plan A—remembering the password. Part two would be trickier. Surely his house was wired with some sort of security system, and just as surely, with him in Florida, he'd turned the system on. But she needed his business keycard. If it was in the same place he'd had it earlier, she could break in, nab it, and jet out before anyone responded to the alarm. At least, that was the plan.

Her palms sweated on the steering wheel. Any number of things could go wrong, but so much rode on her success, she closed her mind to the thought of failure.

She drove her Beamer up the drive to his house. One of the garage doors stood open, revealing a Cadillac Escalade inside. Had Quigley left for Florida without closing the bay? Or was he home and packing the Caddy for the trip? Hadn't he planned to fly?

If he was still home, part two of her plan would bite the dust. She'd have to wing it.

She parked her car at the house, climbed the steps to the front door, and rang the bell.

No answer.

After knocking again and not getting a response, she slowly turned the handle. The door was unlocked. With her lungs devoid of breath, her heart raced rings around her chest cavity. But there was no turning back now. She pushed the door open and peeked inside. "Hello?"

"Who is it?"

Quigley's voice made her jump. Her racing heart skidded to a halt in her throat. She tried to swallow it down.

"It's me, Mary." Her voice quivered along with her hands. She took a cleansing breath and tried again. "Mind if I come in?"

He appeared at the door, casually dressed in khakis and a pale green Polo shirt. His smile was broad, warm, and annoyingly confident, as if he'd expected her return. "Of course! Please, come in."

She stepped into the marbled entryway with her hands clenched in front of her. "I can't stay long—"

"Oh, nonsense. I'm sure you can take the time to have a toddy with me." He slipped his arm around her waist and walked her through the large living room they'd visited in earlier. His briefcase no longer occupied a space on the coffee table. She'd have to look for it. But how?

Quigley waved her toward the sofa. "What will you have? White wine? Blush? I have an excellent Chateau Margaux."

She remained standing. "Nothing for me. I just came—"

He laughed. "I know why you came. Old Rutherford sent you to get the check you left without this morning. He's probably itching to get it in his grubby paws."

That excuse worked. She should've thought of it herself. Dr. Lodge had definitely been unhappy she'd failed her mission—and she had no intention of remedying it now. She nodded. "So you understand."

"Of course I do. Which is why I know you have time to enjoy a drink with me. It was naughty of you to leave like you did." He feigned hurt, but then delivered a charming smile. "Have a seat. Stay awhile."

"Well, perhaps you're right." She stretched her lips into what she hoped was a winning smile and settled on the sofa's center cushion.

He rubbed his hands together. "Now, what'll you have?"

"That Chateau Margaux sounded lovely."

"Excellent choice." He patted her shoulder and headed for the kitchen.

The moment he was out of sight, she twisted toward the door to his office. His briefcase sat on the floor by the desk.

"Are you hungry?" he called.

"Absolutely starved. I haven't had a thing to eat all day," she said, though her burger from Mike and Erma's threatened to make a reappearance.

"I have some tapenade flatbreads left over. They're even better the second day."

"Sounds wonderful." If he stayed away long enough, she could nab his keycard and run. She tiptoed from the couch and peeked around the corner. He had his head buried in the refrigerator. She scurried toward his office. "I thought you were going to Florida."

"I had some business come up ..."

While he droned on about whatever kept him from his fun, she lifted his briefcase to the desk and tried to open it. Locked. She tightened her lips and frantically glanced around the desk for something to pry it open. A letter opener poked up among the pens in the holder. She grabbed it. It felt sturdy enough to do the trick.

She dried her damp palms on her slacks, then set to work prying open the locks. After several fumbles and one broken fingernail, the first lock popped open, then the second. His keycard sat atop some papers, his smiling face gleamed from its glossy surface. Below the picture were the words Robert Quigley. President. Hadley Scientific.

Her stomach churned. Was he the Headmaster? Was he the man who had ordered her uncle's death? She swallowed hard. Would he arrange the same fate for her?

Fury pulsed through her veins. Even now he happily garbled away in the kitchen, thinking he could seduce her with food and wine. He knew Wayne was her uncle! How could he think she'd welcome him into her arms? That diabolical, egotistical—she had a good mind to confront him right this minute and discover for certain whether he had a role in Uncle Wayne's death.

But she couldn't. She didn't have time. She snatched the badge and hurried from the room.

" … of course, it wouldn't have been the same in Florida without you." Quigley came from the kitchen with a silver tray in his hands. "Where are you going?"

The front door seemed a mile away.

"What did you do?" Anger laced his voice.

She darted for the door, didn't break her stride, didn't look back, until she sat safely in her car. As she cranked up the engine, she glanced at the doorway. Red-faced, Quigley trotted down the steps with a phone at his ear, his free hand gesticulating wildly.

Mary floored the accelerator and shot down the driveway. The Hadley Scientific building was nearly ten miles away. The dashboard clock showed seven fifteen. She slapped a hand against the steering wheel. She should've been there by now. They were running out of time—the shipment would be leaving in half an hour.

She kept a heavy foot on the gas.

CHAPTER THIRTY-FOUR

DR. BABSON HADN'T been kidding about the security at Hadley Scientific. The chain-link fence stood seven feet high, eight with the razor wire on top. Flood lights illuminated every square inch of the grounds.

At the loading dock behind the main building, a white utility van backed to the first open bay, and a hulk of a man jumped from the driver's seat. Gunnar slipped behind a hickory tree and lifted his binoculars, bringing the tattoo on the man's neck right up close. This dude was everywhere. Gunnar's hands itched for a few minutes alone with the guy. He then checked the license plate. Sure enough, Florida plates.

Down the dirt access road from him, a BMW fishtailed to a stop behind Sheila. About time Mary showed up. She was late.

The hulk disappeared into the building. No telling what a peek inside would reveal. Gunnar slipped from his cover and sprinted over to meet Mary.

The passenger window lowered. She leaned over from the driver's seat. "Get in."

He settled in and softly clicked the door shut. "Did you get it?"

"Yeah." She held up the badge for him to see. "Quigley was on the phone when I left, but if he called the cops, I never did see them."

Gunnar nodded toward the loading dock. "Our friend Tat-Man is here."

"Buzz-Cut?" She backed the Beamer away from Sheila and eased onto the access road. "Do you think he works here?"

"If he does, it'll make sense of everything." He pointed at the gate. "Pull in there."

The security gate was set to ride on rubber wheels eight feet adjacent to the fence. Mary stopped at the keypad/card-swipe unit and slid Quigley's card through. The gate didn't budge.

"This thing's asking for a code," she said.

"Is there one on the keycard?"

She studied it. "No, just the bar code the computer should've read. I wonder, though …"

She poked on the keypad and the gate slid open. "Same number he uses for his summer home."

"Park it over there." Gunnar indicated the other side of the lot, beyond the few parked cars several yards away from the white van.

She drove into a lined space and killed the engine. "How is this going to work? Even if we get in the building, even if we find Paluxy Man, we have no way of getting it out of here."

"There's always the van."

"You mean steal it?"

"Let's just say we'll borrow it for a while." He looked over the back seat toward the cargo bay. "But first we have to find the skeleton."

Mary crossed her arms. "How? We can't simply walk in and start reading labels."

"Sure we can. And we're going to walk with confidence, just like we belong here. With all this light there's no way we can sneak in."

She blew out a breath. "Okay. You ready?"

"Ready."

Mary pocketed the keys, and they strode across the weathered concrete toward the dock. As they drew closer, Tat-Man and a redheaded guy came out of the building carrying a large gray crate. They were walking toward the open cargo doors of the van. When they reached it, they placed the crate inside and closed the doors.

Mary grasped Gunnar's arm and pulled him to a stop. "That's James Darbyshire," she whispered. "That's the Chancellor!"

Gunnar said, "How much do you want to bet that your fossil is inside that crate?"

Darbyshire spotted them and shouted into the bay. "They're here! Get 'em!"

Before Gunnar could blink, four guards scrambled down from the loading dock, weapons drawn.

"Run!"

They dashed back the way they came, well ahead of the guards.

Gunnar held his hand out. "Keys!"

Mary tugged them from her pocket and tossed them to him as she ran to the passenger side.

They slammed themselves into the car. Gunnar fired up the engine and aimed the Beamer directly at the guards. They scrambled and started shooting.

Mary yelped. She scrunched down in her seat, covering her head with her arms.

Gunnar hooked a left, squealing the tires on the pavement. "Well, now we know who Quigley called."

"He's in on it. They're all in on it!"

A bullet hit the back quarter panel with a metallic thunk. Another hit. Another.

Mary squealed. "Get us out of here!"

"Gate's closed!" He checked the rearview. Three of the guards maintained their shooting stance while taking potshots at the Beamer. The fourth held a radio to his lips.

Backup. Great.

Gunnar whomped over a speed bump. The car rocked; the chassis groaned. He stole another glance behind. The van had pulled away from the dock, headed for the gate. Gunnar kept an eye on them while he drove. When the van got to the gate, he whipped the wheel around, pulling a U, then slammed on the brake.

"Are you crazy? What are you doing?"

"Waiting for the gate to open."

The guards crept toward the car, weapons pointed at the windshield. Gunnar revved the engine. They scattered, two on either side.

Darbyshire leaned from the van's driver side and poked on the keypad at the gate. It rode back on its wheels.

A freckle-faced rent-a-cop raced to Gunnar's side window. He tested the door, pounded on the glass, kept his Glock at Gunnar's face. "Get out of the car! Out of the car! Now!"

Gunnar kept his focus on the gate. Just a few more feet.

"Move! Move! Move!"

"Gunnar, what are you doing?" Mary's high-pitched voice wavered.

"Just hold on."

The van left the lot and pulled onto the service road. The gate began its ride back to the lock.

Now!

He floored it.

A shower of bullets plunked the back of the car. One lucky shot popped a rear tire, and the Beamer swerved through the opening like a drunk sidewinder. The gate slid closed behind them.

Gunnar let up on the gas and limped the BMW toward his bike. "Sorry about your car."

"I'm not sure my insurance is going to cover this." Mary pushed herself upright in her seat, then turned around. "Not even a dust trail. They're going to be long gone before you get that tire changed."

"We're not going to change the tire." He handed Mary her keys. "We're going to ride Sheila."

Mary's eyes widened and her mouth dropped open.

Gunnar opened the car door. "It's either that or let them get away."

He strode to the Harley, plucked his helmet from the handlebars, and waited. But not for long.

Mary approached, tight-lipped, hands flexing.

He gave her the helmet—"Strap it on good"— then straddled the bike.

She climbed on behind him and wrapped her arms around his waist. He turned Sheila to the service road.

A brown Ford Focus with a flashing red cherry on top barreled toward them. Hadley Scientific Security.

Gunnar shouted, "Hang on tight!"

CHAPTER THIRTY-FIVE

GUNNAR AIMED SHEILA at the dead center of the security car's hood. Nothing pumped the blood like a good old-fashioned game of chicken.

Two men occupied the car's front seat, and each shot at them from the side windows, firing bullets as fast as their fingers could squeeze the triggers. The security guards probably hadn't had this much excitement since they started working there.

Gunnar was pretty much done with people shooting at him. He pulled his piece from its shoulder harness and popped a few right in the middle of the windshield. The car swerved in the dirt and ran off the road.

Sheila skimmed on by.

Mary's grip almost choked Gunnar's breath from him. "You're insane, you know that? Certifiable!"

"We're alive, aren't we?"

The service road ended at the black top.

"Which way?" Mary asked.

"I don't know if they're driving the skeleton all the way to Wright-Patterson, or if they're going to load it at the airport and fly it there. Either way, they'll have to hit the Interstate," which was to the right. Gunnar pulled onto the pavement and cranked all he could get out of Sheila.

Ahead, a pair of taillights pin-pricked the darkness. Was it them?

Had to be them. Gunnar clenched his hands on the grips. He wanted to clench Tat-Man's throat.

He pulled closer; the taillights shined brighter. With the lights spaced apart the way they were, they had to be sitting on the backside of a utility van.

Within seconds, Sheila's headlight hit the van's Florida plates. Gunnar slowed, matched speed with them, and waited for an approaching car to pass. Light traffic. Curve ahead. Round the curve. Straight-away.

Time to make a move.

"Hang on!"

He pulled into the left lane, just enough to aim his headlight into the driver-side rearview. The van sped up. Sheila did too.

Another curve ahead. Gunnar moved even with the driver's window and yanked out his pistol. He pointed it at Darbyshire's face. "Pull over!"

Darbyshire glared at him and jerked the wheel left.

The van swerved into Gunnar's lane. He braked and grasped the handlebars with both hands. The gun dropped from his grip, hitting the pavement. The back tire lurched to the right, and Gunnar lowered his foot. He straightened the bike and rolled to the side of the road.

Ahead, Darbyshire had lost control of the van. It veered toward the left shoulder before he managed to pull it right. Once righted, he hit the gas, and the van disappeared around the next bend.

Mary had her head buried between Gunnar's shoulder blades and his shirt knotted in her fists.

He pried her fingers loose and twisted toward her. "You okay?"

"No! How can I be okay? How can you be okay? They tried to kill us!"

Gunnar clamped his lips and surveyed the highway. His gun rested on a center stripe thirty yards back. He dismounted the bike, checked traffic, and jogged down the blacktop.

What could he do with Mary? She was terrified—and with good reason. But he couldn't turn back. He had no intention of letting Darbyshire and his tattooed lackey get away. Still, he couldn't very well leave her on the side of the road. She'd just have to toughen up.

He trotted back to the bike. Mary had taken off her helmet and sat drooped over the seat. Her shoulders shook as she sobbed, and Gunnar's heart ripped in half.

He placed a hand on her back. "Want to go home?"

She stiffened and wiped her eyes with the heels of her hands.

"No. They have to pay." Her voice trembled with determination and a slow-burning rage. "You have to make them pay."

"That's my girl." He climbed on the bike. "Put your helmet on."

Darbyshire had put some distance between them, but Gunnar caught sight of them a few miles from the entry lane to the interstate. He cranked up Sheila's engine until once again, his headlights reflected of the van's cargo doors.

The back right window shattered, and Tat-Man's sneering mug showed in its place. He popped off several rounds—orange flashes lighting the night.

Mary screamed in Gunnar's ear. He wove the bike, trying to maintain control with one hand and return fire with the other. One wild shot cut through the left rear window and sent the van skidding off the road. It flattened tall weeds and took out part of a barbed-wire fence before crashing against a tree.

Gunnar turned around and parked on the side of the road. "Stay here."

"No way." Mary climbed off the bike. "I want to make sure the fossil's okay."

"Stay behind me, then."

"No problem," she muttered.

They picked their way through dirt and weeds until they came to the van. Gunnar flashed a hand to keep Mary back, then waddled in a crouch toward the driver's door. He rapped his barrel against the side panel. No hand gripping a pistol emerged to shoot at him from the window. He peeked in. Darbyshire was slumped over the steering wheel, blood oozing from impact wounds on his forehead. A crack spider-webbed across the windshield.

Gunnar felt Darbyshire's neck for a pulse. "He's dead."

"Did you shoot him?" Mary's asked from behind a tree.

"No, but I must've shaken him up."

He eased to the cargo doors and flung open the one on the right. The interior lights flashed on. He aimed his gun inside, but nothing moved. Tat-Man was sprawled on the metal floor next to a large gray crate. Gunnar holstered his piece and checked the man's pulse. Weak, but there. He rolled him over, dug his wallet from his hip pocket, and drew out the driver's license. Val Gordon. A Hadley Scientific keycard gave his title: Science Tech Director.

Tat-Man was a scientist?

There was bound to be more to that story, but Gunnar didn't have time to sort it out. He eyeballed the floor of the van. Val had been shooting at them. Unless his gun had flown out the window when they crashed, it had to be around somewhere, but it wasn't on the floor. He felt under the driver's seat, then moved to the passenger seat. His fingers wrapped around a rubber grip, and he withdrew a Ruger SP 101.

Once it was safely secured in his waistband, he studied the rest of the van. A collapsible ladder had been secured to one side along with some plywood planks. A silver utility box nestled under them against the wall. He scrounged in it until he found a sturdy nylon rope.

He yanked Val up and tied his hands behind his back.

Val groaned and rattled his head. He raised hate-filled eyes, and a snarl curled his lip. "Gunnar Schofield. Dime-store detective."

"Yeah, and you're Val Gordon, armed science nerd. Now that we've got the introductions out of the way, where were you taking Paluxy Man?"

"Out for a joy ride."

Gunnar jerked on the rope, drawing trickles of blood from Val's wrists.

Val grunted.

Gunnar said, "Surely somebody's waiting for this package, right? Where?"

"I don't have to tell you anything."

"Nope, but it'll go better for you if you do." Gunnar drew his semiautomatic and waved it in front of Val's nose. "One shot. That's all it'll take. That's all you needed for Wayne Oakford, wasn't it? One shot, center mass? Of course you shot from a distance of—what? Five feet, was it?"

Val sneered at him.

Gunnar lowered his voice, spoke directly in the man's ear. "Let's see what a .45 will do to your nerdy little brain at point blank range, shall we?"

"You kill me, you won't know where this crate was going."

He jammed the barrel against the soft spot under Val's jaw. "You know what? I don't really care."

Gunnar's watch ticked off the seconds in the silence that followed. Two. Three. Four.

"All right," Val growled. "We were taking it to Fort Knox."

"Liar. You were headed to Wright-Patterson. I may as well blow your head off right this minute."

"No—we changed our plans."

"Nope, don't believe you." Gunnar slammed the gun butt against the man's skull.

Val's eyes rolled back in his head, and he slumped. He'd be out for a while.

"Why'd you hit him?" Mary stood at the open cargo door, shadowy in spite of the overhead light.

"He was lying. Babson said they took the skeletons to Wright-Patterson, but this guy was trying to sell me on Fort Knox. If he wouldn't tell the truth about that, he won't tell the truth about who he's delivering to, or anything else for that matter." He reached down to help her in. "Want to look in the box?"

"Of course!"

Together, they lifted the lid. Resting on a thick velvet cushion was a fossilized human skeleton.

"Is that it?" Gunnar asked.

"I think it is. It has to be, right? I've never seen it before—well, except for the skull." She shifted, and the cargo light hit the fossil better, giving the ivory bones an eerie yellow cast.

A storage label had been affixed to the side of the crate. "Human Skeleton. Paluxy, Texas, USA."

Mary's jaw slackened. "The label says human?"

"Plain as day. In bold print."

"We've got to get this into safe keeping. It proves Uncle Wayne was right."

"All right, I'll see if the truck will start. If we need to, we can store the crate in my office."

They dragged Darbyshire's lifeless body from the front seat to the back of the van and settled him near Val. Then Gunnar plopped in the driver's seat and turned the key.

The engine started. Fortunate, considering how crumpled the hood looked.

He backed away from the tree, then eased up to the highway and parked in front of Sheila. The ladder made a perfect ramp once he topped it with the plywood. He rolled his bike into the back of the van. With it and the crate in the cargo bed, along with one dead guy and one unconscious guy, there was no way Gunnar would be able to put his make-shift ramp back inside; he left it on the side of the road.

CHAPTER THIRTY-SIX

THE VAN TOOK a deep curve, and the dead body slid with it.

Mary shuddered. "What are we going to do with Darbyshire?"

"Haven't figured that out yet," Gunnar said.

"Maybe we should've stayed at the scene and called the highway patrol."

"And say what? That we were involved in a shoot out with the president of the Smithsonian and his goon? That a wild shot from my gun sent them off the road? And 'oh, officer, by the way, don't lose that crate of bones. It's evidence.'" He glanced at her. "What do you suppose would happen to Paluxy Man then?"

Mary clamped her jaw and shifted toward the darkness out the side window. Her emotions twisted her gut—anger, hatred, fear braided themselves, coiling in the pit of her stomach, threatening to shoot up and choke her. Darbyshire had ordered the hit on her uncle, and that other guy probably pulled the trigger. Darbyshire was dead. Part of her was sorry for him. Another part wanted to pummel Val Gordon until he too was dead.

Vengeance was a dangerous elixir for hate. But at the moment, she'd drink it.

Her cell phone rang, and she fumbled for it in her purse. "It's my boss," she told Gunnar, then answered the call. "Dr. Lodge! You won't believe—"

"Mary, listen." Urgency filled his voice. "You were right about Paluxy Man. It's a human fossil. If what I've heard is true, the company that made the plaster cast for the Smithsonian changed it to look like a lower primate."

"Yes, I know—"

"This is serious business—the military is involved. The United Nations is involved!"

"Operation Remnant," Mary said.

"You know about it?"

"Yes. That's what I was trying to tell you. The reason Uncle Wayne saved the skull was so he could prove the Smithsonian cast is a fraud—"

"The skull! I'd forgotten about it! Do you still have it?"

"I have it and —"

"Oh, thank God! The rest of Paluxy Man is likely gone for good. Someone broke in and stole—"

"Dr. Lodge, calm down!" She'd never issued an order to her boss before, but her nerves were wired so tight, she didn't care. "I have Paluxy Man. Not just the skull, the entire fossil."

Lodge hesitated. "You're kidding."

"Not at all." She told him what had happened, including the fact that James Darbyshire had taken the skeleton. She skimmed over the chase and gunfire. "There was … an accident. He didn't survive."

"Darbyshire's dead?"

"Yes."

"Whoever put him up to stealing the fossil may be after you. You need to get Paluxy Man into safe keeping as soon as possible." He was quiet for a moment. "The Academy has an arrangement with a warehouse terminal over on the east side. It's a secure location, and they'd never think to look there." He gave her the address. "I'm leaving my house right now. I'll meet you. How quickly do you think you could get there?"

She plugged the address into the GPS. "About twenty minutes."

"Excellent," he said. "Back the truck up to bay number six and honk the horn. I'll call and make sure personnel are waiting to assist you."

Mary signed off and filled Gunnar in on their conversation. "He finally figured out Paluxy Man is a human fossil."

"That's a step in the right direction. Now to prove he really lived with the dinosaurs." Gunnar smirked. "The science that's available is so flimsy and contradictory, proving it will be tough."

"Everything I've been taught my entire life ... I feel like I did when I was a child and learned where my Christmas presents really came from. I had always believed what the adults said was true. They were the experts."

"Before he became a private detective, my old boss used to work for the insurance companies, helping them build their cases for trial. The lawyers on each side used expert witnesses. Your side would have your experts, they would have their experts. You can find an expert to say anything. Even the medical doctors. One time he told me, 'the more you learn, the more you lose faith in experts.'"

"Yeah," Mary pressed her lips together. Every person they'd talked to had been an expert, and it seemed like every one of them had a different story.

"You never suspected that maybe the theory of evolution was just a theory?"

"No, but I never really cared. My background is in literature, not science." An old memory tickled her mind. "No, now that I think about it, I did notice some issues. I had a college biology class and it touched on evolution. They had a graph showing how apes had evolved into humans. They started out in the trees, went through various intermediate stages, and ended up as homo sapiens. It was jarring because it totally lined up with what I was learning in a creative writing class. It followed a traditional narrative framework."

"What do you mean?"

"In classical story-telling, you begin with the world at peace and the hero in the safety of his home. That's how they portrayed our ape ancestor, living in the relatively safe haven of the trees. Then the hero sets out on a dangerous journey, acquires various gifts, survives a series of tests, and is finally transformed into a true human being. That's exactly how they portrayed the evolution from ape to human. And when I read it in my textbook, I thought, wow, this scientific information looks exactly like a storyteller spinning a tale. It just didn't dawn on me."

Gunnar nodded.

Mary twisted in her seat to face him. "And there was something else that bothered me. Do you know what homology is?"

"No idea."

"It's said to be one of the strongest arguments for evolution. If you see two species with similar features, such as eyes or limbs, you can see how the organs developed over time from one species to the other. That demonstrates evolution."

"Make sense."

"But there's a problem. Like, in Japan there's a type of dog called a tanuki. It's a canine, but it looks exactly like a raccoon and it fills the same role in the animal kingdom as raccoons. Are they homologous?"

"I'd say so."

"You'd think so, but they're not. Dogs and raccoons did not evolve from a common ancestor. That's the thing. If scientists say that two species share a common ancestor, the similar features are proof of evolution. But if scientists say the two species evolved separately, the similar features prove nothing. They just happened to evolve separately with nearly identical features. That's called 'convergent evolution.'"

"So homology is another case of circular reasoning?"

She sighed. "Yes."

"This whole thing stinks to high heaven," Gunnar said as they turned into an alley. According to the GPS, they were only a tenth of a mile from the warehouse. "The whole science behind the theory of evolution is a charade."

They entered the parking lot for the warehouse. Gunnar backed the van up to bay six and honked. The aluminum door lifted, revealing Dr. Lodge's walrus-shaped silhouette. Gunnar and Mary joined him at the dock.

Dr. Lodge rubbed his hands together. "You've got the fossil?"

"It's in the van," she said as Gunnar walked toward the cargo doors.

"Take a look." He opened the twin doors. His motorcycle had shifted against the side panel. The crate holding Paluxy Man lay open, its cover on the floor.

Sitting beside the crate, Val Gordon gave his head a vigorous shake, then blinked at the light. His eyes shifted to Dr. Lodge. "Headmaster!"

Mary whipped around and faced her boss. "Headmaster?"

Dr. Lodge aimed a pistol at her chest.

A muscular man in a camouflage t-shirt held a gun on Gunnar. Gunnar's hands were up. The man pulled Gunnar's weapon from its holster, then patted him down, finding Val's pistol in his waistband.

None of this registered in Mary's brain—it was too nonsensical to register, too surreal.

She slowly raised her hands, her jaw slack. "You're the headmaster?"

He offered a slight blow. "At your service."

"You let them kill my uncle!"

Dr. Lodge shrugged. "It was necessary for the preservation of science."

Rage spewed through her veins. She lunged at him.

Gunnar yanked her back. "Not now."

"Smart, Mr. Schofield. Keep her in line."

She strained against Gunnar's grip. "All Wayne did was offer an opinion," she shouted. "He didn't deserve to die for challenging a scientific theory!"

"Didn't he?" Lodge sneered. "What do you know about it? Your knowledge of science is confined to meeting rooms and fund-raising. But you, of all people, should understand science is a business. There are billions of dollars at stake in research grants and donations, and one way or another, most of that money depends upon the continued belief in Darwin's theory of evolution. The last thing we need is inconvenient fossils and novel theories that bring the Darwinian theory into question."

"But what if he was right? What if complex life suddenly appeared 6,000 years ago? Wouldn't you want to know the truth?"

"Truth is determined by consensus, and we have a scientific consensus on the theory of evolution. At this point, evolution should be accepted as fact. It's a well-settled truth. It's our truth." He drew his shoulders back, raised his chin. "You act as if Darwin's theory of evolution is some isolated idea, that it's an island you can pluck out of the ocean without any consequence. Evolution by natural selection has been accepted as true for over a hundred years now. It's become one of the foundational beliefs in the life sciences. Do you understand? All of the life sciences! Modern biology can no longer be understood without it." He took a breath, calming himself down. "If Darwinian evolution were falsified, the entire fabric of science would be shredded. The College will not allow that to happen. The theory of evolution will not fail. It's too big to fail."

"What about the truth?" Mary demanded. "What is science without the truth?"

"You disappoint me, Mary." He shifted his eyes to the thug beside him. "I've got 'em, Major Stark. Cut Val loose."

The major pulled a knife from his hip pocket and jumped into the back of the van. In an instant, a flash of t-shirt and denim erupted from the van and tackled Gunnar. Val straddled Gunnar's stomach and swung a powerful fist into his jaw.

Gunnar didn't move.

Mary's heart vaulted to her throat. "No!"

She wanted to run to him, but Dr. Lodge held her back with a wave of his pistol.

Val stood and slapped his hands together as if brushing off dirt. "Payback."

Dr. Lodge grinned at him. "That should make it easier to tie him up. Tie 'em both."

As Val rolled Gunnar to his stomach, the major entered the bay and returned with duct tape and nylon ropes. He tossed a length of rope to Val, then approached Mary. "Turn around."

She backed away from him, clutching her hands behind her to keep them from his grip. He clamped a hand on her shoulder and swung her around, but she wrenched away again. She rubbed the ache of his grasp from her shoulder, and he grabbed her arm and twisted it behind her back.

The pain shooting through her arm made her cry out.

The major growled." It'll go a lot easier on you if you just cooperate."

She held still. Tears stung her eyes as she glared at the walrus on the dock. "You won't get away with this! And you won't get away with having my uncle killed! I'll see you in prison!"

Lodge propped his fists on his hips. A smug grin stretched his mouth. "You can't prove anything about your uncle. As far as the world is concerned, he startled a burglar and caught a bullet for his trouble."

"Howard knows! Howard Sheldon told me the truth!"

"He's dead. And you soon will be."

The major finished tying her hands behind her back. Already her fingers tingled, starting to go numb. He ripped off a few inches of tape and mashed it against her lips. Her tears spilled down her cheeks. The best she could do was to wipe them on her shoulder.

The major turned to Dr. Lodge. "I should get moving. Long drive ahead. The general wants the shipment at Wright-Patt as soon as possible."

"Of course, major." Dr. Lodge clapped him on the shoulder. "Let me know when you've arrived."

"Will do." Major Stark dropped from the dock and jogged around to the front of the van. The engine started, the vehicle pulled away, taking Mary's only evidence of Wayne's integrity with it.

Val straightened from tying Gunnar's hands. "What about these two?"

"You have a pilot's license, don't you?"

He nodded.

Dr. Lodge put a hand on his shoulder and leaned toward him so Mary couldn't hear. But their sinister expressions told her everything.

Gunnar lay bound and unconscious on the concrete floor. With her hands tied behind her back and fear rooting her feet to the ground, there was nothing she could do for him. There was nothing she could do anyway—Lodge still held his pistol.

Terror chilled her bones as she stared at the man she'd once looked up to. No one knew where they were. No one knew what was happening. No one would come to their rescue.

CHAPTER THIRTY-SEVEN

GUNNAR'S HANDS WERE numb, his brain felt sluggish, and his jaw ached. The back of his head had probably sprouted a walnut-sized knot that caused a non-stop throb, no matter how hard he squinted and willed it away.

A monotonous drone filtered through the haze in his mind. The sound aggravated his pain, but as it drove through the fog, it became easier to identify. A plane engine. Wind noise. Not the hum of the road he'd awakened to earlier. When was that? His heart hammered his ribs. He was in a plane. He hated planes. How long had he been in the air? Who was flying? Where were they going?

Settle down. Count to ten.

He eased his eyes open, waited for them to focus. Mary sat across from him, watching him through wide, red-rimmed eyes. Tape covered her mouth; her arms were behind her. Probably tied, as his were.

He was lying on his side on a black plastic bench pad identical to the one Mary sat on. With the exception of Darbyshire's carcass, the rest of the plane's cabin was empty.

"How many are in the cockpit?" He kept his voice low.

Mary blinked.

"One?"

She nodded.

The darkness outside the cabin windows and the open cargo door at the back of the plane told him nothing. "How long have we been up?"

A shrug.

"Hours?"

Head shake.

"A few minutes?"

Another shrug. Her frustration etched a crease between her eyes.

Hard to communicate without a voice. This was getting them nowhere.

He wriggled himself upright, then leaned forward for a look-see through the cockpit door. Val Gordon sat in the pilot's seat with his headphones draped around his neck. The instrument panel was bright, but Gunnar couldn't read anything from where he sat.

He squirmed a bound hand into his right hip pocket, withdrew his Buck knife, and pulled out the blade. He'd never had his hands tied behind his back, and sawing the rope proved awkward. Every time the blade tip jabbed his hands, he winced. A careless fumble slit his wrist just enough to make him grimace.

Mary darted anxious glances between him and the cockpit. She sat still, ramrod straight, as if every nerve inside her were stretched to the snapping point. Her eyes reflected her tension. She amazed him. She'd been through so much, but any sign of self-pity had been well hidden. She'd faced every demanding challenge with barely a complaint.

Just like Becky.

One more drag of the knife across the rope, and it gave way. He shoved it behind the cushion, then crossed the aisle to sit beside Mary. She twisted and gave him access to her bound hands.

He sliced the ropes free from her wrists. "Keep your hands behind you. I don't want to tip him off that we're loose." He offered her a sympathetic smile. "Which means we should leave the tape over your mouth. Understand?"

She nodded. She flashed a glance at the cockpit, rubbed her red, raw wrists, then clasped them behind her back.

Gunnar patted her shoulder. "Good girl. We'll get through this."

He resumed his position on the bench across from her, lying on his right side with his arms behind his back.

Promising her they'd get through was a mistake. He had no idea whether they would or not. He'd promised Becky they'd be okay, and now she was dead. He had no right to promise anyone anything.

He squeezed his eyes shut, shoved away his wife's image. He couldn't allow himself to recede into the dark corners of his mind. Becky died two years ago. It had been a fluke, a malfunctioning fuel injector, a broken seat belt. An accident.

This was now. This was different. This plane had nothing to do with that plane.

Faint squares of light reflected off the floor of the fuselage. The sun was rising behind him; they were flying a northwesterly route, though not west enough to assume they were going to Wright-Patterson. Where then?

Gunnar's gaze slid toward the open cargo door, once again catching sight of Darbyshire's body.

Val's plan became obvious. No better place than the mountains to lose a few dead bodies.

The steadily rising sun continued to brighten the cabin. The plane began a slow descent through soggy clouds. Val stood from the pilot's seat, grabbed a parachute, and emerged from the cockpit. Gunnar snapped his eyes shut and listened to Val shrug the pack over his shoulders as he passed.

He stopped. "Too bad about this. If your uncle hadn't given you the skull, you'd still be happily living life. As it is, by the time the rescuers get to you, you'll be nothing but a pile of smoldering ashes."

He started walking again, the sound of his steps disappearing in the wind noise. Gunnar sprung from the bench and tackled him from behind. Val freed a leg and jammed his foot into Gunnar's shoulder, sending shards of pain ripping down his arm.

Val scrambled to his feet and slipped out of the parachute harness. "I've been waiting for this. C'mon!"

Gunnar put up his fists. His opponent had him by thirty pounds or so and maybe four inches in height. He sent a sharp jab into Gunnar's kidney and a walloping hook into his chin. Gunnar's head snapped back.

Mary screamed. Gunnar stole a glimpse of her. She'd yanked the tape from her mouth and had the presence of mind to nab the abandoned parachute. She scuttled away from the action and disappeared into the cockpit.

Gunnar paid for getting distracted. His opponent sent another crushing shot into his jaw. His head jerked back till he thought it'd roll off his shoulders. He hit the floor, but rose to a crouch and bulldozed into Val's middle, shoving him toward the tail of the plane and the open cargo door. Val untangled himself and sent a right cross into Gunnar's cheek. Fireworks exploded behind his eyes. He swung wildly in return and connected with Val's nose. Val roared; blood flowed from his nostrils.

Val stalked him, throwing punches aimed at his face. Gunnar backpedaled and dodged, watching and waiting for Val to open himself up. He ducked a punch and slammed a pulverizing blow into Val's breadbasket. Val's breath shot from his lips, and he doubled over.

Gunnar jabbed a fist under Val's chin, sending him upright again, then pummeled him with one-twos all the way to the tail of the plane. A solid hook to Val's ear drove him through the cargo door.

Val reached for a hold, for a lifeline, but grasped air. His screams faded into the valley below.

Mary shouted from the copilot's seat. "Gunnar, we're going down!"

He scrambled from the tail to the cockpit and flopped into the pilot's seat. They were rocketing toward the side of a mountain, close enough to tell the oaks from the hickories.

The plane was a Twin Otter. He'd never flown anything bigger than a Cessna four-seater, and even then, he hadn't been able to keep the plane up. Hadn't been able to save Becky. Her screams echoed in his ears. It won't latch!

Mary yelled, "Do something!"

He ran his damp palms down his jeans and grabbed the control column. He tried to slow the rate of descent, tried to bank left. The plane felt sluggish, slow to respond. The tree limbs out the windshield became too well defined.

"Hold on, here we go!"

The Twin Otter tilted, but not soon enough. The plane shuddered as they skirted over the treetops; the bottom of the fusilage collided with several high branches.

Gunnar gritted his teeth, his hands tight on the yoke. The plane vibrated and groaned, but it turned and rose skyward. Within moments, the side of the mountain fell away beneath them. He leveled the plane and shot a breath through his cracked lips. They were past the trees and southbound in the open sky.

"Are we okay?" Mary asked. "Did the trees hurt the plane?"

He shrugged. "The gauges look normal. The props are still spinning. I guess we're all right."

She slapped a hand over her heart. "I thought for sure we were going to crash."

The engine sputtered.

The left propeller slowed its rotation.

Gunnar clamped his lips together, tapped on the fuel gauge. Its needle slapped zero.

Mary stared out her side window. "How far up are we?"

"Three thousand feet."

The right propeller slowed to a stop.

Mary whimpered, a soft sound that shredded Gunnar's heart.

"Let's see if this thing will glide." He flicked a glance at the altimeter, watched the needle drop. His stomach felt tight, his calves cramped. The bump on the back of his head drummed an opposing beat to the throb in his cheek. And his hands were sweating a river.

But he kept the plane level and slowed the rate of descent.

Beyond the trees, a lake shimmered in the early morning sun, reflecting the fluffy pink sky. Gunnar tilted the wings toward it, and toward what appeared to be a golden wheat field beyond it.

"Are we going to land on the water?"

"Not if I can help it." He looked at her. "Tighten your seat belt."

The needle registered a thousand feet. Craggy land lay to the left. On the right, a smattering of vacation homes and an inn. The land at the far side, largely flat and grassy, was the only safe place to land.

Eight hundred feet. Closer to the lake. Too far from the field.

"Are you sure we're going fast enough to make it across?" Mary asked.

"I don't know."

"Can't we just land on the lake?"

"Not a smart idea. We're going over." He clamped his jaw, determined to make it happen.

Six hundred feet and dropping. Ripples on the lake became visible. On the right, smoke puffed from the inn's twin chimneys. Gunnar could almost count the number of logs on the inn's façade.

His heart raced. They were too low, too slow. "Make sure your seat belt's on."

She pulled the strap. "It is."

"Is it buckled all the way? Did you hear it click?"

"It's on, Gunnar! Stop yelling at me!"

Becky's terror-filled eyes flashed in his memory. It won't latch! It won't latch!

Sweat popped on his neck, his face. Stung his split lip.

The fuel gauge laughed mockingly.

He shook his head. He couldn't do this—couldn't think of Becky. Not now.

"Are you sure we'll make it?"

"Yeah." He forced a smile. "We'll make it."

An image of Becky transposed over Mary's face. She looked beautiful. So beautiful.

Suddenly, he didn't care if they made it to the field. Didn't care if he lived or died. To die would take him to Becky.

"What's wrong?" It was Mary's voice, speaking to him through a tunnel. A long, dark tunnel.

"Nothing." He shot a glance her way. Becky smiled at him. "We're fine. Just fine."

"I don't like that look in your eyes. Gunnar, what's going on? What are you thinking?"

He studied her this time, saw the fear in her features. Becky's face, Mary's voice.

Dear God, she looked so much like Becky when they'd first married. "Gunnar!"

He blinked, clearing away the image. "We're fine."

We're fine. The idea of being with Becky again lured him–created in him a strong desire he had to fight to control. But Mary had been through so much. She deserved to live.

He blinked again, hard. Gave his head another rattle. Concentrated on the field ahead. Too far ahead.

Only a hundred feet above the water.

They weren't going to make it.

Sweat drenched his face and arms and trickled down his back and chest. He sucked the salt off his top lip, swiped drops off his face with his forearm. His shoulders tensed. His fingers cramped on the yoke.

How was he supposed to do this? All he knew for certain was to keep the wings level. Tipping a wing in the water at this speed would shear it off. But landing tail first, like he did on the runway, would have the same effect, right? Nose first would send them flipping end over end. He had to slow down, remain level, land flat on the water.

Mary's eyes were wide; she grasped the arms of the copilot's seat in a white-knuckled grip. Fear radiated from her and mingled with his own until the cockpit shimmered with terror.

The plane slowed, but not enough. They hit the water hard, bounced, and crashed down again, tail first. The Twin Otter rolled and twisted. The left wing snapped off with the screech of ripping metal. Water flooded the open cargo door, making the plane tail-heavy and pulling it backward into the lake.

There wasn't enough pressure in the cockpit to create an air pocket. Lake water sheeted the windows and seeped through the riveted panels.

As the tail flooded, the plane leveled. Soon, they were entirely submerged.

Gunnar's lungs burned with his own breath. He fought to release himself from the seat belt, then reached for Mary.

She was unconscious. The water around her was pink with the blood from a head wound.

Panic clawed Gunnar's throat. How long had she been out? Had she been breathing water?

He freed her from the belt and tried to float her through the lake water, but his own lungs were bursting.

Bubbles rose from his lips, but not from Mary's.

What did that mean? Was she dead?

He had to get them out.

But his own frantic movements, slowed by the drag of being submerged, forced his body to suck in a breath of non-existent air. He couldn't cough. He couldn't breathe.

And finally, he couldn't move.

CHAPTER THIRTY-EIGHT

GUNNAR SQUIRMED TO his side and coughed up lake water until his stomach cramped. Between choking coughs, he sucked in sweet pine-scented air.

A black-shirted EMT sat back on his heels, a hand on Gunnar's shoulder. "You're going to be okay. Rough landing, but you're okay."

"Mary?" Gunnar's voice scratched his throat.

The tech shifted and looked over his shoulder. "She's okay, too."

Just beyond the tech, Mary coughed and sputtered, her face red and contorted. But she looked whole and didn't seem to be bleeding anywhere. She gulped air and struggled to sit up against the restraining hand of the EMT who knelt beside her.

Beyond her lay the still, unattended corpse of James Darbyshire.

Gunnar's cough subsided. He sat up with the help of the tech. His stomach roiled, and he clamped a hand over it, settling it with a series of deep breaths.

He faced the tech—Jason Thornton, according to his tag. Thirtyish. Fit. Tan. Exuding a reassuring confidence.

"Where are we?" Gunnar asked.

"Raystown Lake."

"Pennsylvania?"

"Yep." Jason wrapped a blood pressure cuff around his arm. "You've given us something to talk about for years to come."

"I bet." He pointed toward the lake. "Is that one of the wings?"

"Yep. First one to break off when you cartwheeled on the water. Crew's gonna see how to get the plane out of the lake. Don't much think you're gonna want it back."

Gunnar shrugged. "It's not my plane."

On the lake, a crew of divers in a ski boat shot an impressive rooster tail on the way back to the Twin Otter; only the tail of the craft was visible, and it was sinking. Fishermen and recreational boaters formed a rough ring around the watery grave site from a safe distance away, just as the curious on the tree-lined shore kept their distance from the hubbub occurring around Mary and Gunnar.

Not far away, the media surrounded a woman who looked remarkably like Gladys Kravitz of the '60s sitcom, *Betwitched*.

Gunnar gestured toward the crowd. "What's going on over there?"

"Mildred Tomlinson is reliving her golden moment. She's the one who called in the crash." He chuckled. "Biggest thing that's happened to her since her septic tank flooded her yard three years ago."

"Glad we gave her something more appealing to talk about."

Gunnar rose stiffly to his feet, stood for a moment until his gummy-bear legs decided to hold him up. Then he wobbled the few yards to Mary's side and dropped to the sand beside her. "You okay?"

She nodded, but her teeth were rattling, she was shivering. Colin Packwell, her EMT, draped a wool blanket over her shoulders. Jason brought one to wrap Gunnar in, but he waved it away.

From the left, a pencil-slim man in a deputy's uniform approached. He had the health-nut jogaholic look about him—the wiry kind who consumed nine hundred calories in a day and jogged it all off in fear of belly fat. He waggled a finger between Mary and Gunnar and asked Jason, "They good? Can I talk to 'em yet?"

Jason cocked a brow at Gunnar. "You sure you don't want us to take you in? Let them check you over?"

"No, thanks. I'm good."

"Mary? What about you?"

She shook her head. "I'll be all right."

"Then I guess they're all yours, Pat." Jason gathered his equipment and he and Colin strode toward the ambulance.

Pat Melton took his time studying Gunnar. "You get those knuckles from the plane crash, did ya?"

Gunnar fisted his hands, the knuckles were cracked, but no longer bleeding. Bruises colored his fingers. "No, not from the crash."

Pat pointed to James Darbyshire, now stretched under a white sheet on top of a medical examiner's gurney. "That fellow over there catch your punches?"

"No, he was dead before they put us on the plane."

"They?"

Gunnar squinted up at him. "Long story, too detailed to go into here, but if you give us a ride to the inn I saw a few miles back, we'll tell you whatever you want to know."

*

The shower steam followed Mary out of the tiny bathroom and into sunny bedroom suite in Raystown Inn. The small room sported a retro look and what smelled like a recent coat of ivory paint. A star-pattern quilt covered a double bed with an ornate, wrought-iron headboard, and light blue drapes had been pulled back from windows facing the lake. Under different circumstances, the room would be charming.

The concierge had taken her clothes to the laundry, so her choice of attire was limited to the damp oversized towel she'd wrapped herself in and the terrycloth robe hanging in the chifforobe. She shed the towel and slipped into the cushy softness of the robe. The shower had brought some life back into her veins and warmth to her bones, but exhaustion nagged and the bed beckoned. And her stomach growled. The innkeeper had promised to deliver a lunch to her room. Now would be a great time.

Gunnar and Mary had spent four brutal hours talking with the deputy and answering his questions. Mary's raw wrists and the huge knot on the back of Gunnar's head finally tipped the scale for the deputy to believe they hadn't killed anyone. Deputy Melton dispatched a team to search for Val Gordon's body on the mountain, but given what little information Gunnar could provide about where they'd been when they fought, the man wouldn't be found any time soon.

A knock on the door drew Mary from the lake view. Gunnar, also wrapped in a complimentary robe, stepped back from the threshold. He held a tray of covered plates. "Hungry?"

"Starving."

"What do you say we take these out on the balcony?"

"I don't have a balcony. Besides, it's too chilly out and I just thawed my toes."

Gunnar tightened his lips and peeked around her into the room. He shook his head as if dismissing it from consideration. "No one else is in the inn. Let's take this downstairs. We can eat in front of the fireplace."

She closed her door and followed him. Several conversation areas dotted the great room, cozy-looking sofas and chairs arranged around magazine-laden coffee tables or the big-screen TV along the back wall.

They chose a pair of Queen Annes parked near the fireplace. The wood snapped and crackled in a red-orange fire that smelled like hickory-smoked ham. The scent amped Mary's appetite, and she lifted the cloche off one of the dishes. Roast beef sandwiches with gherkins on the side never looked so good.

They ate in ravenous silence. Words didn't even form in Mary's head until she'd swallowed the last bite of a slice of cheddar cheese-covered apple pie. "That was heaven. Sheer heaven."

"I don't even remember the last time we ate."

"Yesterday, early evening. Mike and Erma's with Dr. Babson. Remember now?"

"Oh, yeah. Ages ago." Gunnar grabbed a mug of cooling coffee off the oak table and stretched his legs toward the fireplace. Hairy legs. Muscular, strong. Like the rest of him.

Mary redirected her gaze to the flames. "So, what happens now?"

"Well, I don't know about you, but after I finish my coffee, I'm going back up to my room and sleep until this time tomorrow."

"No, that's not what I mean." The entire time she'd stood under the shower spray she hadn't been able to escape this one thought: "We failed."

"Failed?"

"We failed Uncle Wayne. In every way." She shifted to face him. "I can't save his reputation among his colleagues because Paluxy Man—complete with skull—is sitting at Wright-Patterson Air Force Base by now. I can't prove the Invisible College arranged his death because the only member who'd been willing to talk died of cancer yesterday. I can't bring Dr. Lodge to justice because everyone involved is either dead or … well, involved. It's his word against mine. And face it, this entire thing is so bizarre, no one's going to believe me. The presidents of the National Academy of Sciences and the Smithsonian Museum belong to some secret society that ordered the murder of a lowly paleontologist? Kidnapped us—planned to kill us! Who's going to believe it?"

Gunnar rubbed his jaw and winced as his hand hit a bruise. "It may not be over. Not yet."

"What do you have in mind?"

"At the moment, nothing. Too tired to think."

Mary sighed and leaned back. "No kidding."

Full from lunch, warmed by the fire, exhausted from the insanity of the past several days, Mary couldn't make it back up the stairs if she tried. And she didn't want to try. She snuggled into her chair and watched the flames dance among the charred logs.

Her lids began to droop, until a thought slammed into her mind and out her mouth. "I don't even have a job now!"

The sudden realization stung like a slap across the face. The tears of grief she'd squelched since this whole mess started erupted from her eyes and splashed down her cheeks. Nothing in her life made sense anymore. Uncle Wayne was the last relative she'd been close to, and he was gone, his reputation ruined. Everything she'd worked for had been yanked out from under her. Everyone she knew was perpetuating a colossal lie—one she'd fallen for, believed all her life. And for what? To protect a theory created by a man who had himself denounced it? Or did the Invisible

College members' hatred for God run so deep, they'd do anything—lie, deceive, kill—to disprove his existence?

Gunnar scooped her up from her chair, returned to his seat, and cradled her. "Shh, shh. Everything is going to be okay. It'll be all right."

His soft words and gentle tone calmed her.

Her tears slowed, and she sniffed. "I'm sorry for crying so much. I guess I'm just tired."

"More than tired. You've taken quite a hit."

He kissed her hair, rubbed her shoulder, and she became too aware of his chiseled chest. She scrambled awkwardly off his lap, trying to keep her terrycloth robe closed in the process, and offered him a shy smile. "I think I like your original plan. I'm going to my room and sleep until sometime tomorrow."

"Or until I get hungry again," Gunnar said. "Whichever comes first."

He walked with her up the stairs, stopping at her door.

She clasped the robe at her throat, peeked at him through her lashes. "Thank you."

"For what?"

"Everything. Being so understanding and patient with me."

He studied her eyes, his gaze so intent, her breath caught. When he leaned toward her for a kiss, she didn't turn away—she welcomed it, wanted it. Was disappointed when it was just a light brushing of her lips.

"Sleep well." He strode toward his room across the hall.

*

What was he doing? Mary was a client, a vulnerable woman who'd been through a rough time. He had no business falling for her.

He probably wasn't falling for her. Stress, shared experiences, memories of Becky—they all played on his emotions, and he was too exhausted to battle them. Any other time, the thought of Mary as anything other than a client would never cross his mind. Regardless of how much she looked like Becky.

Exhaustion had probably caused the bizarre episode on the plane, too. Seeing Becky, wanting to join her. He missed his wife, hurt for her daily, but he wasn't suicidal. It must have been exhaustion—or a few too many blows to the head.

He picked up the phone, pressed 9 for an outside line, and called his office.

Cathy picked up on the first ring. "Where are you?"

"Raystown, P. A."

"I don't remember you telling me you were going to Pennsylvania."

"Trip wasn't planned. Long story. Good one though—high speed chases, kidnapping, attempted murder. Plane crash."

Cathy drew a breath. "Another one? What is it with you and planes?"

"I guess I needed a reminder to stay off 'em. What's going on back in the real world?"

"Brody called. He's got everything he needs to proceed with your defense against Dan. He wants to know when you plan to answer the petition."

Gunnar rubbed his forehead. "His place isn't too far from here. I'll go by there before I come home."

"And when are you planning to come home?"

"I don't know yet. Not today."

He signed off and stretched out on the double bed. So many things to do. Top of the list: rent a car. See Dan. Confront Lodge. Find Sheila.

Sounded so easy.

CHAPTER THIRTY-NINE

LEAVING MARY BEHIND proved more difficult than Gunnar expected, but he had to let her go. Had to release her from his realm of protection. But surely she'd be okay. No one in the Invisible College knew they were still alive. She should be safe driving home by herself. Her condo had already been searched, so she should be safe at home too. Still, Gunnar fought the urge to protect her, to keep her with him to assure himself of her safety, even though her resemblance to Becky would no doubt be unnerving for Dan.

Funny how it hadn't bothered Gunnar until they were on the plane. Her voice and mannerisms were so different from Becky's that her physical resemblance hadn't crossed his mind. But he couldn't spring her on Dan.

He turned his black, rented Mustang onto Dan's driveway and shut it down. The tiny tri-gabled Craftsman could use a fresh coat of paint and a new roof. The surrounding flower beds were choked with weeds, and the hedges needed a trim. Did the deterioration on the outside reflect the deterioration on the inside? Had Dan grown worse in the past couple of years?

Gunnar tightened his lips. Might as well get this over with.

A middle-aged woman of Asian descent answered the door and eyed him from bruised cheek to dull leather boots.

"Can I help you?" Her voice was stiff, proper. She regarded him as if he were a street beggar.

He cleared his throat. "Does Dan Henderson still live here?"

"Who wants to know?"

"I'm his son-in-law. Is he in?"

A rattling noise came from behind the door. "Who is it?"

Gunnar tried to peek around the woman, but she eased the door closer to her, blocking his view.

"Dan, it's Gunnar. Can I come in?"

"Talk to my lawyer!"

"I'm not going to do that, Dan. We don't need lawyers to settle this."

The woman glared at him. "He said he didn't want to talk to you."

She tried to close the door the rest of the way, but Gunnar put his foot across the threshold.

"He may not want to talk to me, but I want to talk to him." He forced his way inside, and stopped instantly.

On the other side of the door, his father-in-law stood on shaky legs. Once a proud six foot three, he now seemed he would barely scrape six feet. His shoulders stooped, and both hands trembled incessantly. His clothes hung loosely on a withered frame and his yellow-white hair had thinned. Bitterness had chiseled deep lines around his eyes and mouth.

"You've gotten worse."

"Stage three." He reached out, and the woman helped him return to his wing-backed chair. "Thank you, Ada."

She draped a lap quilt over his legs and fussed among his pill bottles on a nearby table. "It's time for your medicine. I'll get you some fresh water."

As she slipped from the room, the old man focused rheumy eyes on Gunnar. "Why are you here?"

"Why are you suing me?"

He glared. "Why did you kill my daughter?"

"I didn't. And you know I didn't."

"You took her up in that plane, didn't you? Did you bother to check all your gauges? Did you bother to check the seat belts? Did you inspect everything?"

Gunnar dropped onto the flat cushion of an ancient sofa and rubbed his eyes. "I checked everything, Dan. I always ran through the checklist before taking the plane up. Always."

The old man snorted. "Yeah, you 'ran through' it. Maybe if you'd taken more time—"

"I was cleared of all negligence, and the same proof that cleared me of negligence will clear me in a wrongful death suit." He leaned forward. "What is this really about?"

Dan's eyes watered, and he turned away.

Ada brought his water in a blue plastic glass resembling a child's sippy cup. She popped a pill out of one of the bottles and placed it on his tongue for him. He drank with both hands wrapped around the tumbler and returned it to her.

Even after she'd left for the kitchen, he didn't face Gunnar. "Her birthday was last month."

"Yes. She would've been forty."

"And she would've been here, taking care of me. And you would've been here ..."

So that was it.

Gunnar understood loneliness, but his father-in-law's pain must've cut deeper than merely missing his daughter. Braving his illness without family must've been agonizing. Facing the fear and uncertainty as each new stage brought worsened symptoms was no doubt unbearable. Nobody should have to face that alone, or with the cold comfort of hired help.

If Dan had only returned his calls. He never had to be alone. That had been his own choosing.

Gunnar shook his head. Spilt milk. He was here now, and he'd make it a point to return more often.

He knelt in front of Dan's chair and laid a hand on his fragile arm. "I've missed you. As much as I've missed her, I've missed you. You were like a father to me. When I lost her, I lost my entire family."

"I did too."

"It doesn't have to be this way. I mean, I can't stay here, I can't take care of you, but I can come more often. Visit on weekends, holidays. You don't have to be alone."

A tear slipped down Dan's weathered cheek, and Gunnar choked up.

Two wasted years. And with Dan's condition getting worse, who knew how long they'd have together?

Gunnar shifted his head, trying to encourage eye contact. "We can go for rides, pick up some of your favorite meals, and eat at the park. Whatever you want."

Dan patted Gunnar's hand. "Yeah. I'd like that."

*

Mary sat on the edge of her chair in her own kitchen, her hand still wrapped around the handle of a butcher knife. She'd been through the house twice and checked the locks three times. She was safe. No one was hiding in the closets, lurking in dark corners, waiting under her bed. She wouldn't have a Psycho moment during her shower. But the air conditioner clicked on, and she jumped. Her nerves were taut enough for a high-wire act.

The ride from Pennsylvania had been uneventful, except for a few bouts of heavy traffic. Concentrating on her driving in the rental car gave her a sense of normalcy she hadn't felt in days. But parking in front of her condo—the home that had been violated by strangers—shocked her system with a new surge of fear. Unreasonable fear. It had to be unreasonable, right? Like Gunnar had told her before she left, everyone who'd been after her believed her to be dead.

That thought alone made her shudder.

What was she supposed to do with herself now? She'd wrapped herself in her work for so long, she had no friends outside the office.

The office!

Did Celeste know about any of this?

Mary left the knife on the table and went to the phone in the living room, but she couldn't pick it up. She balled her hand. If Celeste didn't know, Mary could be putting her in danger. If she did know, she'd tell Dr. Lodge Mary was still alive.

She crumbled onto the loveseat and cradled her head in her hands. How awful that her closest friend in the world was Gunnar Schofield. Even more awful that she was beginning to find him attractive. And that she missed him, missed his comforting arms.

Ridiculous. She'd hired him. He'd completed his job, and she wasn't likely to see him again. A thought that brought no comfort.

She grabbed the mail off the coffee table. A week's worth of bills and periodicals and junk, all in a neat little pile. A letter from the medical examiner's office caught her eye, and she ripped into it. They'd released Uncle Wayne's body for burial.

His burial. She hadn't even given it a thought. Had he left instructions? Had he left a will?

She snatched her keys and purse and started for the door, but detoured into her office. A tape dispenser sat on her desk, and she pulled a couple of inches from it. Once outside, she stretched high over her head and sealed the tape, part to the door and part to the frame. She'd read it in some book and thought it clever, but she never thought she'd need to develop that much paranoia in her own mundane life. Such precautions weren't necessary for people with boring office jobs.

She studied the street from the safety of her tiny porch. All the cars parked in the cul-de-sac looked familiar. Nothing seemed amiss. Still, she fisted a key between her fingers and hurried to her car.

*

The police tape was gone from around Uncle Wayne's house, but the investigators had left enough debris in the yard to stand as a reminder that Wayne's house, too, had been violated. Mary snagged an empty Sprite can off the sidewalk and plucked a burger wrapper from the flower bed to throw away inside. No wonder cops were called pigs.

She paused at the door. Fear and grief formed a meatball-sized lump and squeezed themselves into her throat, choking her, bringing tears to her eyes.

Uncle Wayne's home had been violated, too—and not just by cops. The reason the cops had been there in the first place was because …

Her legs weakened. She lowered herself to the steps and sobbed. Her aunt and uncle had been there when her parents died. She and Uncle Wayne had held each other up when Aunt Clarice died. Now she had no one to rely on, no one to help her, comfort her. Everything was up to her.

She sniffed, wiped a knuckle under each eye, and squared her shoulders. Yes, everything was up to her, and she could do it—must do it—whether she wanted to or not.

Her hands trembled as she unlocked the door. The air inside was warm and stale. It held the smell of the dozens of men who'd traipsed in and out, looking for clues, burrowing into her uncle's life, and still jumping to the wrong conclusion. It smelled of fear and murder and blood. A call for vengeance hung in the air, but the call would go unanswered. The man who'd ordered this was out of her reach.

She shook herself, tightened her lips, and headed for the office. But she had to cross through the kitchen to get there. Uncle Wayne's blood still stained the parquet floor. Fingerprint dust still covered every surface. More debris from the investigation still littered the counter tops.

It never dawned on her that clean-up would be her responsibility.

She clenched her jaw to keep it from trembling and shifted her eyes to the office. Maybe he had left instructions somewhere in his desk, or a clue of what he wanted for his last days. Undoubtedly, he'd want to be buried next to Aunt Clarice, but Mary needed the details. Who would perform the service? Where? Who would etch his name and dates into the granite sweetheart headstone?

She rummaged through his drawers until she found a safe-deposit key. Not until she clasped her fingers around it did she remember co-signing the card to the box after her aunt died. In case anything happens to me, Uncle Wayne had said. Still too raw after Aunt Clarice's death, Mary had jotted her name on the line and had deliberately forgotten the box and what its existence implicated.

Now she needed it.

She took a moment to flip through the yellow pages for cleaning services and found an ad for crime-scene cleanup. One call got her a recording. The business was closed until eight a.m. Monday—tomorrow. She'd lost track of time.

The cleaners, the bank, the M.E.'s office, the mortuary, all would have to wait until tomorrow.

CHAPTER FORTY

R UTHERFORD LODGE SNAPPED through the channels on the small TV that sat in a corner on the soapstone kitchen counter top. Surely one of the news services had details about Saturday's crash. Saturday afternoon, Headline News reported about a plane that had crashed into a lake in Pennsylvania. One fatality, two survivors, no names released. Not much more had been reported about it yesterday, and today's local news held nothing.

Val hadn't contacted him, and all his calls had gone to voice mail. If Val was the "one fatality," then it would fall upon Lodge to kill Mary and that pet detective of hers. Or find someone else to do the deed. Meanwhile, he didn't know where they were, what kind of shape they were in. One thing he'd bet, if they weren't dead, they'd be after him.

Dorothea patted his shoulder. "You'd better get moving, dear. You'll be late."

"You're right." He rose and set his breakfast plate in the sink. "Can't keep those pliable young minds waiting."

He kissed her goodbye, grabbed his briefcase, and headed toward the garage, then turned on his heel and marched to the library and the .38 he kept locked in a desk drawer. He'd be ready for Schofield if the idiot had the nerve to come after him. He slipped his belt through the holster loops and reset his suit jacket, buttoning it to be sure the gun didn't show. The extra weight of the pistol gave him a strange sense of power, of preparedness. But could he pull the trigger?

In a heartbeat. And it wouldn't be murder. It would be self-defense. Unquestionably.

He patted the gun at his side and left.

Traffic had already picked up by the time he joined the commuters, and driving was slow. He rested his elbow against the door and his head against his hand as he drove. His class was in for a treat today: a nice lecture on Drosophila melanogaster—the common fruit fly.

Mutations were one of the key mechanisms of Darwinian evolution. Most genetic mutations were harmful or had no significant effect on the survivability of the species. But occasionally a mutation provided an advantage to a species that made it easier to survive or to reproduce. Over a long period of time, those mutations could theoretically result in significant change within a species and, at a certain point, could even result in the creation of an entirely new species. And there was no easier and better way to demonstrate this concept than with the four-winged fruit fly.

A four-winged fruit fly hadn't been easy to create. It required the combination of three separate mutant fruit fly strains. But by combining those strains in the laboratory, it was possible to produce a fruit fly that had an extra set of wings., which would appear to an average person to be a beneficial mutation. If one set of wings is helpful, surely a second set of wings would make flight even faster and easier.

A reasonable conclusion, even if it happened to be entirely wrong. But Dr. Lodge wouldn't try to dissuade them from forming such a conclusion. Like most biology professors, he would simply neglect to point out to his students that the second set of wings lacked flight muscles. His students would never realize that the second set of wings, while appearing to be an evolutionary advantage, were in fact a serious disability to a fruit fly and would critically impair its ability to fly. It was extremely unlikely such a combination of mutations would ever occur in the wild; the only time this "superior" fruit fly ever existed was when it was created in a classroom.

But Dr. Lodge wouldn't tell them that part.

And if he didn't tell them, they would never know. His students would never question him. They wouldn't dare. Sure, many of their cars sported bumper stickers with bold pronouncements like *question author-ity*, but most students at top-tier universities accepted whatever they are told by their professors without question. Students were as ignorant and gullible as NPR listeners. Most of them likely were NPR listeners. If any student managed to question whether the second set of wings was an advantage, Dr. Lodge would quickly shoot down that line of questioning with clever condescension and ridicule, accusing the student of being a Christian and worse, a Creationist. Peer pressure and professorial arro-gance were more than sufficient to stop any inquiry into Darwin's theory of evolution.

He loved teaching the Georgetown students precisely because they were so intelligent. The brightest students were used to hearing and believing scientific truths that were counter-intuitive and, in many cases, downright unbelievable. The upshot was that the more intelligent a person might be, the more likely he was to believe whatever he was instructed to believe. And consequently, the more likely he was to believe whatever was popular to believe.

Dr. Lodge smirked as he pulled his Lincoln into his space in the parking garage. Yes, it was as true today as it had always been: it was far more important to believe what was popular than to believe what was true.

Mary should've learned that.

*

Cathy looked up from her work with a smile she reserved for poten-tial clients. When Gunnar smiled back, she put on her usual smirk. "Welcome home."

Gunnar's grin grew wider. That smirk was what he loved about her. "Did ya miss me?"

"Maybe. I didn't hear you drive up. Something wrong with Sheila?"

"Bad guys got her." He flipped through the mail on her desk. "What's new?"

"Got a job for you, though you may not want it after playing super-cop for the past week. It's pretty mundane."

Mundane sounded good right now. "What is it?"

"Another unfaithful husband gig."

Gunnar shook his head. "God bless 'em. If the men in this town ever started honoring their vows, we'd be out of business."

"Want me to set up an appointment?"

"Sure, but there are some things I want you to do first." He fished out his wallet and withdrew Deputy Patrick Melton's business card. "Call this guy and see if he ever contacted DC police. If he has, I don't need to talk to him."

Cathy took the card and tapped it on her desk. "And if he hasn't?"

"Then I'm gonna want to know why." He started for his office, then stopped. "And get me a cell phone, would ya? Office account."

She raised a brow at him, her smirk more pronounced.

He waved her off. "Just do it."

He opened the door to his private office and got smacked with a wave of odors that better belonged in the city dump. Cleaning the space was solely his responsibility. He'd banned the service from doing it when he caught one of the maids riffling through his files. When he'd asked Cathy to take over the cleaning, she'd demanded a raise Rockefeller couldn't afford. So he was stuck with it.

Cathy's voice, asking for Deputy Melton, drifted to him through the open door. He listened to her end of the conversation while he chucked moldy take-out into the trash. The small trash bag filled long before he finished, and he had to grab another. After the third bag, the office was looking a bit better—except for the unmade Murphy bed— and Cathy had completed her call. Apparently Melton had done his job.

Which meant that if Gunnar was going to get to Lodge before the local yokels, he'd better get moving. But he needed to know where to find the man first. He dropped in his desk chair and placed a call to Mary.

*

Mary signed the card at the bank and followed a matronly woman to the safe deposit box. She extended a hand for Mary's key, and put both the bank's key and Mary's into their appropriate slots. The small door opened, and the woman slipped her key out, stretched her too-red lips into a smile, and left Mary alone in the room.

Mary drew a deep breath, slid the box from its vault, and carried it to a service table. There wasn't much inside, papers mostly, and Aunt Clarice's wedding set. She'd wondered what had happened to it.

A white envelope of heavy stock lay halfway down the box. It held a law firm's return address. Mary slipped the will from inside and thumbed through it. As expected, she inherited the bulk of the estate, except for a generous donation to the National Academy of Sciences. Too generous. She clamped her jaw. She'd choke before she paid a single penny to an organization run by Dr. Rutherford Lodge!

A handwritten page in the envelope caught her eye. The burial instructions she'd been looking for. She slipped it and the will back in the envelope and put the envelope in her purse. As soon as she was finished here, she'd make arrangements for Uncle Wayne.

She rifled through several papers and envelopes. Another envelope held his life insurance; another, the deed to the house. These she needed now, but most of the other things she could look at later.

The last, an unmarked manila, held pictures from a dig. The Paluxy dig. Her blood pressure spiked as she flipped through the glossies. The images were of Uncle Wayne, Ted Cranston, the kids from the college, the skeleton—complete with skull. A smaller envelope inside the manila held negatives. Just like Uncle Wayne to insist on an old-fashioned camera. Bless him. Maybe they'd be proof enough that the photos were unaltered.

She clutched her find to her chest. This meant she could prove her uncle was right. That the fossil unearthed in Texas was of a human. Once she showed this to somebody—anybody—at the Smithsonian, they'd have to change the skeleton on display to match the original.

She slapped the lid back on the box and shoved the box into its vault, then all but floated from the bank. Finally, she could vindicate her uncle, and something good would come out of the entire ordeal she'd suffered the past week.

The minute she slid into her rented Prius, her cell phone rang.

Gunnar. How perfect for him to call when she had such good news to deliver. "Gunnar! I've got pictures!"

"Of what?"

She told him of her find. "I'm going to take them to the Smithsonian and make them fix that display."

"Do you think they'll do it?"

"They'll have to, won't they? I mean, Dr. Darbyshire won't be there to refuse me, right?"

"I don't know, but I guess you won't know if you don't try."

"No, I won't." The skepticism in his voice put a damper on her enthusiasm. "What did you call me for?"

"Do you know where Lodge is?"

"He teaches a class on Mondays. He's at the college." She frowned. "Why do you want to know? What are you going to do?"

"He thinks we're dead. I'm going to go haunt him." He chuckled. "I'll call you later."

They disconnected, and Mary stared at her cell. A slow grin spread across her face. She almost wished she could be there.

*

Dr. Lodge opened the windows to let fresh spring air into the classroom, then addressed the thirty young people watching him. "The origin of complex life is an incredibly important question, and it deserves a serious answer.

"Before the advent of science, people were forced to accept religious explanations. The Hebrew Bible told us human beings were created in the image of God. We were unique among the animals—better and more important than the other animals—and we were created for a purpose. And those beliefs made sense to us. They made us feel special. The Bible is a collection of the greatest stories ever told. Its stories made those of the Judeo-Christian tradition feel comfortable with our past, our future, and our role in the universe. There's no question the Biblical creation myths served an important purpose in their day.

"But that was a different time.

"Today the human race is far more advanced. We don't need to rely on ancient writings to understand the world around us. We have a process for discovering truth—the scientific method. It's science that informs modern society about the nature of the universe.

"Science isn't in competition with the Bible. We should honor the Bible for its poetry, its history, and its beauty. But it's not a science textbook and when it appears to conflict with known scientific truths, it must be reined in. The Bible must be constantly reexamined and reinterpreted to bring it in line with contemporary views and values. And certainly the most important area where the Biblical narrative needs to be reinterpreted is the origin of life on Earth."

Dr. Lodge picked up a piece of chalk and wrote fruit flies on the board, then sat on the edge of his desk. "We can learn a lot about evolution from the humble fruit fly. It's one thing to talk about survival of the fittest and evolution by natural selection in the context of theory, but it's another thing to actually see those biological changes happen with your own eyes. Two great things about fruit flies are that they're easy to keep alive in a classroom setting and they have a short reproductive cycle.

"We've all heard the saying 'seeing is believing.' It's true, and I think it's important for every high school and college student in this country to witness the truth of evolution right before their eyes.

"Despite a scientific consensus in favor of Darwin's theory of evolution, there remains a large percentage of Americans who question the truth of evolution. And the best way to educate you is to show you.

"To be fair, when I say 'you' I'm not referring to students in this classroom. Creationism isn't a huge problem here in Washington, DC. The evolution deniers tend to cluster in the South and large portions of the Midwest. Basically, the parts of our country that are best known for corn liquor, feuding, and inbreeding."

The students chuckled.

Lodge smiled. Degrading comments aimed toward the less sophisticated were always popular in elite colleges.

Gathering his thoughts for the next point he needed to make, he strolled to the window and looked down to the street. A black Mustang squealed its tires turning into the parking garage. Two squad cars weren't far behind, hot on the tail of the speeder.

But instead of turning into the garage, they parked near the building.

Lodge studied the insignia on the side of the nearest car. These guys weren't campus cops, but DC police.

Four rugged men exited the cars and surveyed the building.

Dr. Lodge ducked his head back. What were they doing here? Had they come for him?

Impossible. No one could connect him to any crime.

But why hadn't they followed the speeding car?

A student walked toward them, and they stopped her. She pointed them to the building, to the very window Lodge watched from. The men headed to the building's entry.

Lodge's heart began to pound. What should he do? They might not have anything on him, but did he want them to approach him in class? On campus? The best place to settle this would be at his home. Not here, and certainly not the Academy.

He needed to get home. Fewer witnesses, fewer people to realize he'd been investigated by the police.

He faced his students. "Class is canceled. We'll continue our discussion next week."

Whispers from surprised students built to a crescendo. Dr. Lodge shoved his class notes into his briefcase and strode to the classroom door.

"But what about the—"

He silenced the student with an upraised hand and dashed through the doorway and down the hall.

The elevator outside his office dinged. He hustled past it, opting for the stairs. On the bottom floor, he quick-stepped toward the parking garage and his black Lincoln parked three slots in. His face felt hot, his heart raced. He was panting, gasping for breath. A quick glimpse over his shoulder—no one pursued him. He was home free and could slow down.

He unlocked his Lincoln and tossed his briefcase inside.

"Leaving so soon?" Gunnar Schofield stepped from behind a

concrete support pillar, his thumbs hooked in his belt loops. His expression was confident, almost cavalier.

Lodge squinted at him. The cocky imbecile probably felt invincible. He didn't know who he was dealing with.

Schofield leaned against the pillar. "Surprised to see me?"

"Not entirely, no."

"What did you do with my bike?"

"Sold it to the highest bidder." Lodge unbuttoned his jacket and slipped his gun from the belt holster, his motions hidden behind the car. "Got a whole fifty dollars for it."

"You're lying. That Harley was a classic. Fifty thousand couldn't buy it—and you're too greedy to accept anything less." Schofield pushed off the pillar and strode toward him. "You think you're going to get off scot-free, don't you? Figure you're untouchable?"

"You have nothing on me. Can't prove I had anything to do with Wayne's death."

"I don't have to prove you had him killed." He kept coming. His words echoed against the concrete.

Lodge raised his gun and aimed it squarely at his chest. "Stop where you are."

Schofield sneered. "You don't have the guts. You hire assassins—you don't dirty your own hands."

"Don't come any closer!"

Schofield kept advancing, hand out for the gun, a conciliatory look on his face—but a wicked gleam in his eyes. "Why don't you just put that thing down?"

The gun blasted, but the bullet went wild. Schofield dove across the hood of the Lincoln and barreled into Lodge's gut, bowling him over. The .38 went off again as they fell. Schofield grabbed Lodge's gun hand, and a third round rang in his ears.

"Freeze! Freeze! Freeze!" One of the cops he'd seen from the classroom held a gun on both of them. "Drop your weapon!"

Lodge relaxed his hand, and the pistol fell from his fingers. "This man assaulted me. Arrest him!"

Another officer kicked the weapon aside.

Schofield got up and raised his hands. "I'm unarmed." He dropped his arms and clapped one of the cops on the back. "Nice of you to show up, Jake. I was afraid I'd have to hurt him to keep him here till you guys arrived."

"Well, he evaded us in the building. No biggie, though. We knew you had him covered." The man chuckled. "Heck, we should've gone out for coffee and just let you handle it."

Schofield rubbed a bruise on his jaw. "I think I've had enough physical contact for a while."

The policeman standing over Lodge asked, "You Rutherford Lodge?"

"Yes, but—"

Two cops hauled him up, while another held a gun on him.

"Why are you treating me like this? I'm the victim!" He jutted his chin toward Schofield. "It was him! I want to file a complaint. He attacked me! Arrest him!"

One man yanked his hands behind his back. "You're under arrest for the kidnapping and attempted murder of Gunnar Schofield and Mary Dillard. You have the right to remain silent ..."

This couldn't be happening. He was a college professor! The by-god president of the National Academy of Sciences! They couldn't arrest him—he was a pillar of the community!

"Do you understand these rights as I have read them to you?"

"Of course I do. Any moron could."

They flanked him, one man holding each elbow, and walked him toward the garage entry. He caught a glimpse of the satisfied sneer on Schofield's face. Lodge was a man of power. He'd find someone to wipe that sneer off.

Outside the garage, he blinked in the glare of the sun, then focused on a handful of students from his class. He straightened his spine, offered them a judicious grin. "This isn't what it appears. Not to worry. I'll see you in class next Monday."

CHAPTER FORTY-ONE

BY THURSDAY, THE man in the mirror finally appeared rested. The bruises on his jaw and cheek had faded, the bump on the back of his head had finally receded. Gunnar was beginning to feel human again. He had still looked like the loser in a prize fight when he'd met with Mrs. Cambridge about her philandering husband. She had recoiled at the sight of him, but then a gleam sparked her eyes.

"What does the other guy look like?"

"He's dead."

"I wish the same results for Franklyn." She'd given him a wry smile. "Does that cost extra?"

She'd settled for some graphic pictures and the name of a bulldog divorce attorney.

Chuckling, Gunnar turned from the bathroom mirror and paused at the door between the master bath and the bedroom. The smile faded from his lips.

Ever since Becky's death, he had come home only to shower and grab some clean clothes. He spent nights on the Murphy bed in his office. A maid service kept the house clean, but he rarely went into any room but this one, the shower, the closet.

Becky's peach satin robe still lay across the foot of the bed. The dresser still held her hairbrush, her perfume. If he breathed deeply enough, he could still smell her. And if he allowed himself, he could see the curve of her body lying on the king-sized bed. Such a large bed, but the only worn space was in the middle. Even now, his arm ached to rest across her waist, to feel the gentle rise and fall of her breathing.

But working with Mary had gotten under his skin, and their last day together at the inn had elicited a longing in him he hadn't felt since Becky's death. His wife would always hold a place in his heart, would never be far from his thoughts, but maybe it was time to welcome life again.

Maybe it was time to either sell the house or make it his own. He didn't have to get rid of all of Becky's things, but maybe it was time to box a few of them up.

Maybe.

He dressed in his best dark suit and headed out, through the house, through the kitchen to the garage he no longer parked in. That would be too much like a homecoming. But maybe it was time.

The rented Mustang sat outside on the driveway. On his way to the house, he'd stopped for a newspaper; it lay untouched in the front seat, waiting for him to unfold it at a nearby diner. He pulled down the garage door—the remote had been lost with Sheila—and climbed into the car. He rested his hands on the wheel and stared at the brick A-frame.

Maybe it was time to buy himself a few groceries and have coffee and breakfast at home.

*

The funeral service was beautiful. Far more people attended than Mary had anticipated. Many filed past her, offering her hugs, condolences.

Robert Quigley stepped up to her, a Barbie-doll blonde at his elbow. Bimbo, no doubt.

If he hated Mary for stealing his keycard, he showed no sign of it. And if he did hate her, she didn't care. The feeling was mutual.

He reached out to hug her, but she drew back and offered her hand instead. Doing even that much made her want to retch, but she never could prove whether he was in the Invisible College. Didn't matter. He still disgusted her.

Celeste Martling slipped an arm around her waist. "Office isn't the same without you. When are you coming back?"

"Probably when we can go ice skating on the River Styx." Mary hugged her. "The only thing I really miss there is you."

"You don't have to be a stranger. If you aren't coming back to the office, at least we can meet for lunch."

"I'd like that." She liked it more than Celeste could know. The invitation kept her from feeling quite so alone in the world. "I'll give you a call."

Celeste pecked her cheek and moved on, allowing Gunnar to come to her side. Mary caught her breath. She hadn't seen him since they'd parted ways at the inn. He was stunning in his black silk suit and gray striped shirt. His tie looked a bit tight, but to his credit, he hadn't loosened it yet.

Did he realize how attractive he was?

Probably not. There didn't seem to be a narcissistic bone in his body.

He shoved his hands in his pockets as if not sure what to do with them and rocked on his heels. "Nice ceremony."

"Yes, it was."

"You been keeping an eye on the news?"

She nodded. "Disappointing." Dr. Lodge had pleaded guilty, and part of the bargain included having his allocution sealed.

"You wanted him to go to trial?"

"Yes! If he'd gone to trial, he would've had to explain his motive for kidnapping us."

Gunnar grinned. "That would've been a complicated mess, wouldn't it? Possibly even putting the Invisible College in danger of becoming visible. No wonder he avoided it."

"I guess from his perspective, there was nothing else he could do."

They stood together for a few moments, him with his hands in his pockets, rocking on his heels. She studied the ground at her feet, but there was nothing in the dirt to tell her what to say.

He broke the silence. "Did you go to the Smithsonian?"

"Yeah, for what good it did me."

"No go, huh?"

"No, they wouldn't even listen to me." She raised her chin. "But someone will. If I have to present the evidence to every church and home school organization, I'm going to get the truth out."

"So, you don't believe in evolution anymore? You a creationist now?"

She bit her lip and turned away. Did she? She'd been taught evolution as truth since high school. But everyone she'd talked to had chipped away at what she believed. Gunnar himself had debunked a lot of the evolutionists' logic—and he was no more a scientist than she was. His simple logic had cast doubts on the popular means of dating fossils, so it was quite possible for dinosaurs and humans to have coexisted. What she could grasp from her discussion with Babson illustrated there were alternative theories to Darwinian evolution.

But creationism? No.

"I believe in science. Evolution may not be the answer, but maybe Uncle Wayne's theory of spontaneous life is. There has to be a valid scientific explanation for the appearance of complex life on Earth."

"You may be right," Gunnar said. "But if you question the theory of evolution, won't they laugh at you?"

"I don't care." Mary's face hardened. "Let them laugh."

Gunnar grinned. Then he rocked on his heels. The awkward tension returned.

Finally, he patted her shoulder. "Well, I guess I'll see you around. It was good working with you."

Her heart plummeted. The job was over. She had no real reason to see him again.

She tried to smile. "Good working with you too."

He wandered off in the direction of the parking lot.

She watched him for a few moments, then returned to her uncle's grave site and lowered herself onto one of the chairs provided for family and friends of the bereaved.

Behind her, people chatted, engines cranked, tires crunched gravel in the driveway. Soon it was quiet around her except for a few of the cemetery workers talking together around the backhoe.

She sighed. They probably needed to get to work.

She rose from her seat and approached the casket. Rubbed a hand against the glossy cherry wood. "Good bye, Uncle Wayne. I'll miss you so much."

Tears threatened to spill again. She whisked them away and headed for the parking lot.

Gunnar leaned against a black Mustang, his coat off, his tie loosened. He gave her a slow smile, and her heart melted.

He opened the passenger door of his car. "Want to grab some lunch?"

EPILOGUE

MARY ROSE FROM the stack of papers she'd been going through on Uncle Wayne's desk to answer the bell at the front door. After she probated the will, she'd moved into the old Colonial. No point paying rent on a condo in DC when she had a house in Vienna, Virginia. Besides, she had no desire to return to Washington.

She opened the door and invited Gunnar inside where she gave him a hug and a lingering kiss. "Um. I needed that."

"Happy to oblige." He studied her. "Problems?"

"Oh, Uncle Wayne's being mysterious again." She twisted from his arms, but grabbed his hand and led him back to the office. "Now, instead of skeletons and skulls, he's leaving riddles."

She waved him to a wing-back chair and took her place at the desk. She lifted a note from the stack of papers and rattled it in the air. "Just listen to this: 'Mary, I'm giving you one of the most valuable things I have ever possessed. I saved it in 1980. Professor Corey J. Andrews will give you the key. Tell him, "Total pi." I realize I'm being vague but Corey knows the flesh that goes on the bones. The box has huge implications for Christianity as well as for human history.'"

"For Christianity and human history?" Gunnar rubbed his jaw. "Do you have any idea what he's talking about?"

"Not a clue."

"Who's Corey Andrews?"

"Well, that was another surprise." She turned to her desktop and punched a few keys. Google brought up several pictures of different Corey Andrewses. She clicked on one of them, then turned the monitor so Gunnar could see. "I thought he was a professor at Georgetown or something, but come to find out, he's at Liberty University. Are you familiar with Liberty?"

"Sure. The largest evangelical university in the world. Jerry Falwell started it." He cocked a brow. "Are you saying your uncle died a Christian?"

"Of course he did! He was raised Episcopalian, and so was I. Just because he preferred scientific evidence over Biblical accounts doesn't mean he didn't believe in God."

"I always thought you had to buy it all—lock, stock, and barrel—to be a Christian."

She dismissed his statement with a wave of her hand. "Of course not. It's all about who you believe in."

"Well, you're the expert."

She gave him a grin. "So, you want to ride out to Lynchburg with me?"

"What about our trip to Virginia Beach?"

"I want to do that too. Maybe tomorrow?" She circled the desk and went behind his chair to rub his shoulders. "C'mon. Aren't you up for a good riddle? Let's go meet this Corey Andrews."

"Only if we can have lunch at King's Island. They have the best Pu Pu tray on the planet."

"Deal!"

*

Gunnar conceded to riding in Mary's Prius as long as he could drive. She'd liked her rental so much, she opted to buy one instead of replacing the Beamer that got shot up in the Hollister Baird parking lot. And although he bought a new Harley Softail, she refused to ride on it with him. Something about getting shot at and weaving all over the highway had made her swear off bikes for life.

He drove to the end of the street and turned left. A faded green

Datsun pickup turned left not far behind him. Odd car for this neighborhood, but maybe it was some worker—a maid or a gardener who didn't get paid enough to afford a better vehicle.

Mary asked, "What do you suppose 'total pi' means?"

"That's really stretching my memory. High school was too many years ago." He merged into traffic on US 29. "Pi is three-point-something. It's a specific number. Whatever the 'total' of it is, I can't imagine."

"Me either." Mary blew out a breath. "Uncle Wayne always was one for riddles."

Gunnar checked the review. The Datsun was three cars behind them. Was it a tail, or just some old Joe trying to get home?

Dr. Lodge was in prison, but he wasn't out of business. He had connections. Was Mary still in danger?

Gunnar tightened his jaw. He should've strapped on his gun.

*

The Datsun had remained three or four cars behind them all the way to Liberty University, but once they got on campus, the truck turned down a side-street. Gunnar released his breath and concentrated on building names.

Mary pointed. "This is it."

In a few minutes, they were sitting across the desk from Professor Corey Andrews. Professor Andrews sported a full, graying beard and trimmed matching mustache. His steel-gray hair, thick and leonine, was carefully coiffed back from his face, revealing a high, intelligent forehead. He looked like a televangelist, but his hazel eyes held a kindness that denied the image of a Christian shyster.

His desk, typical government-issue oak—even though Liberty was independent from the government—was orderly. Papers stacked neatly on the corner. Blotter clean, except for a few notes jotted on it. Pens in a homemade clay holder inscribed with, "Papaw's the bestest!"

The man seemed to be all right.

He studied the note. "This is intriguing."

"What is he talking about?" Mary asked.

"He's obviously being a little vague here. But when you talk about 'total pi' and Christianity, I believe I know what he's referring to. I'm sure you're familiar King Solomon in the Bible?"

"Of course. Son of David, right?"

"And the king of Israel sometime around 950 BC. He had seven hundred wives and three hundred concubines."

Gunnar raised his brows. "Seven hundred wives? He must have been a very busy man."

Andrews laughed. "I don't think he was close to all of them. Just a few favorites. Anyway, the Bible credits him with building the first Jewish Temple. And inside the Temple of Solomon was an enormous cauldron. In the Book of First Kings, the Bible states that the cauldron was ten cubits across from rim to rim, and the measurement around the outside would be thirty cubits. In other words, it had a diameter of ten cubits and a circumference of thirty cubits."

"So, how big is a cubit?" Mary asked.

"Approximately eighteen inches, or a foot and a half. So the cauldron would have been approximately fifteen feet in diameter and forty-five feet in circumference."

"Why does that matter to Christianity?"

Professor Andrews raised a finger. "It's a problem because many evangelicals believe that the Bible does not contain error, but the mathematical values appear to be incorrect. The total value of pi is 3.1416. Well, roughly. The number after the decimal point continues indefinitely, never repeating. There are supercomputers that have been trying for years to find a point at which the numbers begin to repeat but so far they haven't found it. As far as we can tell, the number goes on forever without ever repeating."

"Strange." Gunnar wasn't a math whiz, but it seemed that eventually the numbers would repeat.

"The important thing here is that the value of pi is not exactly three. It's a touch larger than three. But the Bible shows the circumference of the cauldron being exactly three times the cauldron's diameter."

"So the Book of First Kings contains a math error?" Mary asked.

"Perhaps. There are certainly some people who believe that. Another possible explanation is that the numbers in First Kings were simply an approximation and not exact numbers. A third explanation is that the numbers are precisely correct but that the measurement from rim to rim measures from the inside of the rim instead of the outside of the rim."

"What do you believe is right?"

"I don't know," Professor Andrews said. "But I believe the Bible is inspired by God and that it tells the truth." He paused, staring down at the piece of paper that Mary gave him. "This is such hyperbole. This problem is well known and Biblical scholars have addressed it. It's hard to believe Wayne would find this issue critical to Christianity, let alone history. What I don't understand …" Andrews stared at the paper for a moment, rubbing his forehead. Then, his eyes lit up and he slapped the desk. "Talpiot! It's Talpiot!"

"I'm sorry?"

"I just noticed that the T in 'Total pi' was capitalized." His voice held a breathless excitement, and Gunnar's own adrenaline spiked. Andrews waved the paper in the air. "It's an anagram! Wayne knew I loved anagrams. He rearranged the letters of Talpiot. And he mentions the year 1980. That confirms it. He's referring to the Talpiot Tomb."

Mary's brows were drawn, a picture of puzzlement. "I still don't understand. What is Talpiot?"

"It's the name of a neighborhood in Jerusalem. In 1980, a family tomb was discovered in Talpiot. It contained a number of ossuaries, boxes that hold the bones of the dead. The tomb contained ten such ossuaries. On six of the boxes were inscriptions. Interestingly, the names were in line with the names of Jesus of Nazareth and his family. There was a Mary and a Joseph. There was a Jesus, son of Joseph. There was also a Yose, which is the name of one of Jesus of Nazareth's brothers.

"There was also a second Mary, and a Judah son of Jesus. This fits with the claim some people made that Jesus had married Mary Magdalene. They had a field day with that."

"Do you believe the tomb was used by Jesus of Nazareth and his family?"

"Not at all. His body isn't buried anywhere. When they rolled away the stone, his tomb was empty. Jesus was resurrected and ascended into heaven. If that's not true, then for centuries, Christians have been persecuted for a lie."

Gunnar shook his head. "Aside from your personal beliefs, do you think they could be right?"

"Those names were very popular during the first few centuries of the Common Era. Most scholars do not believe that the tomb was used by the family of Jesus of Nazareth." He looked at the paper again. "He says I will give you the key. That I can do. I'll give you the key to the safety deposit box. But he says I know the flesh that goes on the bones, and that the box has huge implications for Christianity and history. I don't think he's talking about the safety deposit box. I think he's talking about a bone box. The lost ossuary."

"What do you mean?"

"There were ten ossuaries found at the Talpiot Tomb in 1980. Shortly thereafter one of the ten boxes went missing and it has never been recovered. Some believe that another ossuary known as the James Ossuary was the tenth box. Others believe it was a different box with unknown contents. All that's known for sure is that it disappeared. Wayne was there at the time of the discovery …" He hesitated; his eyes lost their focus for a moment. "The more I think about this, the more I'm starting to wonder whether Wayne hid away the tenth ossuary."

Dr. Oakford had hidden a valuable skull, so it wouldn't surprise Gunnar if he'd hidden a box of bones.

Mary tilted her head. "You think the lost ossuary is sitting inside the safe-deposit box?"

"Impossible. The ossuary would be way too large for that."

Gunnar said, "Maybe it contains something that was being held in the ossuary. Maybe bones?"

"Doubtful, but your guess is as good as mine. But there's one thing I know—Wayne Oakford was not a fool or an exaggerator. If he believed it was incredibly important to Christianity and human history, I'm very curious to see what's there." He rumaged inside his desk, found the key, and handed it to Mary. "Would you mind if I come along and watch you open it?"

"Not at all. We might need your help interpreting what we find."

*

Gunnar and Professor Andrews escorted Mary into the bank. The signature card held only Uncle Wayne's name, but Mary reached into her purse and retrieved her Power of Attorney. The woman had her sign in, then took the key from Mary and led the way to the vault. They strolled down the rows of boxes until they found number 733.

"There it is." The woman used both keys to open the box, then returned to her desk.

"Here we go." Mary grasped the metal handle on the box and pulled.

*

Kinza Fayed sat in his Datsun pickup outside the bank and waited for the trio to exit. He placed an international call on his cell.

"What's happening?" The Shiekh's English held a heavy Arabic accent. "Do you have something for me?"

"Not yet, but soon. They're in the bank now."

"Spare no one."

"Allah Akhbar!"

HEY THERE, READER !!!

THIS IS BRAD Seggie and I'm talking to you! Did you enjoy our novel? Do you want its message to spread? Do you want this novel to sell well enough that Linda and I will write the sequel? My friend, I am asking you for your help. I'm asking you to do a few simple things that will help this novel succeed:

1. Write a review on Amazon and Goodreads. Would you please take five minutes and review *The Simulacrum*? You have no idea how important this is!
2. Post about it on your blog, Facebook, and Twitter. And whatever other social media you use. Don't worry if you don't have a large number of followers. Believe me, every little bit counts!
3. Tell your friends about it. Do you know people at church or work who might want to read it? Do you know any evangelicals who enjoy thrillers? You could even buy a couple copies and give them to friends who are avid readers. If they love it, they will tell their friends.

If you do these three things, I am confident that it will be successful. The novel is out of our hands now. The success of *The Simulacrum* is literally up to you. Thank you so much for your help!